THE AUTOPSY OF GOD

WHAT KILLED GOD?

CHARLES ARTHUR DICKERSON

Grace Ink Cle

PO Box 18612

Cleveland Heights, Ohio 44118

www.clifeministriescle.org

Dedication

To Sermonte, you brought me back to life
and you keep me living life.

I love you.

Acknowledgements

My Lord and Savior Jesus Christ.

My wife Sermonte.

My daughter Charmonte-you are an amazing writer.

My mother Lois Smith, my sister Audrey, & entire family.

The Christian Life Ministries Village.

Corey Reilly, my coworker-thanks for grappling with me day upon day.

Dr. Robin Hedgeman, my pastor.

Pastor Ken Johnson, my friend.

Chris Anthony Lee.

Table of Contents

Chapter 1: "Prelim" 1

Chapter 2: "God Is Dead" 17

Chapter 3: "Mount Sinai Hospital" 24

Chapter 4: "Assigned" 27

Chapter 5: "Deacon Twan" 35

Chapter 6: "Unworthy" 46

Chapter 7: "Thump & Grap" 61

Chapter 8: "Honored" 70

Chapter 9: "Resonated" 81

Chapter 10: "Wonder Working" 84

Chapter 11: "The Oasis" 90

Chapter 12: "Eros" 97

Chapter 13: "Branding" 109

Chapter 14: "Insatiable" 136

Chapter 15: "A Jealous God" 175

Chapter 16: "Surgery" 186

Chapter 17: "Concealed" 197

Chapter 18: "A Vibe" 202

Chapter 19: "Tanisha Johnson" 214

Chapter 20: "Born Day" 225

Chapter 21: "Alleged" 255

Chapter 22: "Breakthrough" 269

Chapter 23: "Examiners Report" 276

"Be Encouraged!" 283

"Prelim"

(Between 9:30 pm December 24th and 12:30 am December 25th, 2003)

"Everyone, let's give a big hand to Ru and the crew tonight, said Churchy. They truly set it out. The food was delicious, the hospitality professional, and this amazing edifice was enormously elegant. I mean from the royal décor, the waterfall, the fondu station, the chinaware, the Brazilian rugs, the decor on the spiral staircase, and so forth.

With Churchy finished, Ru placed a mic on the tables of God and B. Guyler. Churchy then went and sat with God at the table of honor.

Yo God, although you are a humble man, you have great taste, fashionable style, and quality service, said B. Guyler.

Shaking his head, God said, Thanks, but all credit goes to the lady of my life. Churchy never ceases to amaze me. Smiling and pulling her closer, God continues. Bro, her way of doing things regularly catches me off guard.

Okay, whatever, said B. Guyler. (Pulling away from his brother. Then scanning the crowd, he continued) Aye, I wonder what God meant by that.

You silly B. Guyler, said God. Naw, let me rephrase it, you are crazy for that one.

The chuckling grows louder. God stood up, looking out at the crowd from a large stage before addressing the room.

Everyone, I, your friend God, am truly grateful for all of you. You have made my born day special, and I can't thank you enough for coming. And, to my Churchy, thank you so much for setting this up. I love you.

In the crowd, some screamed, We know!

Laughing, God picked up from where he left off. Thank you whoever yelled that out. Let me let those of you who aren't aware in on something… (He was again interrupted by someone shouting encouragements. Sure, God go right ahead.)

The crowd gave a standing ovation, claps and cheers mixed with whistling and catcalls. Churchy, who sat at the table of honor, blushed and blew kisses towards the crowd.

So beautiful Churchy, and very thorough, said Div A. Den from the table he shared with B. Guyler.

Thank you, Div A. Den, said Churchy.

God, looking down at Churchy, pressed on. Churchy my love, I know that this took a lot of effort-a lot of time and frustration, but you truly have honored me, going above and beyond. After blowing Churchy a kiss, he called out to B. Guyler. My brother, back over to you.

Sitting down, God puts his arm around Churchy and B. Guyler walked up to the podium to address the crowd.

Thank you-thank you. As God's brother, I know he treats everyone else with the best wines. So…Ru?

At his insistence, Ru walked to podium.

Ru approaches stage from right aisle way. With the microphone in his right hand hanging near his right side, left hand in whisper position, B. Guyler whispers in Ru's right ear.

Yes B. Guyler. Then Ru glances at the crowd and says out loud. You know that your man Ru is here for you.

Ok now Ru, that was corny, it's not the time to be corny. The moment at hand is special, said B. Guyler.

Sorry B. Guyler, how may I assist you? asked Ru.

That's better but miss me with the sorry stuff. Sorry doesn't fix your "cornball-ness."

As the sound of chatter filled the room from attendees talking amongst one another, B. Guyler spoke into the mic.

Hey, is there anyone available to give Ru a few swag sessions, how corny is he?

The crowd gasps at B. Guyler's statement.

Being that he's a light skinned middle-aged black man, Ru's face turned noticeably red as the stage spotlight shined upon him. Nervously rubbing the left side of his face with his left hand, as well as blinking his eyes repeatedly, he looked very uncomfortable.

Again, B. Guyler leans over and whispers in his ear.

Ru, says B. Guyler, how about you have the staff pass out the glasses now? Because I would like to present to God his favorite brand of wine called, The Nu Wine. Also, wipe that dumb look off your face. I just told you that the moment is special, now hurry, gather your team and go handle what I just said to handle!

Ru swiftly left the podium area, calling out and flagging his team.

Fifteen minutes passed and light chatter filled the room. B. Guyler tapped his glass with a fork to get everyone's attention then addressed the crowd. Excuse me everyone, excuse me all. My special moment has come in which I am compelled to lift this toast up in celebration of my brother's born day. The younger sibling turned to face his brother. Yo God, I want to say this openly. We have had our differences, and we still do, but nevertheless you have made a unique legacy and provided a way of life that many imitate for some reason. Frankly bro, I do n't get why they'd imitate such a boring type of lifestyle but to each his own. The crowd gasped and B. Guyler turned to address them before talking to his brother. I just heard that gasp everyone, let me be clear, I'm speaking from the heart, so this is not a roast…God, some believe that you give hope to the hopeless and it's obvious that each one gathered here tonight has experienced something unique about you. Therefore, it was a must for me to pull out your favorite wine and lift a toast to you today. It only makes sense to do such for a person once and awhile who tries to kind of be a leader. You know everybody, it's obvious you feel the same way being that you are gathered here too. We all could've decided to be anywhere but here, so God that means you should be even more appreciative.

As if on cue, Div A. Den now came up to the podium and B. Guyler continues.

Now, y'all all know that me and Div. A Den are busy men, and our time is quite valuable.

Div A. Den leans over and whispers in B. Guyler's ear.

This thing has gone way overboard B. Guyler… I'm in weariness, feeling like a hostage from being present at this long, drawn out, practically uncalled for piece of celebration thing.

I get you, you are totally right my friend. Taking a step over to his right, B. Guyler redressed the audience, his tone gentle. Has everyone had a chance to have their glasses filled?

Up front, Ru and his team finished setting a table up with wine and treats then went to the podium.

Ru's response is fast and curt. Hold on. We all want the toast, but Div A. Den also has a presentation.

Sure Ru, B. Guyler says. I can wait Ru, Div A. Den is my guy.

Hey everyone, Div A. Den has purchased some complimentary treats for this occasion, Ru said. Me and my team have them prepared for you at this table up front to the right (he points to the right to show them where to grab the treats). Churchy, requests that no one leaves empty-handed, said Ru. And God, here's your special bag (one of Ru's crew members give God the special bag).

Thank you so much Ru, God says. (God grabs mic from the table him and Churchy are sitting at and speaks) I really appreciate this kind gesture Div A. Den, said God.

If any aren't aware, this is God's favorite bakery, said Ru.

Aww wow, that's timely Div A. Den, said B. Guyler.

Thanks, my friend. Everyone, I already know that you agree but I have to say it, says Div A. Den. Had it not been for a servant like God, where would this world be? (Facetiously Div A. Den says this) That's all I would like to say, here's the mic B. Guyler.

Thanks, my friend. Everyone you may come forth and grab your wine and treats, Ru says.

About 10 minutes later. Everyone has been served by Ru and his team:

Well, finally my moment has come so everyone please stand at this time, said B. Guyler (B. Guyler turns to God). God, we raise our toast to you in honor of your born day. Being that actually this day has no true importance, as well as this sort of, but not really impactful type of work you attempt to do for people, has either, we acknowledge you (gatherers gasp). Regardless, we unfortunately raise our glasses to this meaningless moment and make this toast to you anyway, my brother (gatherers are heard grumbling).

(God stands) Thanks B. Guyler and thanks everyone. Be not alarmed my friends, I have heard worse. Hey look though, I know that the hour is getting late, but before you exit, come take some pics with ya boy, said God (God looks towards the dance area). DJ Heavenly Host, you know I see you over there and you know I can read your mind. (God laughs).

God, you surely can.

Well, don't hesitate my friend, make it happen DJ.

Say no more my friend. Now everyone hit the dance floor and rock out to 'Mary Mary's the God in Me,' it's ya boy whose blessed the most, DJ Heavenly Host rocking the ones and twos (crowd yells Ayeeeee!).

People move swift to the dance floor. God is still on stage and points to Ru to come to him. God has a look of pain on his face and has his hand over his stomach:

Ru, go get Churchy for me quick.

Sure thing God, says Ru.

(Churchy comes to the stage) Churchy Bae, said God.

Yes, here I am handsome. Ru told me you wanted me.

Yes, Bae, I'm having some stomach issues and feel a bit woozy. Please cover for me Churchy. Things are winding down, I'm not feeling well,

I really need to head to the executive restroom right now. I'm unable to greet anyone who's leaving, so please cover for me.

Sure, my love, I can greet everyone leaving.

Thanks Churchy, you are very special to me (Churchy blushes).

Are you going to be okay, my love? I can send Ru to look out for you if you want.

No need Bae, I'll be fine. Just make sure all who are leaving receive my blessing and gratitude. I just need to maybe use it and then sit down. I feel dizzy and woozy.

Churchy heads upfront near the front door to greet those who are beginning to leave:

Hey Ru, hey Ru.

Yes Churchy.

Make sure you keep an eye out on God. Suddenly, he's not feeling too well. He went to the executive bathroom. Keep watch until I finish greeting the people as they exit. He's adamant that I do so.

No problem, Ma'am, I got it under control.

Gatherers are beginning to file out. Churchy is chatting with them as they head out:

Churchy, very impressive, says a woman named Hanna.

Thanks Hanna. By the way, that velvet dress and the pumps are eye-popping, said Churchy.

B. Guyler and Div A. Den are on their way out the door.

We are headed out, Churchy my friend.

Thanks for coming, B. Guyler.

No problem. I had to show my face, he said.

I'd say you showed more than your face, but that's another topic for another day, she said.

Anyway, tomorrow, we have a huge meeting with some of the largest businesses and nonprofit organizations in the world, said B. Guyler.

We're excited Churchy, said Div A. Den. A major breakthrough is on the cusp and the plan to free the citizens of the world from generational poverty is soon to be in effect. Churchy, come close (Div A, Den leans in to whisper in her ear). Pretty one, you so sexy and intelligent. I can't keep my eyes off you.

Div A. Den, I will call you later tomorrow, she said.

I'll be expecting to hear from you. Don't play me. I want you Churchy and don't you ever forget that, ever.

I know you do and I feel a strong vibe to be with you. I can't keep you off my mind, she said. By the way is that Versace cologne that you are wearing Div A. Den?

Yes, pretty one it is.

This cologne does something to me every time I smell it on you. I really need you to please leave Div A. Den. I feel like I can't control my feelings about you right now and this is not the time or place for me to go deeper with you. I will be calling you Div A. Den.

As team members of Ru are cleaning up, Churchy flags one to get their attention

Hey, hey you, said Churchy.

Ma'am are you speaking to me, says the gentleman cleaning?

Yeah you, come here. I know that you are cleaning things up butler guy but make a quick run near the executive restroom and tell Ru to come here.

Yes ma'am, I'll get Ru over to you.

Thanks so much butler, said Churchy.

Churchy turns back around to greet the leaving guests

Oh, now look at you two says Churchy. That platinum Rolex and those luxurious pearls complement so perfectly together, you two. Aren't you from the mayor's office?

No Churchy we are not, but that's where you saw us at that day when we were with Div A. Den, said the woman. We're his cousins.

Oh, that's right, now I remember where I saw you both. Div A. Den has told me so many great things about you two. What's your name again?

We're the Pharisees, the woman said.

That's right Mrs. Pharisees, it's all coming back.

Churchy, we run a financial firm called Love Mammon, said Mr. Pharisee. We both once worked in the city's finance department and then branched out to launch our own company, he said.

That's amazing you two, amazing, she replied.

Yes, Churchy it truly is a blessing, said Mrs. Pharisee.

Don't tell me that you two happen to now be allocating city funds to your account, questioned Churchy?

(They both laugh) Shhhh, don't say that so loud, Mrs. Pharisee replied. (They all laugh).

Churchy our hearts break for this city, he said. The employees in this city, as you might know, are barely getting salaries that extend above the low-income rate.

That's terrible, said Churchy.

Cleveland is the poorest big city in the nation unfortunately, he said. Therefore, with this new initiative and partnership we're about to unfold with the mayor, we'll provide lucrative venture capital opportunities for Cleveland residents to prosper.

Churchy, I see you're wrapping up the party, let us not keep you, said Mrs. Pharisee.

No ma'am, this is interesting.

No, seriously Churchy, we should go, she said.

Okay, you two are right, but before you go may I ask how did this vision evolve? Div A. Den spoke briefly to me about your company, and I just need to hear right now from the horse's mouth. You two, I'm just excited about the city.

Churchy, we get it, said Mrs. Pharisee.

So, one day Div A. Den and B. Guyler were burdened by God's lack of ability to increase wages for Cleveland residents, said Mr. Pharisee. All four of us knew crime is a direct symptom of poverty and this city is top rank when it comes to incarceration numbers, welfare, plus it's the murder capital of America currently, he said. After being saddened by this continual reality, we were motivated by B. Guyler to end the crisis.

Churchy, Div A. Den told us that you are passionate about ending this suffering as well and so we'll be in contact with you very soon, said Mrs. Pharisee. In our partnership, we see this initial focus as a pilot for the world at large.

Again, this is amazing you two. This vision is solid, said Churchy.

Us Pharisees don't play when it comes to judging things, and we are about tired of God's empty promises, said Mr. Pharisee.

Pharisees, I'm so in agreement with that, she replied.

We know God has tried to make change, but his methods are horrible, said Mr. Pharisee. We are just about tired of seeing you unfairly being pointed to as the blame for his ineffectiveness. You shouldn't be swooped up into this because you have a pure heart for the people. C'mon woman of God, you know how the struggle is. God's obvious shortage of integrity and unproductivity does not live up to what should be expected from him, he also said. God is a hypocrite if you ask me.

In pure amazement Churchy, the world is about to be caught by surprise by what we are about to unleash for them, said Mrs. Pharisee.

Well, Mr. and Mrs. Pharisee, I'm fully convinced that it is going to be life changing.

It is Churchy, said Mrs. Pharisee. B. Guyler and Div A. Den are doing some things that go beyond the norm and it's time for the crown to shift from God to Div A. Den. Now is it true Churchy? I heard some hot things about you and Div A. Den, hint hint.

Quit it Mrs. Pharisee and hush please (all three of them laugh). Mrs. Pharisee, he is sexy I must say though.

Churchy, be on the lookout because this rollout plan is about to be released. Things are going to be a pleasant shock to all, she said.

See, let me explain further. As this shift pivots the world away from that 'pie in the sky" approach that God provides, which does nothing for people, we will give people what they really need. No disrespect to God, but the former order in which he reigned in, will rapidly pass away and the new order is about to land any day now.

I look forward to it you two, said Churchy. Please send my regards to the mayor.

Will do Churchy, and thanks for the invite, you did such a loving surprise for God, she said. I don't know why you did it, but it truly reveals the grand character and love that you possess. He'll remember this act of love throughout eternity and beyond.

In a frantic manner a crew member of Ru swiftly approaches Churchy as she is talking to the Pharisees:

Hey Churchy, hey Churchy, I'm sorry to interrupt, said this crew member.

(Churchy turns around to face him) Yes, butler guy, where's Ru and what is it that you want?

Churchy please step over here.

Yes, butler guy, what is it?

Ru wants you to come now, it's an emergency happening in the back of the building, please come now.

Okay, I'm right behind you, take me to him.

Churchy turns back around and face the Pharisees.

Hey you two, I have to go but it was nice talking with you. Thank you for coming out tonight and I look forward to meeting up with you both soon, said Churchy.

Farewell, we look forward to meeting up too, said Mrs. Pharisee.

Churchy walks off with Ru's crew member. They swiftly pick up the pace and he directs her to the rear of the edifice.

God, God oh no what is... (Churchy arrives at the back of the edifice). Why is God laying here, asked Churchy? PLEASE CALL AN AMBULANCE NOW! (Churchy yells loudly)

RU! RU!

Yes Churchy.

Is God breathing, she asked?

I can't tell. Maid Laquita checked his pulse, but it's not moving. Should we move him, he asked?

Are you kidding me Ru? Why would you say something stupid like that! We don't want to do anything that will add further complications!

With tears falling from her eyes, Churchy gets down on the ground and speaks into God's ear.

My Lord, my Lord please wake up, please wake up, don't do this, don't do this, she said. NOOO DeVine, NOOO, (she yells, while she is loudly crying!)

Please go and get Churchy some tissue and her coat Laquita, it's chilly out here, said Ru.

Where exactly were you Ru, asked Churchy? I told you to keep watch over him.

I know you did, I practically watched him for…

Don't you, DON'T YOU PLAY WITH ME RU!

Churchy I've been pulled in all types of…

DO NOT GIVE ME ANY EXCUSE RU. I GAVE YOU STRICT ORDERS AND YOU DID NOT LISTEN.

I am so sorry, he said.

Sorry, can't change anything now. Please miss me with that bull Ru.

Loud sirens and flashing lights enter the parking lot of the edifice:

Thank the Lord, here is the ambulance pulling in, said Churchy. Ru, I will find out where they are taking him and go there. Head back up front and give the farewell to everyone leaving out.

Ok Churchy, I am heading there immediately.

Is anyone out here aware of what happened, asked Churchy? Are you aware butler guy?

No ma'am I am not fully aware of why he is lying here. When you sent me to get Ru, God was exiting from the restroom with this bag in his hand.

What bag?

The bag of Nu Wine and bakery items that B. Guyler and Div A. Den presented him with, he replied. I guess he was heading outside towards the dumpster. That's the only reason I can think as to why he was going out that door. Ru was in the hallway opposite the restroom, and he called out to me, as soon as I turned my back away from God to head towards Ru, I heard God collapse down the stairs of the back door.

Laquita, who happened to be coming from the dumpster saw God fall, ran to him, and immediately began checking his vitals.

How long has he been lying here, asked Churchy?

Not long, not long at all. Once Ru got a clear eye on him lying on the ground, he sent me to get you. It all took place in a couple of minutes from when Ru told me to get you.

A paramedic approaches.

Ma'am, ma'am, said the male paramedic.

My name is Churchy sir, approach me with dignity.

Sorry about that, my name is Enoch of Quicken Ambulatory, we will rush him to Mount Sinai Hospital. You may head there now to be with him.

Okay, I will Enoch.

Hey butler guy, go get my car now, said Churchy! (crew members of Ru are gathered around) Everyone, please pray for God because this incident is heart-shattering, and we need God, she said. I need my Love.

CHAPTER 2

"God is Dead"

(Between 12:25 pm and 12:50 pm, December 25th, 2003)

As I was brushing my teeth while looking for my laptop frantically, my vintage Supersonic boombox radio was playing Teddy Pendergrass' Love TKO softly. As the song began to fade, radio personality "Marie-Izzz-She," of local station 86.1FM started mentioning flattering remarks about DeVine Shepherd, better known as God. Enthusiastically, she acknowledged him for being kind and generous throughout the community. Annoyed and angered by those remarks, I rushed over to my nightstand, toothbrush in my mouth, and unplugged the cord abruptly.

My day was not starting well at all. Seems as if my hot water tank wasn't working properly due to the lukewarm shower experience. Also, I didn't realize that the toaster oven was turned to the highest level, so my bagel burnt. Plus, when I went to take the garbage outside, there was a leak coming from the bag. So, a stream of putrid liquid made a trail on the kitchen floor all the way down the hallway stairs until I made it to the outside can.

Despite it being my off day, I left out to head to my happy place, Judah Café to get a jump start on some work for an important upcoming meeting with my team. Although a proud and highly acclaimed investigative reporter for Channel 12 News, I should've taken advantage of my bereavement and combined vacation time. Since today was a difficult day, I tried to take my mind off my devastating reality. Six weeks ago, I experienced a crushing life-altering moment. Therefore, I used my current work project to attempt to redirect my mind from the deep pain. Before heading out to Judah Café I picked up the golden framed photo from the fireplace and kissed it. It was a pleasant memory of our trip to Niagara Falls. I greatly miss my wife, Destiny. Destiny unexpectedly died peacefully in her sleep just about a week before Thanksgiving. A heartbroken experience, and paralyzing anguish, this pleasant memory quickly shifted into nonstop tears as I stared at the picture. Recalling the day of her death, it so pained me to witness the funeral service staff transporting her body out of our home. Before heading out, I kissed the picture and gently laid it back down on the mantel over the fireplace.

Today's weather complemented my mood. Typical December weather in Cleveland, cloudy grey skies and blistering wind. The brisk temperature made me instantly put down my briefcase and zip up my Cleveland Cavaliers Coat. I exited my home and got into my charcoal-colored Buick Enclave SUV. Weakened and numb from my grief, I was unable to put the key in the ignition and pull off. Without hesitation, I broke out in tears, propped my head on the steering wheel, and wailed loudly. I was in disgust and disdain at the very thought of God being kind and generous per Marie-Izzz-Sher remarks.

Ever since the passing of Destiny, to me, God was a liar who did not care. Frankly, God became null and void to me. Overall, hatred toward God was an understatement. He was a byword to me. And, although we as a family were growing in relationship with him before Destiny's death, I no longer had any more desire to acknowledge, speak well of, or recommend anyone else to get to know Him. Many assumed that I remained in fellowship with Him. Yet, to avoid the "why not," "what happened," or "was it because of your wife's death," questions, I would change the topic. I couldn't stand it when someone said, "God's going to help comfort you in your sorrow." I resented God, but for professional reasons, I would hide my true feelings so that my employment would not be jeopardized. I managed to disclose my anger and remain professional when, or if, a case would need further details about Him. Not to mention, his lover Churchy, nor person affiliated with her altruistic work, nor God, reached out to me since the funeral to check on me. Therefore, I no longer returned to worship or serve the community with them, since the funeral. When reflecting on their behavior, that saying, "out of sight, out of mind," lived up to its meaning. I once heard those were common actions of "believers." Therefore, I was no exception to the rule of what I call, "membership forget-them-ness." Probably was a good thing though. I wasn't interested in hearing from "the believers" anyway. Heck, it saved me from the extra headache of rejecting their offering to remain coming to their gatherings. Kudos to their lovelessness, it was to be expected anyway. I've met a bunch of people who bear witness to those facts.

After this heavy cry, I was finally able to start the engine and get moving along with my day. A huge sports fan, I turned on the local sports station, to hear the "Ron & Juan Show." Again, my team, the Cleveland Browns took a loss this past Sunday, however our arch-enemy the Pittsburg Steelers did too. In a drunken stupor by halftime of the game, a concerned couple sitting next to me paid for me to take a cab home.

Listening to today's sports talk show calmed me as I headed to the café. A frequent caller named Art the Fart; gave a stupid comment which had me laughing. The dude was funny, and he is football illiterate. This mornings' exchange between Art the Fart and Juan was hilarious. As funny as it was, such remarks are actually common for a Pittsburg fan.

To get to Judah Café was a little over a 15-minute ride from where my wife and I had purchased our lovely eastside suburban home. Thus, I had a smooth ride in and even got a great parking spot when I arrived at the cafe. Entering through the front door, I looked towards the left corner of the café, and saw that my favorite seat, the one by the window of the café, was available. I loved this seat because it was where the picture of the evening skyline of Cleveland hung.

Jay, a physically fit, middle-aged Italian guy that always had his hair slicked back yelled out to me. Smitty, aye Smitty, don't order the entire cheesecake today! I'm sick of not getting a piece Smitty.

Whatever Jay, I hear ya.

Still flapping his jaws as always, Jay went on to say; I surely need a hefty slice because this is about to be a busy work week for all of us reporters! Anyway Smitty, you need to get your butt in the gym bud. It looks like you've put on 50 pounds since I saw you a week ago Smitty, sheesh man!

I agree Jay, but hey, I don't know which is worse, being overweight or being a starving reporter for Gossip Central. Jay, your journal firm is pitiful for all the cheesy content you guys have been releasing in the last year or so. All I can say is thumbs down Jay, thumbs down.

Save it, Smitty. Smitty, may I ask you something though?

Sure, Jay, I wonder what this "something" could be?

It is Smitty, I really want to know how many elephants you are eating nowadays bro?

As Jay was still running his mouth, Lady Liz, a longtime waitress, gently placed my usual cup of vanilla cappuccino on the table. One thing that I enjoyed about Judah Café was the décor and ambiance that gave me peace to do my work there. Normally, I arrive in the early morning and do my work. Therefore, I usually catch Jay on his way out the door at that time. Typically, my departure from the cafe is around noon or so. Yet, since I was off today, I had to stomach a longer conversation with him than normal.

Although located in downtown Cleveland, and typically busy around the noon hour, surprisingly, today was not packed. The wood-finished walls, parquet flooring, and picturesque glossed tabletop décor were awesome. On my favorite table it shows journalist-oriented images like newsletters, typewriters, magnifying glasses, ink containers, and feathered pins that were in sync with my profession. As a middle-aged black male, and a workaholic with high blood pressure, high cholesterol, and borderline diabetes, plus stricken with much grief, emotional eating was a constant form of self-medication for me. To no surprise, I was experiencing headaches and panic attacks on the regular. So, no doubt about it, my health was faltering rapidly. Although Jay never fails to get on my nerves, his remarks struck a chord today. Moreover, because of his remarks, I said to myself, *it's time I look for a therapist and begin working to cope healthily.*

As I waited on Lady Liz, my favorite server, I began removing my coat and sitting my briefcase on the chair to my right. Lady Liz was a retired African American nurse of 35 years. A sweet lady and a people person. One day she told me that what she enjoyed about working at Judah Café was serving people. She explained that it didn't feel like work to her. For Liz, working at the café paid for her self-care practices. Her café paycheck allowed her to do her regular thrift store shopping as well as keep spa days on her schedule. A fit woman of 58 years old, she also told me that working this job for the last five years kept her in shape. Liz knew my usual, the "BBLTT," (Browns bacon lovers tomato touchdown) so without asking, she went to put that order in for me.

As Liz walked off, my body went into one of those strong yawns with the simultaneous arms in the air stretch. After the stretch, I pulled my laptop out of my black leather briefcase. No sooner than I opened my laptop, and clicked on the Microsoft Edge browser, a big black bold headline covering the background of a Mount Sinai Hospital picture read, "GOD IS CURRENTLY UNRESPONSIVE AT MOUNT SINAI HOSPITAL!"

Now it clicked to me what Jay was referring to about this week's workload and busyness. I noticed in the lower details of the post that he had been in Mount Sinai Hospital since early this morning. I thought to myself, *"this is unreal, let me get to the hospital immediately!"*

Thus, I popped up from my seat and told Lady Liz, to pack my BBLTT asap.

Hurriedly, I gathered my briefcase, left the money and tip on the table, grabbed the brown bag from the front counter, jumped in my car, and sped off like a bat out of hell.

Located in the midtown area of the city, which is about a 10-minute drive through the city from downtown Cleveland, you could see my exhaust smoke literally covering the front entrance of Judah Café. As I was weaving through traffic, I turned to the local 840 AM news radio station and listened. This moment was quite surreal. Enroute to the hospital, the broadcaster sounded greatly saddened and monotone. This breaking news about God was shocking. This was a major and shocking situation. I was completely stunned. I'm thinking, *"Wow, what has happened to God?*

CHAPTER 3

"Mount Sinai Hospital"

(1:00 pm December 25th, 2003)

Within the walls of the hospital's emergency room, I would later learn that the ER medical team began to attempt an emergency operation when God was rushed in around 1:00 am. As told later by one source, once God was rushed in, the atmosphere became frantic, highly stressed, panicky, and nervous energy consumed the medical staff. Nurses and doctors were literally shaking. Maybe it was because of the magnitude of who the patient was? The gargantuan measure of the inability to save God would surely lead to a great investigation since the resident doctor's emergency surgery was unsuccessful. What's challenging is that it could have been a saddening realization from the emergency room medical staff that reviving God was impossible from the moment he was wheeled in by the paramedics. Later reports found it to be true. All emergency efforts to save God's life were unsuccessful. They failed to do the hopeful which was to revive him.

When I parked my car and jogged over to the east side of the hospital campus, where the emergency room was located. I heard noise from the people that were gathered outside. Many people were anxiously anticipating the doctor's update about God. I witnessed people ranging from the young to the old. Some were huddling in prayer circles. Some were pacing in circles crying with tears rolling down their eyes. Others were hugging and trying to console one another. The emotion was heavy and you could feel the sadness in the air. Local and national news cameras and reporters were spread throughout the perimeter of the scene. I had my notepad and recorder out, detailing the scene and asking gatherers their feelings about the shocking news. Honestly, as angry as I was at God, this sad atmosphere was difficult to experience. During this moment my ill will towards him kind of subsided and I focused on keeping my composure. This was sure to be a huge story even if God didn't die.

Greyish skies, brisk winds and cloudiness remained as it were earlier. Truly not surprising for a December forecast in Cleveland. Yet, in the past couple of years, December weather was unusually mild. Escalating though, I now saw snowflakes descending as I looked upward towards the sky. Yet, despite all these factors occurring, when the doctors came through the sliding exit doors of Mount Sinai Hospital and approached the news-press podium, their report was so anticipatory, you could practically hear a pin drop.

Hello, my name is Doctor Leroy Jackson. At 12:38 pm, on Monday, December 25th, 2006, DeVine Shepherd, better known as God, was pronounced dead. He will be transferred to the medical examiner's office for further examination. Currently, details are unknown of the cause of his death. Throughout the morning we attempted to perform several procedures to revive him. Yet, all measures of care did not produce the hope and desire we equally wanted. As a medical staff, all of us are heartbroken. God brought forth a magnitude of positivity in our world. With deep sincerity, his family, and his dear companion Ms. Churchy Selah are asking that cooler heads prevail so that his honor may be celebrated, and his legacy continues forth in an honorable way.

CHAPTER 4

"Assigned."

(From The Hospital to Home, December 25th, 2003)

Over the nineteen-plus years that I worked here at Channel 12, I, Deshaun Smith earned my way up the ladder to become a well-respected investigative news reporter. Many of my colleagues and viewers attested that I reported with integrity and avoided the appeal of notoriety in exchange for controversial hardline sketchy reports. In this line of work, up-and-coming reporters attempting to make a name for themselves can be tempted to release sketchy reports. Quite a lucrative industry to say the least since viewers and listeners religiously seek to know the "scoop." With that in mind, reporters go beyond quality reporting standards, in hopes to get the recipients of their story to "Drink the Kool-Aid." In contrast, my standard is to always put myself in the shoes of the families who would, in their grief, be daggered by the media reels swirling throughout. Media reels that promote lies. Public opinion is a monster. Due to lies that are purported, family and friends of those involved with the tragic outcomes become forced to defend themselves against family members, coworkers, classmates, neighbors, and close peers regularly.

My conviction from the moment I began as an investigative reporter, was that it was never worth selling my soul to tickle the ears of the public. I never sought to receive a bonus, career advancement, or an esteemed accolade. I never will do it for those purposes. I care about families and communities and our world needs truth and security.

Being that this case about God was significantly sensitive to me, because of my disdain for God, I was hoping that my manager would not select me for this case. But with that being said, it would be cool if I was the on to crack this case. I would bet my bottom dollar that God has blood on his hands and that his death was not by accident nor natural circumstances. I am confident of that. I'm confident it was behind something shady that he did. Shady has its name written all over it and shady loves to wear fishy perfume in which the smell can be detected from a mile away. No one knew of my ought with God. I did a great masking job to conceal my true feelings towards him and with the hot-button case that my team and I were working to break soon, I felt my editor/producer would not seek to suggest I hop on this case.

Post the pronouncement of God's Death:

No sooner than Doctor Jackson could finish his final word, many media outlets both local, national, as well as world news reporters were covering the scene. You can see reporters speaking to cameras and conducting interviews with gatherers who remained on the campus of the hospital. This, by far is the most famous death in human history. From here on out, I expect nothing less than a flurry of wide-ranging reports flooding the news. The world is going to be constantly inundated with reports associated with God. Biographical documentaries on his life, people who were close to him being interviewed, controversial reports from anybody's mama to attempt to uncover skeptical actions of him. You're talking a big money grab for ratings, career stardom for up-and-coming reporters and writers, and media acknowledgements from businesses to keep his name buzzing and gain greater attention to their products.

I was already working on a hot-button cold case that was gaining traction with the Akron Police's homicide unit. New forensic evidence was discovered which is why I was preparing my briefing on my off day so that my journal team could position to break this story. Anytime a passion murder goes cold and then later resurfaces, it becomes a heralded day for any investigative reporting staff. Success in cracking a number of these types of cases is how me and Channel 12 News got put on the map as a powerhouse investigative reporting station.

After shaking hands with fellow news anchors and friends, and grabbing a couple of audio recorded interviews, Deshaun hops in his truck to head home.

Dug, whoever the heck is texting me nonstop is going berserk. Jay this bet not be you. Let me pull over and see who the heck this is. "Oh geez, Holy Bologna I am not ready for this piss" Alrighty then, all cap letters...

Whenever I receive text messages with all caps, I know without a shadow of a doubt that it's my boss and that I am being assigned to a case. So, before I could even reply, John Davis, my editor/producer, in all caps typed,

SMITTY THIS IS NON-NEGOTIABLE. YOU ARE ASSIGNED TO THIS CASE! SMITTY, I KNOW YOU WERE DOWN THERE AT THE HOSPITAL; I KNOW YOU PULLED THAT NOTEPAD AND RECORDER OUT, AND THERE IS NONE OTHER FROM CHANNEL 12 NEWS THAT WOULD BE BEST FIT FOR A REPORT OF THIS MAGNITUDE!

Continuing, but without more caps, John encouraged:

You know your work always ran laps around locals like Gallic and Monday. As well as the national reporting hall of famers and future ones from Walters, Chung, Sawyer, Jennings, Brokaw, and Rather. You did excellent when uncovering President Bush's Iraq war announcement, the unfortunate malfunctions that led to space shuttle Columbia exploding, as well as the documentaries of the 7 brave astronauts on that shuttle. Smitty, you touched the world with that report. The phenomenon of the East coast Blackout and all the work you did reporting on our radio affiliate 840 FM. Our city was also affected by it too, yet you brought notices and updates during the moment it was happening, and people felt supported. Smitty, you are the only one I see reporting on the death of God. So Smitty, get on this case immediately! Begin interviewing, digging, and compiling the facts of the soon-to-be-released police reports. Smitty, thank me later.

My reply text: Okay John, I'll get on it.

In a unique sense, as obsolete as I wanted the name God never heard again through my eardrums, today's shocking news of his death did veer my grief and pain from the low place I was in. I do not know if in my subconscious I was gloating over the death of God, but his death began to feel as if the end of his life was a movement toward closure for my pain.

I ended up arriving home from the hospital scenery at around 3:30 pm. For one who has expanded his investigative reporting, it is more than just science for nailing facts, but for me, it is an art as well. To draw the puzzle of God's death, like a seasoned artist, my eyes would be focused closely on the finessed reporting from other journalists in the days and weeks ahead. I sometimes found it beneficial to preview this finessing from other reports before I dove into my report. I do this to get an outlook on how God would be colored. Which reporter would shoot for painting him with an assortment of boundless highlights, in other words, God's accolades and public impact. Some who reported this way also complemented it with a dark outline to make the negative facts pop and easy to depict. I believe this style enabled them to stretch their story out and gain more long-term attention to their reporting. Now that strategy from a business point of view kept the viewer seeking to hear about the report more. This strategy keeps the viewer on edge and tunning in regularly. From a storyline tactic style, I likened it to having a sweet and sour piece of candy. You buy it because it's candy, but you feel the cringing effects of the sour flavor, which shocks and sticks with you every time you eat a piece. I'm a student of the game and so I ear hustle and watch closely to see if I see something substantial for me to dig deeper into as I build my case.

I do not know why, although my stomach was touching my back, what Jay said earlier at the café resonated with me. Realizing that I left my sandwich in the car and knowing that the tomato would soggy up the bread, I ended up throwing my BLT away. With strong hunger pains still in effect, I got back into my SUV and drove to the nearest grocery store that was enroute to my home. The grocery store in mind was located on Damascus Street. Uniquely, it was located near Churchy

Selah's elaborate home. DeVine Shepherd really loved Churchy, and she appeared good to the public.

This was the neighborhood I grew up in. An impoverished, high-crime, drug-infested area. Driving through it now, again produced heartbrokenness because still to this day, nothing has changed. I would say the biggest reason I intentionally avoided this area, unless working on a case, was not because of the continual degradation of this area, but because of the obvious spirit of hypocrisy. This reality made me bitter because Ms. Selah paraded her love for God. Frankly, this parade was sickening to my stomach. Churchy was so fake when it came to serving the neighborhood. The expectation from neighbors was that Churchy would represent God's mission and presence here. Yet, she was rarely seen with her sleeves rolled up. Unless it was an opportunity to pose before cameras and take photo ops to provide empty promises regularly. Although I had relatives and friends in the area, when my wife died, I made it clear to family and friends how they were to meet me elsewhere or at my home if we were to spend time with each other. Although they agreed with these arrangements, none of them knew what I was harboring, because again, I masked my disgust about God from all.

As I browsed the grocery store, I had trouble figuring out what I should feast on tonight. My habitual action to eat poor food was an ingrained norm. Making it more tempting to begin this journey of changing my eating lifestyle was what that light-skinned sister had piled in her shopping cart as she passed me. I'm up here grabbing some tomatoes and she is sliding past me with Edy's cookie dough ice cream, a family-size bag of Doritos, a 12-pack of coca cola, Fruity Peebles cereal, and a Lemon Pound Cake. My growling stomach was salivating over those items I just witnessed. I do not know how, but in a laser five-second scan of her cart, I stored a gorilla glue/plastered picture of all those items in my brain. Why did I do that? But allowing myself to be challenged and warned by the voice of Jay, which never fails to be loud and annoying, did lead me to grab a ton of veggies and fruit. Motivated, I was able to grab a variety of items to enjoy what I call a "boss salad."

Once I arrived home and got comfortable, I switched on the television and started crafting this masterpiece of a salad. Those who know me, understand that whenever I did make a salad, a "boss salad" I might add, came alive because of the wealthy amount of fixings I would dress it up with. After smashing my boss salad, I instantly got in bed and fell right asleep. What a rollercoaster of an emotional day.

CHAPTER 5

"Deacon Twan"

(December 26th, 2003)

After watching various news reports about God's death and scribbling notes till the early morning, I happened to wake up energized today. Sunny this morning, it felt good to see a slight change in the weather. The sun's rays bled through the white and gold-outlined curtains of my bedroom window. Destiny had such an eye for elegance. Our cherry wood dressers, cream-colored lamps, nature-themed pictures, extravagant mirrors, and handmade Brazilian rug made the room warm, romantic, and cozy.

Yesterday was such an emotional rollercoaster. Going from utter sadness to complete shock, was so polar. Today my goal was to level out from the experience. Tough to put my finger on how I was energized this morning, so I pondered a few reasons for what it could be. I started thinking it may have something to do with subconscious satisfaction. Like a personal justification that God was dead. As the reporter of 840 AM was talking about yesterday's surprising news about God's death, resentment was void in my heart. Catch me about six weeks ago and I would've been celebrating that he was dead. Untethered now, I soaked up any information about his death that made sense. So focused and in tune, it was beginning to feel like I had bionic senses. Most are surprised that this is one of my tactical approaches to journalism but who cares. My journalism philosophy has always been basic—whatever works, work it. Although God was someone that I had no care in the world for, my career calling, superseded my overall disgust for him. Because of the magnitude of this case, the workaholic in me and from the pressure my boss gives off, I immediately ended my bereavement/vacation to begin working on the case.

As normal, I headed to my place of peace, Judah Café to start building my case. As I entered the door, I was greeted by another waitress named Wanda. She had a powerful redemptive story about her life. She overcame a 35-year addiction to crack cocaine which at one point in her life landed her prison time and separation from her three sons. Out of all her self-imposed trouble, she obtained her GED and eventually got married. Each of her sons obtained higher education degrees and is doing well for themselves. Wanda was about five years older than me and was celebrating her 50th birthday in a few weeks. She loved small talking about hot button reports with me and giving brief takes on her choice for the "whodunit" award. As she led me to my favorite seat, she shook her head and lowly whispered.

Smitty, you got your hands full with this one.

Wanda, this is a big deal. You are right, I surely got my hands full with this one.

You surely do Deshaun, but you'll do fine as always. Well, I already told Lady Liz to get your cappuccino ready as I saw you approaching the door. Therefore, get comfortable Smitty, it'll be right up shortly.

Judah Café was so my speed when it came to producing critical thinking and pinpoint research of crimes. Being a city landmark with good food and even greater service, the variety of things like low lighting and cleanliness never failed to ignite my investigative juices.

Hmm, that looks like that's Deacon Twan walking in the door. That's my guy. I have to go holler at him.

Deacon Twan happened to be one of the few "believers" that I enjoyed fellowship with. He was a laid-back guy, late 60's, onyx skin complexion, bald head, and one who you'd never catch wearing tennis shoes because he always dressed sharp. He kept his slacks cuffed, and no doubt, Deacon Twan had every color of Stacey Adams shoes to match any color outfit he would wear. Deacon Twan's bass voice pitch could be likened to the voice pitch of Michael Sean McCary from the R&B group Boyz ll Men. He was the type of old' school guy that kept a toothpick hanging out of his mouth as he talked. Long white goatee with the gold crown on a single tooth located on the right side of the top row of his teeth. In shape and stocky build, Deacon Twan was the coolest.

Ever since Destiny's death, there's been times when I've spotted a "believer" from a distance, like when I'm out at the mall or gas station. In those instances, I either went another way or waited until they left to pump my gas. Yet, Deacon Twan is my guy and I have to say something to him.

Near the front counter by the entrance of the café.

Hey Deacon Twan, it's me Deshaun Smith, how are you doing today?

Hey Deshaun, long time no see sir. I'm quite sad and in shock, ya man Deacon Twan is not doing too well. Deshaun did you hear about God's passing?

Yes, I did and like many, I'm utterly shocked. I can only imagine how you feel. The entire world is in pain. The news about his death is all over the news stations, Deac.

I know Deshaun, tell me about it.

It's so good to see you Deshaun.

Aww, thanks Deacon Twan.

I expect you to do well on this case, Deshaun. Young man, it really looks like some type of foul play happened to God. You know that Div A. Den and God's brother B. Guyler had competing views against God.

I agree, you are so right about that, so right, said Deshaun.

Yeah young blood. Although I'd see them around Churchy's edifice, to me, something didn't smell right between her and Div A. Den. I just never trusted them dudes, you know what I'm saying, said Deacon Twan.

I do Deacon Twan, I do.

It's funny he says this, I feel the same way about God, I couldn't trust him.

Deshaun, ya boy Deacon Twan has been around the world and back and I know when two people are digging each other out.

Experience is wisdom, said Deshaun. But Deacon, tell me something, what do you mean by "two people digging each other?"

C'mon Deshaun, you didn't know sir?

Naw Deac, I don't, I've been out the loop for a while now.

Well, there you have it. That mess will be a good place to start when you dig into the details concerning this case, he said.

Yeah but Deacon Twan, I know that B. Guyler is one who walks in total control and persuasion. So, do you think he'd really approve of his business partner Div A. Den getting with his brother's companion like that? The reason I ask is that I'm sort of confident that B. Guyler would have not wanted to further stain the strain of his relationship with his brother God?

Deshaun, let me help you to understand something young man. Deshaun, revenge is a dish best served cold. If you ever want to hurt another man, get with his woman and you will break him into pieces.

Ouch Deacon Twan, that is a cutthroat move on B. Guyler and Div A. Den's part.

Yeah, I know, but remember it takes two to tango.

Hold up one second Deshaun, Lady Liz is saying something. Yes Lady Liz. I missed that Liz, can you repeat it again?

Yes Deacon Twan, I was saying that I put extra salt and vinegar in your bag per your request.

Thanks Lady Liz, I really appreciate your quality service because you always make sure I'm together.

You know I got you, I'm Lady Liz and you know what it is (she laughs).

Deshaun, I'm about to head out. I have so much on my plate right now. I have to start making calls to get the funeral arrangements going and I want a moment to enjoy this BBLT sir.

Hey Deacon Twan.

Yes, young blood.

How much was God's life insurance policy?

I'm not sure. At this point I am unaware, but I can already see you in "motive sniffing mode."

You bet I am, he replied.

Deshaun, please get to the bottom of this because this reality hurts and it's a hole growing inside my heart every moment. I think about the fact that God will no longer be with us. Do the job well young man. I haven't seen you in a moment and I know you are probably still experiencing deep pain at the loss of your wife. I know you got to still be hurting my friend.

I am Deacon Twan, I am.

Deac, I appreciate you and thanks for the encouragement about this case.

Yes indeed and know that I am praying for you and if you need me for anything, your boy Deacon Twan got you!

Check on Churchy Deshaun or better yet, look in on Churchy if you get what I am saying…

Deacon Twan leaves. Deshaun goes and takes his favorite seat and begin to think things over:

Interesting that Deacon Twan would say that. From the day I first met Churchy, it was easy to understand that she was all about pomp and circumstance. Churchy was very easy on the eyes. A light-skinned, voluptuous built, black woman with green eyes. She favored the actress LisaRaye. Churchy is surely one who turns heads when she enters a room. I mean she is stunning. About 25 years old, sassy, witty, and intelligent. Destiny didn't really care too much for her though. Destiny was one who parents raised her to enjoy fashion but remain professional and dignified because of her noble occupation as a teacher. She simply thought that Churchy was too attention seeking by the way she dressed. Destiny felt that Churchy was always too loud in public gatherings, and could be snobby, anal and arrogant most times. Churchy was a successful woman who had went through some character challenges in her past, but her atypical personality and creative mind attracted onlookers to become followers of her and God's vision for the world. When it came to putting on a huge showcase, she never slacked in any area. You always knew when Churchy was in the room. Churchy valued the outer appearance of herself and all things she was associated with. She so valued things that if there was something out of place or seen as not admirable, that person, place, or thing was ex'd quickly. Yet, Churchy was also a masterful schemer. She has a gift of gab that is manipulating, eloquent, and magnetizing. Churchy is one who can draw and command the attention of others through her speech and well-put together outward appearance.

I remember awhile back when me and Deacon Twan was chatting, he said he never will forget when she was providing a Thanksgiving outreach meal for the homeless. Deacon Twan went on to say that when this volunteer arrived without wearing his ministry t-shirt, he was dismissed from the event. She then sat this person down from his other duties in the ministry such as the parking lot ministry and the cleaning ministry. Her reasoning was that if the local news station would've interviewed the gentleman during the thanksgiving event, he would've embarrassed God and the fellowship because no one would've seen that she, referring to Churchy, was decent and in order.

Learning that this event was coming up, I heard that she'd be pulling out the whole shebang, Deacon Twan said. In that, I can only imagine the fear of those who were serving at the party, he also stated. It's things such as this that gave me a bad impression of God, as I reflect on what Deacon Twan told me about Churchy. If God was so humble, how could he be in love with someone who's so flamboyant and prideful? It just doesn't make sense to me. There's no way to consider it logical that God would be obsolete of having none of those similar character traits. Traits equal or even worse than what he told me about Churchy. Yes, God is a smart dude, but I am no fool by a far stretch. Thus, I was furthermore convinced that God was also caught up in a show-and-tell presentation. A flaunting, a lifestyle of the rich and famous, a big baller shot caller, and a bougie show-off way of doing life.

Heralded for being sacrificial, loving and forgiving, (at least that's all the jargon that is being reported about him thus far, and I'm about to throw up if I keep hearing it) it is tripped out to know that God would be lifting toasts and breaking bread with folk that really don't care for him. Jay and Gossip Central are already pounding out the headline reels with as much controversial stuff as there is possible. Their headlines don't shock me. The fact that those who oppose God, Div A. Den and B. Guyler would in the first place attend the party, and then provide God with quality heartfelt gifts like his favorite deserts and wine. Such gestures as these, alone raise eyebrows to me. The Father's memoir states how "love covers a multitude

42

of sins." Respectfully, I once accepted this but was extremely far from accepting that to be a true reality after Destiny died. He didn't love my Destiny. Churchy and those under her ministry didn't care. Heck, if they would've found it necessary to invite me to this celebration, the only thing I would come out of my pocket to pay was to pay God no attention and give 2 cents about the matter.

What stuck out to me about Gossip Central's report was how God was very overjoyed with the acts of kindness and gifts from his brother B. Guyler. As well as the gifts from Div A. Den, his arch enemy. Jay from Gossip Central caught a quick interview with a partygoer who attended God's born day celebration. The partygoer told Jay that you could feel all in the air, the "phony-ness" of B. Guyler's and Div A. Den's presentation. Jay reported that those he interviewed that night stated that Churchy, although overly self-exalted from the grand extravaganza, did quite superb in surprising God. Oddly though, towards the winding down of the party, Churchy was not seen with God, said a few people that Jay interviewed. Nobody knew where God had gone, but what was blatantly noticeable was this exchange between her and Div A. Den that seemed to be more than just a hi and bye. Those who Jay interviewed said it crossed the line.

After watching and hearing all of these headlines, I must be fair with this thing though. Churchy has always been under a lot of scrutiny. Scrutiny is such a heavy load on those who are in relationships with high-profile people. Honestly though, I can admit that there's no other relationship that can be greater scrutinized than an intimate relationship with God. With God, one who's in an intimate relationship with him must be seen as nearly perfect, it just comes with the territory. Many want the limelight until the heat from it beams nonstop. Surely, Churchy has that desire to want such *attention, however, I'm not convinced that God has the "stud-ness" per se to appease her public wish for attention.*

On the other hand, there's Div A. Den. Div A. Den is, has, and possesses the resources that will forever exist as long as the earth remains. The money alone that Div A. Den gives makes the dreams of everyone's desires become a reality. You only want more and more and more of the money that Div A. Den provides. That resource provides an unending lavishing of excess in whatever area you seek excess in. His money and resources buy you friends, power, and love. Div A. Den's money and resources will buy you any and everything. Top it off with the influence and notoriety that his business partner B. Guyler gives freely to everyone, the drug that fame and fortune gives provides an unmatched pleasurable high. And, if those are things you lustfully want, well, God is not the answer for obtaining such provision. So, when Deacon Twan shared with me about the interaction he saw between Churchy and Div A. Den, my eyebrows raised because of the controversial things surrounding Div A. Den's life, and the chase for notoriety Churchy desires.

The biggest leak that ABC said sources reported was the whispering by Div A. Den inside Churchy's ear. A whisper, kiss on the cheek, and hug that was way too sensual. ABC's report exclaimed it was so freaky that it's easy to comprehend that they did not want to let go of one another. Div A. Den was quite brut, and aggressive to the point that he wanted people to know and to see their interaction. A source interviewed by ABC, said that God was not to be found and the last time he was spotted was like 15 minutes prior to Div A. Den and Churchy openly cutting up like this. Per source, the last time God was seen was during B. Guyler's toast presentation. God had drunk a couple of glasses of the wine, ate a few of the sweets that Div A. Den gifted him, hit the dance floor, and then disappeared. ABC's source said it looked like God was really enjoying himself. The source said that the party had ended soon after. So, this source thought it was strange that God wasn't there to greet people as they exited the party. I just think that God not greeting people as they headed out was interesting…

As the days moved ahead, I upped my attendance frequency at Judah Café especially as I awaited the public record releases and police pressors.

CHAPTER 6

"Unworthy"

(October 30th, 2002)

Currently happening at the Narrow Path Smash Spot.

Shep, you know I've been knowing you for a long time. Everyone knows you by your surname, but we were neighbors growing up and to this day we remain close, said Wiz.

God reflecting to himself about Wiz.

Wiz is one who I greatly adore. She and I grew up together in the Oasis. The Oasis community named her Wiz which is short for Wisdom. Wisdom Charity is one who is simply down to earth. She per se "knows it all" and my Father felt it necessary for her to be on earth so that she could guide people in ways in which they'd maximize their earthly experience via the guidance of his memoir. Extremely smart, those from the Oasis that was affiliated with B. Guyler tagged her as one that seemed abrasive, but she is just wise in all areas. She is a short caramel complexion woman. She has had a dreadlock hairstyle like forever and her hair color is grey. Like myself, Wisdom enjoys a variety of things such as food, sports, music, dancing, traveling, and serving people. She has worked in the profession as a teacher for many years. She loves youth. Wiz is a definite extrovert, very outspoken, and one who has always been overprotective of me. She's the type of person who sincerely has your back and has always been generous.

It's Wednesday evening, God and Wiz are at their favorite place they like to link up and talk, eat, and enjoy some entertainment. A colleague of Wiz told her that a jazz band named "David's Harp" is playing and that they're a must-see.

Shep, please put the phone down. You know the drill; we go off the grid on Wednesday evenings to enjoy a mental break from the hustle and bustle of our busy lives.

Okay Wiz you're right. Now what were you saying, he asked?

Shep, you know I've been knowing you for a long time.

Indeed, you have. You my girl and one who I know will be down with me to the end and through thick and thin. Wiz, you my ride or die.

Oh, ok Shep so now you got barz?

Wiz is my girl. She always got jokes, she's cool like that, and her dry humor always invites people in, whenever she gives people guidance. Being that my Father is the most powerful person in the universe, as his son, I take on much pressure. I don't know how I'd handle it all without Wiz.

Whatever ma'am, and yes, my rap game been dope and you are just a hater. My proverbs be on rewind out here. Check my Father's memoir and get with it, ma'am.

Whatever Shep (She laughs). I'm glad you be giving me shoutouts throughout your "proverbs album," but you still can't rap. Anyway, Shep I was saying…

Ok Wiz you got me anxious about what you are about to say since you got all deep with your opening statement "you know I've been knowing you a long time."

Shep, you are too all-knowing for your own good. Your sis is just trying to shoot you something to think about.

Okay now, here you go again getting all deep, he said.

But naw dude, in all seriousness you're one I have depended on to be a voice of reason and a guide to my feet, she said.

Wiz, I know where you are headed with this conversation. You threw a bug out in that text last week. Hold up, Wiz.

Excuse me Shanae, he said.

Yes sir, how may I help you?

May we get some extra napkins?

Sure, how do you like that fish, she asked?

It's the bomb, Shanae.

Aye, didn't I tell you so. I told you I know what I'm talking bout.

Yes, indeed you do and I'm glad about it, he said.

How are those loaded nachos Wiz, asked Shep?

Delicious, you already know it's my fave.

The Narrow Path Smash Spot always comes through, said Shep.

Yes indeed it does, and that's why I always suggest people to go this route because they'll never be disappointed, she said.

Is it me Shep, or is it blistery in here? I should've followed my first mind and grabbed my coat.

I'm good, the temperature is just fine with me, he replied. Do you want me to go grab your coat out the car for you though?

Naw, I'll be alright. So again Shep, why you…

Aww here we go Wiz I will…

No Shep don't interrupt me, you won't be. I'm always worried about you dude because you are overly generous.

It's all good, I will be okay, he said.

Yeah, but Shep…

But nothing Wiz, all I know is blessing people. I would not be able to live with myself knowing that I could support someone but didn't.

Yeah I hear you, but why her though?

Shhh, Wiz. You are screaming loud (Shep laughs).

I know my dude, but the band is rocking out, and it's loud as ever in here, she said.

Yeah, they gettin' it in on that Motown Wiz.

But any who, you got me on one when it comes to her Shep. You know I don't play about my peeps.

Yeah I know, but you are too overprotective though. I'm a big boy and can handle my own.

I'm not letting you off the hook with this. Therefore, before we dip out of here, it'll be dessert on me, said Wiz.

Thanks my girl, you the realest, he said.

Excuse me Shanae, said Wiz.

Yes, can I get you anything?

Yup, we'd like dessert, she said.

Sure, what are you having ma'am?

I'll take that strawberry cheesecake Shanae.

Awesome, good choice. And you sir? But before you answer sir, are you DeVine Shepherd?

Yes, I am.

I figured that was you. DeVine your Father is amazing, she said.

DeVine, my son attended one of your outreach events in the past and it really did something powerful to him from that point onward. I was having a tough time with him. Sir, you know how teens are. I almost lost my mind trying to get him on the right track. I know we've all been teens before, but I never thought he'd be sneaking to the point of smoking weed and cutting class under my nose. DeVine, I believe that since the day he lost his Father, which was a year prior to attending your event, it took him down that rebellious path. My son was hurting from the loss of his Dad. But now he is a college graduate and is excelling in his career. He often encourages me to say prayers and read your Father's memoir. I do sometimes but I just can't seem to be consistent.

It's a blessing to hear about your Son, Shanae. It's my Father that all the glory goes to. As a community, we must be here for one another and I'm grateful to hear the testimony of your faith. You saw it necessary to get him to the event Shanae. That shows a lot of endurance and faith by you, he said.

It's my child Mr. Shepherd, it was a difficult time in my life but the work that you do truly did help me get through such a rough patch. Trey had just lost his father. I was in depression from the pressure of being a single mother and raising an African American male in the inner city. I didn't have much income coming in. Mr. Shepherd it was tough. I really thank you. I thank you for what you did.

It's okay, it is okay Shanae. Wiz, hand me one of those napkins, please. Is it okay that I hug you Shanae?

Yes, please do so Mr. Shepherd.

So, Shanae tell me, how have you been doing lately, asked Shep? I've been okay but I feel like my purpose is greater than what I'm currently doing in life. I have a passion for single mothers raising children in the inner city. Mr. Shepherd, I know the struggle, but I don't know where I can begin walking out my purpose.

You know, the world we live in is difficult, but it's passionate people like yourself who feel the weightiness of serving others, he said. Shanae, it's a heavy burden that is laid on the hearts of those with a spirit of sacrifice. If it's okay with you, I'd like to get you linked with someone who's very special to me, he said. Her name is Churchy Selah. She would be good in helping you with your spiritual journey which will lead you towards ways of how you could carry out your purpose. Do you think that'll work for you?

It certainly will, she said. I thank you so much for what you did for my child.

The Father is good, Shanae, thank you for acknowledging his goodness.

I'd be remised if I didn't Mr. Shepherd.

Okay Wiz, what were you about to say, asked Shep?

Wiz is staring at me hard with her eyebrows scrunched and her hands folded. She always looks at me this way when she is ready to say something deep.

Shep, do you not know the preying lion that this woman is, Wiz asked?

C'mon Wiz I...

No Shep! Destiny Smith aggressively and unashamedly destroys anyone who'd dare pushback at the way she treats her staff and students. Shep, you need to wakeup sir. I've seen this lady spitefully flunk kids because of those kids' parents raising an issue with her about various challenges she's posed in our school.

Wow Wiz, that steak over there that that brother just got brought to him looks tantalizing. Wiz, look real quick look.

Oh yeah, you are right but stop trying to change the subject, Now answer me Shep. Why Shep, why? Why do you think it is necessary to link with her?

Wiz, I wish I knew. The memoir speaks of things that describe me in ways that I'm humbled to know. You know Wiz, I'm learning more about myself through the memoir. For instance, while yet people are in their worst form, I seek to take on their challenges in order to help them not suffer. I get why you could feel that way about Destiny, Wiz, but...

Shep I don't think so, you really don't know her like that.

Wiz, people who got things going good for themselves—like their character and willing soul to follow the ways of my Father, aren't the only people that should have my fellowship.

No Shep I disagree, and I don't want to hear it. Miss me with that bull sir. It's people who do right by others, they are the ones who are worthy, not mean-spirited and shady people like Destiny Smith.

Wiz, listen to me.

No Shep, I have more to say! Shep, they are not alright, she said.

What do you mean by that, he asked?

Look around in this place right now, she said. Look around. Their family's well-being is enroute to being shattered if you are not able to help them. These are the ones who would most need your help. So many in this world have worked hard to keep the honor of their bodies, and live respectable lives yet their bodies are racked with excruciating pain, she said. What I'm getting at is… It's these ones that could be made better by your fellowship and leadership. They are the ones who would truly appreciate it sir.

Wiz, you don't know any of these people from a can of paint. The memoir talks about how the heart is deceitfully wicked and yet you act like you know the hearts of men, said Shep.

Ok, whatever Shep. But listen, I'm just saying that you and those who serve the community with you, should save yourself from people like Destiny. See, these who are gathered here at this restaurant are the ones who deserve your fellowship and not Destiny. Destiny doesn't appreciate a thing. She'd just use it to glorify herself sir. So, I just want to know something.

What Wiz, know what?

I want to know, did your previous acts of generosity warp your entire way of thinking? Are you naïve dude? People will still die even if you go to their aide. You are endangering yourself and your reputation to accomplish something with this one person, Destiny, who I believe, after receiving fellowship, will be even more arrogant and conceited than she already is, said Wiz.

Wiz, I believe she will maximize the situation once we link. I believe she has a good heart.

Not at all, Shep, her heart is wicked. I'm not feeling you on this one, she said.

Wiz, I'm not sure why you are so stressed that things will turn out so negatively. I think this effort will revitalize Destiny and it will make me feel good that I did it.

Yeah whatever. I can't imagine the type of monster she'd be once she receives it. Friend, all I'm saying is watch your back dude.

Don't worry, it will be all good. What I want you to understand is this principle here: It is not those who don't need help that I focus my effort on. It is those who need the most help possible, he said. I understand the course of struggle that will culminate for the families of so many that will suffer without what I and Destiny can do. Think about it.

About what, Shep? Think about what, sir?

About this, sis. There have been various efforts and forms of impact from connections that have blessed your life. As a matter of fact, not just yours, but many in this world. Those involved in those efforts weren't perfect, yet because of their willingness to try to do something together with you, many benefited from it, ma'am. That's why I decrease so that my Father may increase.

Yeah, but, the memoir says what fellowship does darkness have with light, replied Wiz.

Yeah Wiz, but…

But nothing Shep, but nothing!

No Wiz, you are not thinking straight in no type of form or fashion. See ma'am, my Father so loved the world that he gives me as his best so that others may live forever.

I can't tell Wiz's body language now. Sometimes when she sits back and folds her arms, she starts coming into agreement. However, at other times when she looks like this, it means she has tuned me out.

Wiz, unity in things that are the Father's will is power and the power of love is unending. So let me say this to you. You can't proclaim to love someone and not be willing to make sacrifices for them, Wiz.

Oh, so you "judgey" now Shep? Really? You trying to go there like that dude, Wiz asked?

Chill, sis. You a little extreme with it now. I'm simply trying to say that it's not right to hold back something that will impact future generations from now.

Yeah Shep, I get all of that, but why risk it with Destiny? She is completely selfish and will take all the credit.

Naw not true. If me and Destiny's effort together is a success, it will become life-changing, he replied. The reason I believe in linking with

Destiny, is similar to the extent that you do for your worst-behaving students, sis. See, you know the seriousness of the outcome if you just let it be, he said.

What do you mean by "let it be," asked Wiz?

What I mean is this: You've felt at fault by feeling and asking yourself what you could have done better when you see or hear about any of your students getting in trouble. Bad news like that, pains you to the core. It pains you because you care. You would not have received a unique name such as Wisdom Charity if your parents didn't believe you'd walk in wise ways. See, the students who are performing well, don't cloud the space of your mind and emotions, like the ones who are in trouble. So why would you go above and beyond to help those troubled students of yours, Wiz? Oh, let me guess why. Because you know they are going to do well if you go the extra mile to help them, sis. The course of their life will flow well because, by you going the extra mile to help them, eventually they get it. See, for the challenged students, you know the power and potential excellence that they can possess because of the extra support you carry out to provide them. You have receipts from those previous efforts. You have a proven record my girl. You were and continue to be willing to join in the cause, even when other teachers don't think it's worth trying to do so. If the effort failed, you could've jeopardized your own performance standards that are expected of you to meet. But guess what sis?

What bro?

You have never been stuck on measuring your performance standards. You know how systems can pad things. What matters most to you, is that students are given the time and support that they need to succeed.

You are willing to face the music so that all of your students have the opportunity to excel. I don't have to say it. Sis, you know that that effort, when achieved according to those measurable standards, will bring better resources. Yet, if you never had one extra resource, you'd take it on your shoulders to figure it out and get whatever your students need to make it in this world. You pride your passion in serving students who are from the roughest neighborhoods. The ones that lack support—both emotional and financial. Sis, you are a teacher who is not steered by achieving quotas and all that type of stuff. You are one who feels that it's worth losing it all—all the accolades and wage increases, for just one student's academic success. So why am I passionate about connecting with Destiny?

Shep, I'm surely trying to understand why, she replied.

Well, it's because I liken my effort for Destiny to the effort you have for the worst of your students. Like you, I believe I will get to see that "Kool-Aid smile" that you see every time you give me an update about how they turned out. Am I correct when I say, those types of results are priceless for you, Wiz? Priceless in the effect that the largest form of salary could never take the place of how those results make you feel, said Shep.

You are totally correct. No dollar amount or public accolade could ever compare to me feeling what I feel when a troubled student of mines flourishes.

Sis, you know that I know you know you, he said.

Shep you do.

Yeah so stop playing with me sis, I always know what I'm talking about, no cap.

Shep, I say all of that but…(they both smile and chuckle)

Shep hands Wiz a napkin off the table to wipe her eyes.

To you it's priceless because of how they were once a thorn in your side but, because of your sacrifice, they now experience prosperity, he said. For you sis, it's the trouble students who are role models and substantial community figures. Even the most annoying of class clowns that you've had are now walking in your footsteps and have become educators. Destiny Smith for me, is a prime candidate for that comparable type of result, he said. So Wiz…

What Shep.

Why did Chevrolet let you purchase that brand new car from them when your credit history is trifling, he asked?

What? Here you go again, Shep. Now you coming for me and all I'm trying to do is look out for you bruh.

Huh, Wiz, what did you say? I couldn't hear that, he said.

The sound in the room is loud. The band is rocking out and the people in the room are clapping and shouting.

Shep, I said…

Huh Wiz. What did you…

SHEP I SAID.

Oh Okay Wiz, now I hear you. Wiz, all I can say is wow. David's Harp is getting it with that Aliyah Rock the Boat mix with that Michael Jackson I Want to Rock with You, he mentioned.

I know, that's a banger, they sound really good, she said.

I saw your lips moving and your face scrunching up. It appears you were on some trash trying to comment, he said.

Oh, whatever, you heard exactly what I was saying, you just don't want to face the music, pun intended, she replied.

The music level comes down, you can hear multiple voices chattering.

Naw Wiz, for real, what were you saying, he asked?

Again, oh, here you go again Shep. I asked you why you are coming for me and all I'm trying to do is look out bruh.

Well, once again, why did Chevrolet let you purchase a brand-new vehicle from them? Sis, your credit is jacked up. Wiz why? Why did they do that? Oh, I got it Wiz, let me answer that. Because they were willing to take a risk on you, despite you having bad credit. That is why they did it, he said. Out of that act of favor, in which you did not deserve, you were given a chance to purchase a new vehicle. Because they believed you would do right, and you did, you got a chance to prove your commitment. Look at it now Wiz. Through doing what is right towards their company, who took a risk on you, you now own a stewardship testimony. You did Chevrolet right, you did yourself right, the economy right, and those who experience hearing your testimony of financial irresponsibility right. So again Wiz, your testimony is a reality because you maximized the risk that Chevy took on you when you did not deserve it. I hear your heart and concern for me about my dealings with Destiny, but think, thousands of people didn't make the mistake you made when you faulted on your loan with Chevrolet. Millions have faulted though. But you have become a beacon of change through your story. Wiz, because your story has come alive, all who have the opportunity to hear it, can believe that financial redemption is possible. So, in a comparable sense to your question why. Why would I connect with Destiny? Wiz that's my why. That's why Destiny and I must connect. Destiny's success in this, unbeknownst to her, is way bigger than her. Her betterment is for those way down the road that will experience my Father's grace and mercy. Mercy beyond their challenging conditions, which is minor in the grand scheme of things. As well as grace for their broken souls in which they are the accomplice for their own brokenness. Wiz, ya boy Shep, will gladly risk taking a loss if it will result in a gain. Therefore, end of conversation, sis. I hope you'll understand my why. I got to bounce, but I'll be talking to you, he said.

All right Shep, much love and success to you and Destiny. Be easy my dude. Peace, Shep.

Same to you, my girl. Peace Wiz.

Oh wait, no dessert Shep?

No dessert Wiz, maybe next time my girl.

CHAPTER 7

"Thump & Grap"

(A Few Days After December 25th, 2003)

"Hello regions of heathens and the genius, this is podcast episode 48 of Book Six Six, where the real spiel gets squealed.

I'm Thumper.

And I'm Grappler. And you can know one thing, or maybe a million, yet either way, you will always get what's heard you herds.

Good evening to you Thumper.

Good evening to you Grappler.

How are you today Grap?

Slow motion Thump, slow motion. I would ask how you are doing, but it's easy to figure out because you're like a headless chicken dude.

Whatever dude, you got jokes Grap.

Well Thump, it's time for the formalities, and time to get the show moving, my friend.

Ok Grap, well, here we go bro, I got this.

Dear heathens and genius ones, it's ya boy Thump and today we have an inferno topic on hand.

And what is that inferno topic, replied Grap?

Hold your horses, Grap. Hold them, said Thump.

Hold your breath Thump, man dude, are you sure the inferno topic is not the breeze of hot funk coming out of your jaws man?

I think not bro, it's most likely your ear drums, Grap. I'm totally convinced that it is my friend, you'll need a Q-Tip the size of a telephone pole to clean them boys out, Thump replied.

Anyway Grap, the world is in complete shock regarding the death of DeVine Shepherd, better known as God.

Wow my dude, before we go any further, get the bills paid Thump.

Most def sir, Thump replied. It's ya boy Thump again, and, like every single time we do this podcast our sponsorship is by Manna Meats, "Where a taste from heaven falls fresh to each."

Also, heathens, make sure you tell everybody you know about our show. How come, you ask? We are trying to get paaaaaaid!!!

Thanks, Thump. You say weirdo stuff but God Bless the weirdos, said Grap.

Now before we go any further bro, I need to mention this to you, said Thump.

Mention what?

Grap, we need a new spot, sir. I enjoy our "odd cast" but dude, your grandma's basement is too ritzy and does not match our gritty news deliveries. I got to say this, and not delay this. Bro, this plush white couch, Brazilian rug, Paris depicted mural upon the wall behind us and these gold-plated beverage coasters we use for these designer glass tables are way too much bro, c'mon man.

Ok Thump, so now you're a rapper? Dork myster did you just try to rhyme as if you're a mainstream lyricist? Sir, your receding hairline, greyish/blackish blending beard and those generic clothes and shoes you wear are just not appealing to the Hip Hop culture, Grap said. Further may I add, you are a fifty-two-year-old, five feet/three-inch, two-hundred and forty-eight-pound white dude who grew up in Boise, Idaho. Need I say more, Thump? Oops, there's one more thing I forgot. Rep your hood Thump, rep it, Grap said.

Grap whatever sir. Bottom line, this setting is just not it.

Whatever Thump, suggesting we go to the backroom of your friend's barbershop isn't appealing either..

Grap you mental.

I'm what?

I said that you are mental. Mental, Thump said?

Thump, what the heck is mental?

My point exactly, Grap. You got mental issues bro.

Never that, said Grap.

Thump you are the one with mental issues bro. But anyways, we'll revisit this convo at another time my friend. I refuse to delay our viewers any longer. I got to get out of here anyway because if I delay any longer, your acidic breath will melt my entire being into a clump of green-ish glob.

Huh, not you talking Grap. If I take too many more whiffs of your trash heap ear wax, I will croke from putrid inhalation. So bro, let's get to today's inferno topic.

And Thump, that topic is…

Today's topic is about the death of God.

Well, this is a subject matter that is already mind-boggling. Regarding God's death, there is no suspect or determination of what killed him yet, Grap. All kinds of speculations are swirling out there and many are calling his death a homicide.

Bro, the guy made a huge impact on the world, why would anyone find it necessary to murder him, said Grap?

I know bro. Honestly; I was a little saddened by the news. My aunt loved him greatly and she always felt that calling forth his name in a way, helped her to overcome challenges and receive blessings, replied Thump.

Huh? C'mon now that's hilarious but hey, whatever works for her is not my business. Nevertheless, let me read this excerpt I found in the Alpha Omega Post that speaks on God's character, said Grap.

It reads: "You must consider this a known matter as to why God's life has been snuffed away. His Father's memoir points to this guy named B. Guyler, a brother of God that their Father aggressively threw out of the place called the Oasis."

Interesting take. I want to speak to this Grap.

Go right ahead bro, he said.

They both are residents of the Oasis, but God also has property here. I'm sure B. Guyler must have a bad taste in his mouth and that anyone who was of God's Father's empire would be the first to be targeted for revenge, said Thump.

Bro, what could be more satisfying than to take out the enemy of your favorite child? And if that wasn't enough evidence for the pre-meditated murder of God, how about his lifelong lover Churchy Selah, Grap?

Churchy Selah, replied Grap?

Yes, my friend, her.

Why her my dawg, asked Grap?

You ask why? I'll put it to you plain and simple, passion murder is why.

But with who bro? Who is she creeping with, asked Grap?

This guy named Div. A Den they say.

Is that the guy we interviewed like a year ago Thump?

Yeah man. It sure is.

You got to be kidding me dude.

Naw, this real talk, Grap.

Bro, I knew I felt something about that cocky conceited prick who drove that midnight black Lambo, said Grap. Aye, he did have some amazing financial strategies, though (they both laugh).

Yes, he did, replied Thump.

Yeah, some good friends I know went to some of his seminars and took his online classes. Thump, they are shooting up the financial ladder.

That's dope, my dawg, replied Thump.

Yeah Thump, but go ahead with the rest of the story.

Sure. Div A. Den is being identified as one who could have blood on his hands too.

Why, Thump?

Because God often spoke openly against him in his Father's memoir. Div A. Den's influence and resourcefulness have been in existence since time began. Many in this day and age are turning away from God to obtain anything they can get. Dude got money and dude is lavishing it upon folk. Bro, folk are beginning to come around to it. His offer to freely provide seemed too good to be true, but word on the street is it's no cap. Heck Grap, even Churchy prostituted herself, did obscene things, and chased desperately after Div A. Den, per word on the street too (Grap laughs).

Word on the street, Thump? (Thump laughs)

Yes bro, word on the street.

Thump, you are the Goat sir. Dude, why you say that? With all that funk coming out your mouth, fire breathing dragon breath, your trash compactor of a mouth contains all the hot scoop, dude. (Thump laughs)

Yeah right dude, you the real MVP. How so? Sir, the way your ears are compounded with all that wax, it's a miracle how you can stuff more information in them grocery store vanilla caramel looking things, said Thump (they both laugh).

But for real Thump, I can see how a motive for a passion crime can be established. I'm no investigator or nothing, but it's obvious this love triangle, or better yet, love scandal, has passion crime written all over it. God was found dead at Churchy's location. God is a jealous God they say. The writing is on the wall. He didn't want anyone following Div A. Den more than they followed him. The dogmatic point was made about that in his Father's memoir, Thump. (Thump looks awed) God's Father made it clear in the memoir about how dangerous Div A. Den can be to those seeking to fall in love with his riches.

Div A. Den has big time bank, said Thump (Grap head shakes left to right).

Bro, that statement doesn't even do justice in explaining how much money this dude possess, replied Grap. (Thump's head goes up and down relaying agreement with Grap) Thump, it's strongly stated in the memoir that Div A. Den encourages people towards the love of having the root of all evil.

Which is money Grap, right?

Bingo, the love of money, he answered.

Thump, again, I'm no investigator, but it's reasonable to say that Div A. Den more than likely got tired of God attempting to block him out of people's lives. After all, the memoir says he's a "jealous" God.

Man, oh man bro, there are so many twists and speculations about God's death, said Thump. But, due to the lack of evidence, I see it becoming a cold case afterwhile.

Huh Thump? Now you acting mental again sir, said Grap.

Whatever dawg, but be aware my friend. Know that the same ear wax that can make you hear, can make you deaf, replied Thump.

Bro, I just broke down in theory what led to God's death, how are you so polar to first comprehend and now, be in disbelief, said Grap. Look my friend, you who have a chicken egg smelling mouth. I am no investigator, but this is all the way plain as day.

Grap, you know this.

Know what Thump?

You know there's always a different angle about any and everything. Don't be so sure of your theory Grap. After doing this work for a while, I'm sure you'd agree that there are always two sides to the story.

Definitely, Thump.

But, check this testimonial out, said Thump. Marie from Bedford Ohio wrote: "God was one who was trustworthy. I believe what made him so remarkable is that he was willing to walk with me during my difficult experience of divorce. I fell into such a deep depression, but I didn't have to go through it alone and God encouraged me through his Father's memoir with encouraging words." Grap she goes on to say, "words like, 'weeping may endure for a night,' but joy comes in the morning." As well as "God is my refuge and strength a very present help in a time of trouble." And also, "God regularly went to his Father to intercede on my behalf. I felt comforted that he requested help for me," she said. As well as, "I tell you, I come to know that God is a burden bearer, and his burden is light, and his yoke is easy."

That's alright, said Thump, I'm glad that this lady had a positive experience with God.

I also would like to share a message from Kimmy. She states that her son was stricken by a rare disease and the doctors were unable to find a solution. She explained that God went to the hospital where her son was admitted and laid his hand on her side, said Grap. Bro, she said that God proclaimed that her boy was healed. Later that evening she said that she had received a call from the nurse station. Then unfortunately, things quickly turned for the worse when she received a follow up phone call stating that Dr. Shaquille Greenwood, was unable to save her son from the rare disease that attacked his body, he also said.

Grap, I can see why there was disdain, said Thump.

Bro, God's death is such an anomaly and as the days ahead continue, more will be revealed to express God's true character, said Grap.

CHAPTER 8

"Honored"

(March 16th, 2002)

Inside the ballroom of the Cleveland Convention Center. Formal event. Meet and Greet hour. Local jazz quartet playing softly. Attendees gathered about. Some individuals and some groups of people conversating with one another and gathered throughout the ballroom.

Hello, hello. How are you guys doing today, he asked?

Well before I answer that, let me recommend that you try the pepper jack cheese squares on that tray over there to the right, he said. I'll let you try those first, and you'll know how we are doing today, sir. (Both the guy and the gentlemen he was speaking to laughed).

Oh yeah sir, you mean those cheese squares over there, the gentlemen replied.

Yes sir, I mean those cheese squares. See, I hate to be a pig out in public, but I had to have eaten nearly 5 of those cheese squares from the moment I entered the door, up till now (the gentlemen he was speaking to laughs again).

Well, you deserve it, sir. And I must say, you have escalated my craving so, let me go get a taste of the cheese squares to see if you know what you're talking about, the gentlemen responded. And let me also say jokingly sir, everybody don't know what good food really is, (he walks to the table, grabs a cheese square and eats it.) Man, oh man, these cheese squares are the truth, the gentlemen said! These squares should be charged with a felony (the gentlemen's' face is in astonishment), I feel like I'm committing a theft case, my fingers will be on these for the rest of the night.

Well, I think you now understand how we are doing (the gentlemen laughs). I'm sorry we didn't introduce ourselves before we went over to the table. My name is Deshaun, and this is my wife Destiny. We are the Smiths, said Deshaun.

Well, nice to meet you Deshaun, and Destiny. My name is DeVine Shepherd, but I'm mostly referred to as God.

Do you prefer we call you God, says Deshaun?

Please do. Deshaun and Destiny. I'm glad to meet you guys.

Oops, watch it, those utensils can be slippery at times God, said Destiny.

You got that right Destiny, I don't want my cherry tomato to roll like a bowling ball on the floor, this place is nice looking, replied God.

Deshaun, sometimes I'm somewhat clumsy with things, but with the exception of preventing some people from falling away from their purpose, said God.

I like the way you put that God, said Deshaun.

Thanks, Deshaun.

So, tell me Smiths, what do you both do?

I am an investigative reporter for a local news station, said Deshaun.

I'm a school principal at a nearby school, said Destiny.

Awesome, I like to teach others myself Destiny, God replied. For me, it is a personal joy to see people grasp the information and maximize the principles in which they've learned.

Still gathered by the appetizer table:

Hey God, how are you?

Hey Div A. Den, how are you? I'm doing great today. Sir, I must say, that's a nice suit and pair of shoes you have on, said God.

Thanks, but would you expect me in nothing less than an Armani suit and gator skin shoes, God? But anyway, that's a humble little red tie you are sporting. Walmart special?

Yes, Div A. Den. Yes, indeed, Walmart Special.

I thought so. So cheap. I believe you can do better than that. I hope that you realize how much your outer appearance means to those looking for inspiration, said Div A. Den. You need not to be ashamed to look good. Matter of fact, if you ever think about upgrading your wardrobe, I know just the person for you. This what you need to know though. My appearance is not by accident, it's intentional. Plus, I have the income to show for it. Do you know why I say this God?

No, Div A. Den, I do not, tell me why?

I believe we all ought to look our very best all the time. Now, these outfits can get a little pricey, so I hope you have the means to purchase them. It costs to be the boss. I know all too well about what it means to be a boss, and my hope is that others will see the importance of the love of money. God, let me leave you with this nugget of wisdom; love money and money will love you back.

Thanks for your input and insight, said God.

Most definitely, and next time, I hope to see that you've put it to use. Just so you know. The game I give is meant to be sold, not told, said Div A. Den.

God turns his attention back to the couple:

Excuse me for that Deshaun and Destiny, I'm expecting to run into a few folks here today.

Oh, no problem at all, said Deshaun.

So, tell us what it is that you do, asked Destiny?

Thanks for asking, Destiny. What I do is make impact in the community simply by giving up my time, support and a number of my possessions to help assist people throughout their journey in life.

Wow, why go so far with-it, she asked?

Frankly speaking, it's my passion. I do it so that they are able to experience an everlasting well-being. My focus is to completely heal people, but sometimes people desire that I give them help for specific issues. I don't reject their requests. But if they don't care to want me to sacrifice regarding other challenging areas in their life, I let it be. Sis, I care for the soul since the pain within the soul permeates throughout the entire body, said God.

Can you elaborate a little further before the program begins, this is fascinating, Destiny asked?

Sure can.

You two, the soul is the spirit of the body. The spirit is where our standards are housed. The soul places the standards in our hearts and mind. The mind wills and the heart feels. They work in tandem to produce our actions and reaction to the way we view and live out life. Let me go a little further with it you two, God asked?

Sure God, go right ahead, said Deshaun.

Yes sir, this tandem per standard establishes our worldview and that worldview defines the way we conduct our choices, via what we believe is objective. Now, abstract concepts such as love are subjectively defined, said God. Yes, you two, we all think we know what that concept means but do we collectively agree?

I for sure know I don't agree, said Deshaun.

Thanks for being honest sir, said God.

Who has the authority to define it, and can it ever be objective by those who are imperfect when the Perfect One is Love itself? You two, the only objective truth that the imperfect can acknowledge is that a Perfect One has designed anything that is objective, whether concrete or abstract, said God.

How is Perfection objective God, asked Deshaun?

Thanks for asking Deshaun.

Perfection is objective because anything created by the One who is perfect defines what perfection actually is. Let me go further you two.

Sure God, I have questions, but I'd like to hear more, said Destiny.

Ok great. Take the sky as an example. Meaning the sky and all the contents in the sky may I say.

Sure, says Deshaun, I'm listening.

Ok follow me. The sky and its contents are perfect (Deshaun and Destiny are nodding their heads). No person that is imperfect can objectively establish, nor define if the sky is or isn't perfect, explains God. Why so? (God, questions himself) They aren't the maker of the sky, just the benefactor of what the sky and its contents produce. Only the Perfect One can define its objectiveness because the Perfect One designed it to perfection, states God.

Oh, I get it, any invention that is created is objectively perfect by the inventor, replied Destiny.

Umm kind of but, not really, said God.

Destiny, the reason I say this is because, only one person is perfect so the purpose for which he or she defined it is objectively perfect, explains God.

Oh, okay God, then we humans are perfect beings because we were designed by a Perfect One, states Deshaun.

Kind of sort of but not fully bro, answers God. The Perfect One had an ambition, an intent of His original creation regarding humans. Yet, humans who are gifted with a soul and heart thought and felt differently about their purpose. So, by doing so, the results are loud and clear and easy to see. Why? (God questions himself again) Because the world is imperfect and humans in a sense govern it?

Is that a proper assessment, God?

Yup, it is, Deshaun.

Follow me further. When first created, humans were perfect and perfect in their purpose. The good news though is that my purpose is to restore humans back to their original purpose and then everything that they are graced to invent will be objectively perfect.

How, asks Destiny?

Oh, that's easy, sis. Because they will be in the perfect will of the Perfect One, God answers.

Okay, hold up, hold on, God said. (God laughs and is looking back and forth to Deshaun and Destiny). Why are you guys looking at each other like that, questions God?

God…

Yes, Destiny.

I have a question, she says.

Ok, let it rip, sis.

What does this philosophical discourse have to do with anything, she asks?

Well. My work is purposed in encouraging the imperfect to believe in the Perfect One. Perfect One, being my Father, that is. Without such belief, one's worldview will be guided by those who are imperfect. In that attempt, they'll gravely struggle by defining concepts through their imperfect knowledge of what those concepts mean or are established to be. Sis, the imperfect had no part in the creation of the concept of life, therefore the imperfect cannot objectively determine life's concept properly. Whenever I've introduced a soul to my Father and that soul accepts my Father's will. Through his infallible memoir, the concept of life through love is the reward. Sis, souls that grow in adhering and agreeing to the direction stated in the memoir, reap, replicate, and reproduce the benefits of the concept's perfection on the earth.

Wow, that was a mouthful, said Deshaun.

I agree hubby. I'm very interested in learning more about your Father, said Destiny.

Me as well, said Deshaun. How do we go about learning more, he asked?

Smiths, are you familiar with Churchy?

Yes, I've heard of her but don't know much about her, said Deshaun.

No worries. I'd like you to go to her and she will be the one to point you toward the Perfect One. My Father, The Perfect One, is the lover of your souls.

May we have her contact info, asks Deshaun?

Yes, here's her card. On it you'll find her physical location and meeting times.

Cool. I look forward to checking her out and learning more about your Father's memoir, said Deshaun.

I'm curious to know. Upon what I just told you, do you accept it as truth, asked God?

Meaning the worldview of a Perfector, asked Destiny? Well God, I do.

I do as well God, said Deshaun.

Good for you both. Your soul has come to life now.

Are you telling us that our soul wasn't alive, asked Deshaun?

Yes, Deshaun, replied God.

God, how so, asked Deshaun?

Imperfection creates ruin. So bro, anything ruined cannot benefit anything. What's ruined is not alive. Perfection creates what can't be ruined. Anything that is not ruined is beneficial for everything. Whatever is beneficial is alive. What's alive is eternal and eternality does not have an expiration date.

God are you imperfect, asks Destiny?

Destiny, I'm not. Destiny, I am a part of the Father and we are one. My Father's memoir explains that. Are you familiar with my Father's memoir?

(A guy comes over where they are standing) Oops, excuse me, sir, yes the napkins are here. Here you go (God gives the guy some napkins).

Thanks sir, appreciate it, replied the Guy.

You're welcome, sir, replied God.

Okay, where was I at, Destiny? I told you guys that the cheese squares are the bomb. (Deshaun and Destiny both laugh)

Where was I, oh, I remember now, said God. Are you guys familiar with my Father's memoir?

Yes God, I heard of it but don't know much about its story. All I ever heard was that it was written by men, said Destiny. I was told it was not to be trusted because man wrote it. Therefore, my question to you is…how can the imperfect define who and what is perfect, she asked? How can they? This a little pushback because you said that they are incapable of doing such a thing.

Yes, you are right, I did say that, God replied. But here's how. See, the imperfect cannot define the perfect. Only the Perfect One knows what he created the creation for. As a comparable example think about it this way. Say you are perfect and therefore; you created the curriculum for the school you work at. If I was imperfect, I would be unable to properly judge, assess or define or determine if the curriculum is good or not. Follow me here you two as I take this point a little further.

I'm following you sir, Deshaun said.

Me too, said Destiny.

Awesome. Let's say I'm the composer of the content in the curriculum. My only task would be to compose the contents of the curriculum and not create what the actual content is. Now Destiny, according to the standard that you've created the curriculum to be and do, it's not my job to define the meanings or reasons of what you put in or determined the curriculum to say. Why so, you may be thinking.

I am, she said.

Here's your answer. Because I'm simply the composer, the scribe of what you laid out for me to compose, states God. Thus, Destiny, I have no authority to question what and why you wanted me to compose what you've established for me to compose. I'm not the one who properly knows how the curriculum is to fully work for your students.

Although I may attempt to interpret it the best way I can, only what I've been informed to compose protects the dignity and accuracy of the invention. My opinion or what I think it should say or mean is not included because I'm simply composing what I'm told to compose. No subjectivity can infiltrate what I'm instructed to compose word for word. So, in like manner you guys, my Father chose to use the human agent to compose his perfect memoir. As the memoir states, *All Scripture is God-breathed and is useful for teaching, rebuking, correcting, and training in righteousness, so that the servant of God may be thoroughly equipped for every good work.* Thus, the content of the memoir remains true to its perfection and is not tainted by the handling of anyone imperfect. Interpretation of the memoir can be imperfect since only the inventor has a perfect understanding of His own content creation, states God. Despite that the memoir has been given as a source to point humans towards the perfect plan. Moreover, that's a plan that both of you just received by your confession and belief in him. Only through acceptance of my Father's will can it benefit them, despite being imperfect. As you have just accepted, the overall counsel of the memoir desires only the best for humans and how they may obtain that best, explains God.

What a mouthful, said Destiny.

Thanks God, said Deshaun.

You both are welcome.

Looks like the program is about to start God, she said.

Well Smiths, it was a pleasure to meet and talk with you today. I'll see you around.

Yes, we'll see you around God, said Deshaun.

CHAPTER 9

"Resonated"

(March 16th, 2002)

Wow, only in Cleveland during the spring season, will you get bright sunny skies and warm temperatures. Then on another day, experience a hailstorm and nearly below freezing temps, said Destiny. Even more so, while only hours apart from each other. (both Deshaun and Destiny laugh). Ugggh so sick of our weather.

Here bae, come close and let me cover you, and let's pick up our pace, said Deshaun. We are almost at the garage, beautiful.

Ouch, she said.

Oops, excuse me for stepping on your heel, said Deshaun.

No worries. Bae, I thank you. I'm so grateful to have you as my protector, she said.

I love you, Destiny.

I dearly love you, she replied.

Dear, my back is getting leveled by this hail (Destiny laughs). Bae, we're 10 ft away from relief, he said (as he laughs). Here let me get the door for you, sexy.

So sweet my King. Keep it up, I'm enjoying your chivalry. (They get in the car) Whew, my King turn up the heat fast. I'm shivering and should have listened to the Channel 12 weather woman.

I know, that is what we get, he said.

(Destiny looks over her shoulder as Deshaun backs up their car). Be careful pulling out, these folks are driving recklessly through this garage. Ooh, watch it, Deshaun!

Thanks, Queen, I see them.

You know, what God said earlier really resonated with me, she said.

What resonated the most, he asked?

That worldview part.

Queen, it struck me too. Another thing that struck me is how that lipstick makes your lips look tantalizing. Give me a… (she kisses him before he could finish the sentence). Oh, thank you for beating me to the kiss he said.

You smell good and you look clean today my dear hubby. Okay, back to the conversation, where were you at?

Yes, the whole worldview thing challenged me to rethink what I've chosen for standards, he replied.

Really? In what way?

From that conversation, I feel like the standards I live by are pointless and not prosperous, he replied.

I agree. Due to our imperfect nature, aren't we incapable of creating anything objective King? I'm guilty of putting too much stock into people.

Me and you both, he said. Our human ideas apart from the guidance of the Perfect One who inspired the contents of the memoir, do not have any legs to stand on fully.

I can't argue with that, she said. I too was intrigued, and I would like to meet his dearly beloved Churchy. Those brief minutes of impact were convincing enough for me.

Well, baby, I'd like to meet her too, he stated.

I believe it's going to be life-changing to come into a relationship with God, she said.

Destiny, I totally agree.

CHAPTER 10

"Wonder Working"

(Easter Sunday, 2002)

Someone, please hurry, please hurry fast, please help my mother she just collapsed. Frantically Deshaun yells out!

(God starts praying) Father, I am your son DeVine and you said by your Word that if we lay hands on the sick they shall be healed. Father touch Mrs. Smith's body and restore it fully. You are Jehovah Rapha her healer and she trusts in you.

Emergency Room of Mount Sinai Hospital:

Excuse me, excuse me, Nurse Davis yells! Please exit the room, Mr. Smith, exit now, (Nurse Davis says this loudly to Deshaun and God).

God they are telling us to go, said Deshaun.

(God is still praying). Father, you are the maker of her body and therefore you know how you've designed it to function. I trust in your power that her body is being restored at this moment. Yes, we're grateful for medical care and what you have graced us through medicine and science, but our hope is in you, and we are dependent on your healing hand Abba Father.

Please exit the room sir, yelled Nurse Davis.

It's going to be alright nurse, she's just sleeping, replied God.

What do you know? This is serious, and I need to administer care immediately so exit now or I will have to call security she yells! Go I said, GO NOW!

No problem, replied God.

Code blue, code blue, Nurse Davis announces over the PA System. PA Dr. Miller, Nurse Cheryl.

Ok, I'm doing it right now, said Nurse Cheryl.

Nurse Cheryl Sends a PA announcement for Dr. Miller

Dr. Miller to IC unit 6, Dr. Miller to IC unit 6.

Sandy, check her pulse while I give chest compressions, says Nurse Davis.

(Sandy checks pulse). I don't feel anything. She's not breathing.

Okay, grab the defibrillator and start oxygen, I'm starting CPR, states Nurse Davis.

Nurse Cheryl details patient's identity

A 75-year-old woman African American Woman, 5 feet 6 inches tall, two hundred and twenty pounds. Patient encountering chest pains about an hour ago. Blood pressure rate at…

Unresponsive, Nurse Davis yells. Apply shock, Sandy.

Shock compression applied.

She's now breathing, says Nurse Sandy. (Dr. Miller arrives to the room).

Dr. Miller, what do you have, asked Nurse Cheryl? I confirm that her pulse is now normal. (Nurse Cheryl documents per Dr. Miller's assessment of vitals)

In the waiting room

God, I don't want to lose her, said Deshaun.

I believe that everything is going to be fine with her Deshaun, I believe it will be. My Father is a healer. Here, take some tissue my friend.

Thank you, God.

Oh, here comes the Doctor, said God.

Mr. Smith, I'm Doctor Miller, how are your today?

Hi Doctor Miller, I'm worried.

Mr. Smith, your mother, Mrs. Smith is stable now, Doctor Miller said.

Thank you. I am so glad to hear of this news. I was deeply worried about her, said Deshaun. I appreciate you and your staff.

Mr. Smith, we're monitoring her closely but she's stable and is doing abnormally well after experiencing such trauma.

Abnormally well?

Yes Deshaun, very good. In my 30-year tenure, I haven't witnessed anything like this before, God said. Regarding patients at her age, the recovery speed after a cardiac arrest is a slow and steady process.

Excuse me, Doctor, please meet God.

Hello God, said Dr. Miller

Hello Doctor Miller, nice to meet you.

Dr, Miller, God was in the room with me and during the emergency, he administered care, said Deshaun.

I want to give my apologies to your staff for any hindrance during that frantic moment, said God. I know the power of prayer and so I don't hesitate to release my prayers during such situations.

No worries at all, replied Doctor Miller. My staff also has never witnessed a person deep in prayer while seeking to stabilize a patient. Normally, witnesses of a sudden health challenge like the one Mrs. Smith experienced, are despondent and frozen. Yet, you were actively administering care in another form, and we thank you for it.

Mr. Smith since there are no detectable complications and Mrs. Smith is in good spirits, per protocol we'll keep her overnight and run a few more tests in the morning, said Dr. Miller. I'm confident she'll be able to leave tomorrow or the day after. Once again, in all my tenure, I haven't witnessed any recovery speed like this for someone her age.

Wow, that's amazing Doctor Miller, he replied. I'm certainly glad my mother is doing well now. I appreciate you and your staff, said Deshaun.

Thank you, we appreciate you as well.

I must return to a patient of mine; you gentlemen enjoy the remainder of your day, said Doctor Miller.

You as well Doctor Miller, said Deshaun.

Deshaun, I'm going to have to take off as well, said God. But here you go, please accept this gift. Get you some lunch on me. Also Deshaun, go and get some rest too, we'll get together soon.

I appreciate all that you have done today, said Deshaun. Thank you for coming up here to check on my mom. I'm very grateful.

Much love to you and make sure to tell your wife I said hello, said God.

Sure, will God. I'm about to give her a call now.

Okay, go ahead and do that. Take care, I'll get with you later.

You too, he replied.

Deshaun calls Destiny

Bae, I am so sorry I missed your call, we had an emergency board meeting, and I didn't have my phone on me, said Destiny. I left it in my office. So, what happened with your mom? I just read your text a second ago.

She's okay bae. She asked me to take her to the hospital because she was feeling heaviness in her chest. Not sure why, but I reached out to God to let him know. I guess I wanted someone there with me. You know love, he actually beat us there, said Deshaun.

Really? That was so kind of him, said Destiny.

Yes, indeed it was, he replied. During the visit, my mom went to use the restroom and, on her way, out of it, she collapsed. I was in complete shock Destiny, I yelled and cried out for help. While I was doing that, God kneeled and laid his hands on her shoulder and started praying. When the medical team entered the room, they asked us to immediately depart. I departed but God remained there and continued in prayer. Destiny, it felt like a million years had passed before God exited the room. I was so in a fog. But at some point in time, God came out and met me in the waiting area. Queen, it was frantic, and I surely was fearing and believing the worst would happen. God prayed over me in the waiting area. His prayer over me gave me some peace for a minute, but I became anxious again, right after his prayer. Mom had a cardiac arrest but came through miraculously the Doctor said. Doctor Miller, the resident doctor, said in all his tenure he had never seen such recovery speed for an elder faced with a cardiac health emergency. I tell you baby, I'm touched by God, Deshaun said. We're surely going to meet his companion Churchy and learn more about the mission they are doing, he said.

My King, I'm with you, it's so amazing that in only a couple of encounters with God, he felt it necessary to be by your side. That is true selflessness because he could've been doing anything else.

Yes, I agree bae, true selflessness, replied Deshaun. He also gave me some money for lunch before leaving the hospital. I'm going to head over to Judah Café' and get my favorite, he said. I'll see you later this eve.

Ok love, see you then, I love you, she replied.

I love you too, Destiny.

CHAPTER 11

"The Oasis"

(An eternity ago)

Email to Mr. John Davis-Chief Editor of Channel 12 News

Greetings Mr. Davis

Please see the opening report of my findings and let me know what you think.

Sincerely,

Deshaun

Opening Report

In consideration of the magnitude of who God was, the medical examiners took their time before releasing the autopsy report to the public. There was so much buzz around the world about God's death. All media outlets were covering this story. There was great anticipation awaiting the cause of God's death. Various early morning radio and television shows were suggesting that retaliation was the cause. YouTube influencers and propagandists were drawing conspiracy theories that God committed a murder-suicide. These claims came about after statements from anonymous insiders claimed God was responsible for global proportions of euthanasia. The assumptions about God's death were endless as the world awaited the toxicology report and other potential causes of his death. Moreover, Div A. Den was being looked at as a prime suspect. Many loyalists in the Christian community, a set of people who followed "Shep" God's nickname, raised eyebrows. Due in part because of the relationship that Div A. Den had with the lovers of money. Div A. Den happened to be a key factor of good and bad in God's Father's memoir. The generosity of God's Father, from using Div A. Den brought an impact on people's lives. But, as the memoir informs, Div A. Den's money could lead anyone who became a lover of money to destruction.

In an evaluation of God's Father's Oasis, his main physical dwelling place, some pundits believed the Father needed Div. A Den to make this immaculate place. Yet, the memoir plainly explains how unmatched the Father's intelligence is in comparison to anyone. The Father was a master architect and possessed an unlimited amount of income.

However, the memoir strongly suggested that the Father had an eternal ought with the lovers of money. Why so? This in part was due to humans' desperate dependency to rely on money for everything. Many humans were convinced that having money was the key to happiness, security, and the most supreme and eternal experience for true quality of life. Div A. Den in a sense was one and the same as money. This realization was central to why lovers of money were lovers of Div A. Den. Therefore, it is a no-brainer why they put him above God's Father.

God's Father stated in the memoir how he's a Jealous God and that no other god was to be placed before him. What does that mean? In other words, he wants all things to have an intimate relationship with him, and him only. If not, their relationship is broken, and they have become the Father's enemy. His unrelenting desire to partner with all beings could seem obsessive according to the memoir. The Father goes above and beyond to wed humans and his pursuit for the covenant is constant. In contrast though, it does show that he honors humans' choice to reject him. Nevertheless, in rejecting him, the cost of that would be detrimental.

God's Father has established that he owns everything. That he knows all things. And that he regards the Earth as his footstool. God's Father is one who monopolized the market of life. Thus, an anonymous source created a blog and dug deep into an important asterisk in the Father's memoir that point to his Son, God, and his legacy.

Many around the globe who never cared to read God's Father's memoir were unaware of his initial parental relationship. Figuratively, with this exhilarating and brilliant figure named B. Guyler. According to this investigative reporter, God fearfully created and appointed this son as a high rank in the family's business. This son, B. Guyler, witnessed the building of the earth and had residency in the luxurious estate of the Oasis. A very mesmerizing Oasis, historically the Eden Garden, as it is technically referred as, is quite envied amongst all yuppies. Located in the continent of Africa, God's Father's estate has been regarded as incomparable to any known lavish estate in the history of Earth's existence. Stylish, euphoric, serene, appealing, and richly saturated with the Earth's finest jewels is an understatement. Plus, with the purist ecological landscape, Eden revealed a hallmark of God's Father's illustrious wealth. But, according to God's Father's memoir, a violent fallout occurred between his Father and his son B. Guyler.

God's Father set B. Guyler in a reverenced center stage-like position. It is safe to say that all things associated with God's Father were endowed to B. Guyler. Which meant a limitless and impeccable number of blessings. However, this anonymous source's blog, dug deep into God's Father's background. As a target of attention, he may have uncovered the root of this scandal. These potential facts could've led to his Son, DeVine's tragedy.

Angry Father, Banished Son

At some point in time, B. Guyler was made COO of the Paradise Oasis. Before building Eden from the ground up, God's Father fully designed and built the Oasis. He also brought forth into existence these uncanny beings to which he gave everlasting residency in his Paradise Oasis. God's Father, the supreme intelligent being, always saw fit and important to allot trust and responsibilities to his community of residents. With all his brilliance and majestic appearance, his son B. Guyler was a quality and skilled leader. More skilled than any of the Father's Oasis family. B. Guyler grew in stature and morale among all residents. Capable, effective, and influential, his partnership and brilliance with Oasis residents flourished under the governing of God's Father. Before the collapse of their partnership, many believed that so much was contributed by B. Guyler and his staff to enhance the Oasis dwelling. This anonymous source was able to gain insight into the richness of the Paradise Oasis.

Many years ago, the memoir states that a guy named "P" from Tarsus obtained an inside view of the Oasis. He was hand-selected by God's Father to observe its illustrious environment. "P" was so awed when he returned to earth, that it left him speechless. "P" was so taken aback that he really couldn't tell if he was hallucinating or in such a slobbering and fascinating rem sleep. Yet, despite this prosperous atmosphere, the obvious success, the culturally thriving community, and impeccable quality of life, disruption arose. Which led to a brutal and vicious incident. The residents of the Oasis witnessed an aggressive banishment of B. Guyler by God's Father. Why such actions? What was so egregious that reconciliation for B. Guyler was eternally voided? What happened and why? As the anonymous source dug deeper into God's Father's memoir, he discovered that a power trip ignited the entire reckoning. How could a fallout of this magnitude occur over what seemed like a menial and commonplace disagreement? Vastly, a great portion of people who read God's Father's memoir attribute a great deal of jealousy and anger issues to God's Father. Their consensus argued that the Father was a control freak. They testified he was a dictator who was full of tyrannic ways. They suggested that the way he governed the Oasis was borderline narcissistic. Was envy the reason for God's Father's reaction?

Although a masterful inventor, was he stressed and nervous about the following that Oasis residents were having, because of B. Guyler's leadership? No doubt about it, the Father's ability and skill set are incomparable and unmatched compared to anyone in existence. However, was his inner consciousness and inner esteem resulting in personal insecurities? Insecurities that presumably were overboard in his actions to banish B. Guyler? Was the all-powerful one not all-powerful and struggled with the power that others possessed? Did he feel there was a threat to his kingly position? Is his memoir biased, one-sided, and leading others to believe that his actions were justifiable? That his actions were necessary for protecting citizens in the Oasis? Was God's Father's viewpoint arriving from the perspective that one being's influence in the Oasis was a threat to all beings of the Oasis?

Some Oasis citizens agreed that the Father's actions were noble. Noble in the understanding that the Father was sacrificial by protecting Oasis residents. Knowing that he loved B. Guyler, but he had to kick him out for their benefit. In a selfless act, many struggle to give up their benefits for others to be benefited. Like a lioness willing to defend her cubs against a pack of vicious hyenas. Like a person offering their kidney to save another person's life. Like a soldier willing to give his or her life to defend the well-being of their society.

Selflessness is generosity and generosity is heroism. Many would argue that it's asinine to create anything that could oppose its creator. Yes, creative things do backfire but who intentionally creates anything that could potentially raise up against them and overtake them? Could it be that God's Father always understood that relationship harmony could dissolve? That his supremacy could be opposed by anyone? Did the Father understand that to provide true freedom, he would have to risk his freedom? Again, did he arrive at the understanding that it's abusive to hold someone hostage or subject them to a sunken place of ventriloquist-like robotics, to maintain his dominance over them? Was his creative vision figuratively exemplifying an owner-to-pet comparison, in which the pet needs full dependence on the owner for its livelihood? Was he threatened by anyone wanting liberation from his ideology? Did he create the Oasis with an ulterior motive about how the culture should function? A motive that was non-negotiable by any resident so that his ideas could not be challenged?

If we're looking for an enemy of the Father's Son, DeVine Shepherd, one could arguably voice his murderer to be his brother B. Guyler. It is reasonable to think such. It's easy to see why B. Guyler would be upset with his Father. The feeling of injustice is a penetrating pain that never ceases until justice is accomplished. The adage states that "revenge is a dish best served cold." So, for B. Guyler, killing his brother God might be a sweet and savory quenching of that taste.

Oh, how the taste of blood satisfies the predator of flesh. It's a very dirty game—referring to the passion to accomplish retribution. Yet, it's even more satisfying to gain "get-back" after feeling wrongly penalized and excommunicated for modeling leadership. Is not leadership a requirement by God's Father for all residents of the Oasis?

Some would agree that it's one thing to be demoted or graciously let go, but to be flung and thrown out in front of everybody is something else. Especially, because it was B. Guyler, a person who was obviously adorned because of the distinctive way the Father created him. Some would suggest how B. Guyler would feel. In a sense like, "Oh sir, you want me to do a huge portion of work, you get all the praise and credit, I'm sorely neglected by you for my effort in the success, and so you get defensive about my proposal to get a higher position on the hierarchy chart of The Paradise Oasis?"

B. Guyler could feel he was treated with unreasonable disdain and disgust because he voiced his mind about being a supreme ruler. Some argued that he had the resume qualifications for that rulership position. Head tilting for me, was the shock factored body language of this anonymous sources' analysis of God's Father. Overall, this blogger's report of the Oasis, strongly assumes that B. Guyler had a complete motive to end God's life.

CHAPTER 12

"Eros"

(February 14th, 2002)

Churchy and DeVine at the park having quality time.

DeVine, the most beautiful image besides you is this nature experience. I love coming here with you to hear the birds sing, the wind whisper, the calming sound of the water flow, and the hypnotizing scent of the fresh air that pulsates from the plants we're surrounded by, said Churchy. Also my Love, your Father is such an intelligent designer. He fully knows what's pleasing to the core of our being. You know I love the way that you make me feel. I truly feel loved and empowered. I feel wanted and acknowledged. I feel at peace and loved, says Churchy. DeVine, nothing or no one in this world has ever done nor compares to who you are and what you bring into my life. I'm not sure why you'd even desire a relationship with someone like me because of my many many flaws and imperfections. As you are well aware, I've had relations and intense passions towards destructive people, places, and things. I'm widely known for my whoredom. I have a challenge with my attitude, and I have found power in controlling people, manipulating them, and using them for my selfish gain.

Yeah, Churchy but…

King, hold on, let me share further with you, she said.

Wow, but before you do, take a quick look at that yellow canary. Isn't that pure beauty over there, he said?

Yes, indeed it is. Now, take a listen to this ugliness, said Churchy. I have lied, gossiped, swindled people out of money plotted to have, and coveted things from people I called my friends. I have lost dignity and treated my body any old type of way. I was promiscuous and walked lewdly. I lived in so much guilt and shame and I was so deep into it, that I was numb to its power over my life. I hated myself and felt no purpose at all in this world. I felt I had blown the opportunity I had, by doing all of this. Please don't think that I'm yelling at you right this moment, this band of young folks running a few feet over behind you is exuberant and I want you to hear me fully, she said. BEING RAISED IN AN URBAN SETTING, PRODUCED A DESPERATE LIFESTYLE THAT I ADHERED TO. I ALWAYS WANTED TO FEEL SECURE, THEREFORE, I DID WHATEVER I COULD TO ACHIEVE SECURITY AS I DEFINED IT TO BE. Whew, I hope me yelling that to you wasn't annoying. They are gone now.

Baby, I love staring at your eyes, they are so beautiful, said DeVine. I'm sorry if I'm rude. I hear your heart expression and I'm fully in tune, but I just had to share that with you as I gaze deeply into your eyes. Queen, what you are doing is welcoming me into the depths of your soul and I love everything that comes along with it so please continue, he said.

Sure handsome, thank you.

You look adorable blushing right now, said DeVine. Sorry, Churchy I couldn't resist saying that either (DeVine chuckles). Now continue for real this time, my mouth is zipped (DeVine chuckles again).

You are so funny but romantic bae, she said (Churchy chuckles). Okay, where was I? Oh, so King, if I had to steal, cheat, lie, hurt, fake, or whatever, I did whatever it took. I was hurting deeply. Even when someone or something came my way or landed in my possession, I did not know how to keep it. I was unaware of how to treat it properly. Even in my conniving way of life, she said. For example, say for instance I obtained a load of cash; I'd splurge it at practically cyber speed. Anything good to me, I treated it as unbelievable, and because of it, I became a horrible person. I never believed anything good was real or everlasting. DeVine, you should have been given up on me, left me, forsaken me, and kicked me to the curb. Yet, you endured, didn't count my wrongs against me, or were easily angered. The way I treated you should have made you rightfully insensitive, and unfaithful. Heck, I was certainly all of that to you (Churchy says emotionally). It is difficult to believe you are that good without an ulterior motive, she said. Having an ulterior motive is just the habit of most people in the world. With humans, it's always a catch. Unconditional love is your regular expression and action step in my life. You love me and you sacrifice for me, says Churchy. Excuse me, I'm choking up. DeVine, I can't say enough because honey, you are gentle and sweet to me, strong and merciful, mighty, meek, supportive, and burden-bearing. Why such ambition my DeVine? But before you speak let me prepare our lunch spread, she said. I have strawberries for us.

Mmmm, baby, remarked DeVine.

I also have grapes and tuna wraps to go along with the fruit, she says. For drink, I have fresh-squeezed lemonade.

Yes, Queen, and I like those tumblers bae, they blend with the beauty of this scenery, he said.

Check this out DeVine (Churchy reaches into her basket), I have your favorite crackers.

You sure do, the Ritz is the bomb.

I know what you like, don't play with me, she said.

You laid it out bae, as usual, he said.

King, what's in that bag, she asked?

You know what it is. How could I not? (DeVine reaches to grab it out the bag). Brace yourself beautiful. It is Momma Donna's Famous Apple Pie.

Now you know, DeVine, now you know that....

Yes, I know. I know it's your favorite, I know it takes us back to our first date here. I know that you cannot resists them, even when you are watching your calories, he said. (They both laugh)

Yes, I'm trying to watch my calories now, but heck this beautiful moment will not allow me to constrain myself. (As she reaches to grab a piece) Let me announce to you that I am cheating today, (they both laugh).

Don't think that you are alone on that calorie thang. I'm counting mines right with you, but as of now, I just can't seem to do addition problems so… (they both chuckle).

Can I tell you something, he asked?

Yes, you can. Yes, your eyes are beautiful too DeVine. My King, those waves in your hair are immaculate, and your caramel skin tone is phenomenal. But go-ahead Love, let me not interrupt you.

In response to all that you said to me when you poured out your heart, I want you to know that you are worthy of my love. You are my everything and I only see who you are and not who you were. You are very beautiful, intelligent, full of charisma, and a true companion, he said. We align perfectly because I knew the faith, you'd have in me. Such faith is monumental and pleasing, which in turn, allows me to know that eternity with you is experienced now and for our future. Let me say this too. Every bit of pain and trouble that you've gone through has made me motivated to do all I can to sacrifice so that you may have a better life. My Queen, you deserve it. Yes, this world has trouble. Yes, there are agents and devices of evil that come to steal, kill, and destroy you. Yes, I know who I am, and I know I'm the relationship that you desire to experience fulfillment in. Baby, it's all-encompassing in me. Me and you are the perfect match.

That deep voice of yours is melting me right now but go ahead my love, she said.

Thanks, he said.

But wait a minute before you continue. I got one thing to say to you. I love you, DeVine.

I love you too Churchy.

My heart adores you, she said. Oops, didn't mean to cut you off, but then I really did. Umm, you were telling me something.

I…

Sorry, I couldn't hold my tongue, she said. You are the finest.

I appreciate you Churchy. Okay, where was I at, he asked? Oh, bae, what type of love would I really be expressing if I choose not to love you unconditionally, see the best in you, protect and defend you at all costs, lead and lavish you with every gift in the heavenlies that is eternally abundant according to my riches and glory, he said? My Father owns it all, and I only desire that you share in my inheritance. You are nothing less than the best for me. Churchy, you fully deserve my peace, hope, joy, love, kindness, goodness, patience, rest, and provision. I will never hold that back from you. I do not ever want to live without you. Here's a tissue love, he said (Churchy is choked up).

(He starts to choke up) Please pass the tissue back, I need some myself, he said. I give my all to you because to you I owe it all. My inspiration is to show you that nothing can love, support, and treat you as you should deserve, but me. Nothing can and no one can Churchy. Let me be specific bae, no one, no place, no drug, no money, no achievement, no material possession, no other! I did, I have, and I will continue to give you my all. There's nothing you can do to gain my love, and there's nothing you can do to lose my love. I am love. I love you and I'm convinced that you love me too, he said. I'm convinced that you will never walk away from such a love as this. We look good together, many see our power flowing as a power couple and many are influenced to walk in the ways that we walk, which makes our love even more gratifying. Our love is the catalyst for all to have access to eternity with my Father. To experience the everlasting Oasis in which we already, but not yet have. The love that we have for one another will draw all who are willing to accept such a gift.

So much is in this world that is corrupt and egregious, despicable, disturbing, distasteful, disastrous, and full of death, expressed DeVine. Churchy, all my Father has ever desired for everyone is the fullness of life. That life is in him, and we show and reveal by our actions what his goal for creation ought to look like. Don't allow anything to separate you from my love. Beautiful, let me rephrase that. I will never allow anything to separate you from my love, he said. I love you unconditionally and I will die for you. I will die for all because everyone in this world is worth dying for. It doesn't matter the burden, pain, betrayal, abandonment, or evil that is done. I will sacrifice my life because it is my Father's will that everyone is saved from this world's system, and its mentality of destruction. If it costs me my life so that those in the world are eternally free, made new, and rebirthed through such belief in my sacrifice for them, it is well worth it because my Father's memoir communicates so. We as one, is our purpose my gorgeous one.

See, your example of love for me, points people to the need to have me in their life, he said. Queen, I am change, newness, restoration, hope, and truth, and that defines that I am all love. I relate to people, I cure them, empower them, build them, lead them, and guide them as a model of true life and livelihood. What else do they have if they don't have what we have? Churchy, Div A. Den is a lie, B. Guyler's influence is a lie, faith in this world is a lie, and trust in people or even self is a lie. Nevertheless, such lies are persuasively and daily being communicated as truth and are leading many astray.

I want so much more for people. I want them to know my Father, to live in my Spirit, to grow through and know me, said DeVine. I place trust in you my girl, because you know what life is with me and have overcome by the word of your testimony.

DeVine, I love your intimacy with me.

You do, he asked?

Undoubtedly, I do.

You bring me daily riches and you are making me whole again my God, my King, my DeVine, she said. Never remove your love, your arms, your covering, your eye, your power from me. No one or nothing can ever attract me to them or to it because you have done more than enough, and no love compares to the love you have given me. Take me higher my King, wider, farther, and larger. Bring me to your righteousness and make provision for me so that I may carry your will throughout this wicked earth. You make me glow And I believe if people knew you in various ways that I do, they'd know that absolutely nothing compares to the love you deliver. Use me, DeVine, I want to give myself away in a manner of sacrifice for the least, the lost, the lowly, and the left out. Isn't that what you desire, she asked?

Yes, Queen, it is, he replied.

Regarding the aforementioned challenges, I once was those things and I know the pain it brings. On the flip side, I have experienced, and I know what your love will do and how it transforms and heals, she said.

You help the poor, save the widow and orphan, confound the wise, heal the sick, restore sight to the blind, make the lame walk, and strengthen the weak. There is nobody greater than you. I've searched all over and couldn't find nobody, nobody greater, nobody greater than you. I'm clothed in the finest by your Spirit's design and I walk in your authority, gaining victory every day.

We can devour the locust and the cankerworm from eating away and destroying, he said. The world is hopeless, helpless, and hapless yet we are the source to guide their treasures to where rust and moth cannot destroy. I only want what's all good, for all.

That's deep, break that down further for me, she said.

Sure, what I mean is the following: l want prosperity for all. All joy for all. All strength for all. All love for all, he replied.

I am in agreement with you, and will help bring, and share attributes of your love to this world, she stated. There's no doubt that your love can't be denied if anyone experiences it. So bae, I'm in this battle with you Almighty One. I am your true soldier to the cause of new life for dying souls. Help me help them, DeVine. They need to experience what I've experienced. They're our offspring. Let's bring them to their true self, she said. To be clear, I mean to whom and whose they are. I mean the promises that they be empowered in experiencing. They are redeemed and their stain of pain and error is removed. They'll receive the everlasting inheritance stored up for them. They'll never have to thirst again. They are saved and healed. And those outcomes are found only in you, my King.

My Queen…

Yes, DeVine.

Can we head out to our other spot, he asked?

Don't say where it is. Bae you've created for us a ton of spots. Let me guess though. Do you mean Cookie Wookie's Ice Cream Shop, DeVine?

Queen, I sure do.

Okay, I knew it. I totally accept your invite, she said. (Churchy is enthusiastic) What are we waiting on let's go. Now DeVine, can your supernatural strength, still swoop me up into my arms and carry me (Churchy kisses DeVine)?

(He tosses her swiftly into his arms) Oh wow, I see that you still can DeVine. By the way, I love that cologne that is on you, she said.

I love that perfume you have on, he remarked.

I know what you are ordering Bae. You think so, she said.

Which kind, he asked.

Tell me if I got it right. Is it that Chunky Monkey Cream, she asked?

Yes, you already know, said DeVine.

What am I having, she asked?

Hmmm, (DeVine hums).

I knew you wouldn't know, she said.

I know it all Queen. I know what you're going to want and need before you know it, he said.

Oh really, DeVine?

Yes, really, he said.

What am I having then, she asked?

You are getting that Very Berry Strawberry Cream this time and not that Coca Mocha Shake, he said.

How did you know that, she asked? I guess you are correct, DeVine. You need to get out of my head. (Churchy laughs).

CHAPTER 13

"Branding"

(October 31st, 2003)

At a Grocery Store on the Eastside

Hey hey, one minute young man, one second, please. I just want to thank you for what you've done, it was kind, said the old school gentlemen. Thanks for purchasing all of my groceries. Do you do this all the time, old school asked?

Yes, I do. I do this quite often, said the young man. I tend to go above and beyond a bit much, but heck, that's what I do.

Young man, I see. Sir, because this world has so much division in it, are you from another planet, said the older gentleman? (The two gentlemen laugh) Like, I'm quite curious to know, lil bruh, where are you from?

Well, since you asked, I'll say it like this; I am located throughout the entire earth and a great deal of what I provide is with some people and some of it is with others, said the young man. However OG, I'm confident that people on the earth desire what I can do for them, and for you, this is a small token. But, let me be very clear about this, no person on the earth should live without me, said the young man. OG, it is my understanding that generally everyone on the planet wants me in their life all the time.

Well, young man, I see exactly why everyone would want you in their life, given the fact that you are going around buying carts full of groceries and what not (they both laugh).

As an OG, I'm pretty impressed with how well put together he is. These young guys where their pants halfway down their butts and most of them talk ignorant and are disrespectful. Yet, this lil homie's waves in his hair are banging. His coordination with his clothes is solid and not sloppy. His Gucci fashion with the Rolex and Cuban link chain is a perfect match. The cream leather and fur coat and cream-colored timberland boots set it off. And the Versace-tinted frames make bro look like a famous rapper. He can't be any more than 25-30 years old max. Deep voice, million-dollar smile, approachable and generous. Who is this young man?

Wow, but again young man, let me say thank you, sir, said old school. Now, please excuse me for failing to do so. I'd say it's very rude of me to hunt you down and not tell you, my name, lil homie. Lil homie, it's shocking that what you did even exist in this crazy world. Anyway, young man, my name is B. Guyler.

What's good B. Guyler, my name is Div A. Den (they give each other a cool handshake).

Your name is Div A. Den, asked B. Guyler?

Yes it is.

I like that, it has a money sound to it, said B. Guyler. Let me give you a little background of who I am. I'm a worldwide influencer and therefore I engage so many people and so many people around the world engage me. I bring motivation to people, and it leads them to action, said B. Guyler. Not only that Div A. Den, my influence brings encouragement to people to get them to understand that they can be independent and self-sufficient. That they can be in control, and without borderlines that oppose their free will. People are great and I believe in them, said B. Guyler. Can I hit you with something else Div A. Den?

Go head OG, hit me with it, he said.

Dope, lil homie. Let me tell you this, said B. Guyler. My influence encourages people to hold their destiny in their own hands. And, because of the way that they see themselves, they can gain wisdom, find fulfillment, and enjoy unending pleasure. Lil homie, I help them discover complete love for themselves without judgment. From my expertise, they grow to know it's perfectly fine to only care about themselves.

Care about themselves, asked Div A. Den?

Yes, care about themselves. Lil homie, if they don't care about their own self, who will, asked B. Guyler?

Well OG, the reason I asked that was because those tenants of life have been what I stand on and they have brought me recognition and a better quality of life for people who obtain what I bring to their life, said Div A. Den. Heck, no matter how cutthroat it may sound, the value of what I give requires that folk exercise all measures to have a part of my brand and the wealth I provide them. Therefore, and likewise, my motive is that all people throughout the world exercise freedom for themselves too, said Div A. Den.

I get it lil homie, said B. Guyler. See, what you are doing is out the box and very very important for the world to prosper and for folk to boss up out here (Div A. Den laughs).

Old school B. Guyler seems pretty dope. Looks like he's about 55 or 60 years old. I see he wears gator boots and that the red trench he got on is fire. Dope corduroy pants and a pimp hat, with the sideways tilt, says something about the dude. Instantly, big game comes to mind. Old school could surely sell water to a whale and strips to a zebra. His high-pitched voice surely stands out and his lil grimaces when he talks reels me in. I see why folks could be drawn in. He just has that "IT" factor when it comes to the eloquence of speech and appearance. Really, in all my life I haven't felt a vibe like his. Although I'm very adamant about wanting people to win, I can tell in this brief encounter that his passion might be equally the same. Dude seems wise.

Div A. Den what's so funny, asks B. Guyler?

Bruh people crazy out here, he said. I know you have your back turned, but that old lady just wacked that lil kid with her cane and then her wig fell off. Oh my God, you just missed it again (Div A. Den laughs louder). Anyway, sorry about that, tell me more, B. Guyler.

Sure. I just believe that when we are controlled by standards not set by us personally, we are controlled against our will, said B. Guyler. As a result, that control forces us to adhere to standards that we don't agree with.

Now that's real. Now that's the truth. That's what I'm talking about, you truly make a powerful point, said Div A. Den.

I know that I do, and I'm glad you feel the same way, replied B. Guyler.

Yes, I do, he replied. I think in the same manner of passion that you do. I want everyone to have an abundance of what I offer, said Div A. Den. Especially those who barely possess what I so generously want to release unto them. OG, it seems with that being the reality, those that have none of what I bring to their lives, don't have any opportunity to experience freedom. Thus, they are limited in maximizing true freedom and those tenants that you mentioned, said Div A. Den.

Let's walk over here, said B. Guyler.

Ok, Div A. Den replied.

Now over by the entrance/exit way of the grocery store

No one is truly living if their house is shotty if their car is a lemon if their clothes are cheap, said Div A. Den. Let me put it to you plain and simple, I am needed. I am a game changer. I am a trendsetter. I am a trailblazer, and I am pained that the world is in shambles when I know I can make the greatest difference in it.

I agree, you are. I'm feeling your confidence, said B. Guyler.

What kind of sense does it make to be standing by the door, the woman said?

Oops, pardon me, miss (lady trying to get around B. Guyler).

She aggressively stated the same words over again.

LOOK WOMAN I SAID PARDON ME, ARE YOU DEAF, yelled B. Guyler?

Dag, why is she tripping with that stank look on her face, asked Div A. Den?

Old dum bum, said B. Guyler. Some folk out here will never change.

Whoops, excuse me, sir.

A young dude also trying to get around them at entrance door

Fool, keep looking at me like that and I will…, said the young dude entering.

What? What dude, what you say to me, yelled B. Guyler? Red rooster clown you…young sucka you better keep it moving.

Oh, okay old school, I…, I…, I was…, stuttered the young dude.

Oh, I know you will. Keep it moving lame, said B. Guyler! (B. Guyler pulls out his gun)

Dag old school why you got to go all the way there, asked the young dude?

Young and dumb bum, I don't play any games; I keep my 9-millimeter on me at all times, said B. Guyler. This is my world, and all will bow down to me either voluntarily or by force, he said.

Young man walks away hurriedly.

Excuse me Div. A. Den, I hate disrespect.

I understand B. Guyler.

Wow, this dude don't play no games. B. Guyler is the truth, and to be a protector of what is right, proves why he carries so much influence. I got the money, he has the power and the world needs what we have. Dude has a calm but quiet stormy way about himself. It's like I can feel the sincerity he has to make people's lives better. Glad I paid it forward for him, he truly deserved it even though it's obvious he didn't need it.

An older lady enters into the store and is trying to get around them.

Ya'll shouldn't be blocking the door like this, the old lady says.

Ma'am, yes you are correct I should not be blocking the door, said B. Guyler.

Aye, let me get to where I'm going, said B. Guyler. Div A. Den, I really hate going to shop on an early Saturday afternoon near the first of the month. People lose their minds because they have some money in their pockets. It's raining out here and everything and these people piling into this grocery store like flies on shii-yucks…, said B. Guyler.

I got you B. Guyler, don't even raise your blood pressure. You know poor folk don't got no sense when they get a few coins in their pocket, said Div A. Den.

Real talk, real talk, replied B. Guyler. This the hood, this that St. Clair mindset all day.

You right, but also from my experience, this poverty mindset extends far beyond a geographical location; it's in the burbs and backwoods too, said Div. A Den.

Young woman walks in the store with a revealing outfit on.

See what I'm saying, look at her coming in Div A. Den, she thinks it's club night already by the way she is dressing just to buy some milk, eggs, bread, and cheese. But, that would be too responsible for her to buy those thing. I'd say she's about to purchase some shrimp, steaks, lobster, and ravioli, said B. Guyler.

Why ravioli? What the ffu-rankfurt, said Div A. Den?

Chill Div A. Den, cool it, sir, said B. Guyler.

Naw, B. Guyler you crazy for saying that ravioli part, where in the world does that fit with them high-class items she is about to grab?

Man, you are crazy, said B. Guyler (B. Guyler laughs). You know folk ain't got no sense when they get a few dollars in their pockets. I can't go broke, so, I stay grabbing all kinds of stuff off shelves when I go shopping. It's raining cats and dogs and folk up in here going for broke, said Div A. Den (they both laugh).

Lil homie, there needs to be a solution to this. Some folks get it. That's why you see some who have riches and power. Others don't and so in an effort to keep up with the Jones' they splurge as if they living a rich rapper's lifestyle. They are so numb to my influence in certain ways, said B. Guyler. Some go to jail because of my influence, others drink and drug themselves to death, others steal, others take it far and beyond when it comes to promiscuity, others pop babies out of their womb-like they are popping popcorn, etcetera. Only a few know how to maximize and understand how my influence is best worked. It's not that those who run wild with their ability to be free are ill-equipped to have a top-notch/high-class lifestyle, they just refuse to fully rock with me and walk out the directions I give them, lil homie. These fools just find contentment in a poverty mindset, B. Guyler explained. We got to link because your resource power is the catalyst that will bring forth healthy ambition in the world. When folk have more than they can spend, they spend more in a holistic manner to provide other folks with that abundance. People like doing charity. It does not take a rocket scientist to understand that.

I feel ya OG. I am that solution and all I wish to do is put money in people's pockets to end this thirstiness and poor/survival mindset, expressed Div A. Den. I just realize I'm missing what I need to pull it off which is worldwide power that influences people's minds. How about I give you a call then, asked Div A. Den? It seems that a great partnership can arise between us because you have the influence, and I have the money and resources. With the power that we possess, if we lock arms in unity the world can practically become perfect. Matter of fact, the world will be perfect. Do you have a number I can reach you at?

I certainly do, said B. Guyler. Are you ready for it?

Yes, he said.

Ok, call me on my cell at any time at 216-666-0666, said B. Guyler.

I will do so soon.

Dope lil homie, I'm looking forward to hearing from you soon. We have a mission and purpose to accomplish, stated B. Guyler.

Yup, I agree that we do, he replied!

A Few Days Later

Hi, thanks for calling. You've reached the voicemail of B. Guyler. Leave a message at the beep.

Uggh, not the voicemail again. I know old school people don't be on the up and up with cell phones. Let me try one more time and if no answer, I'll let it go and remain doing my own thing, said Div A. Den.

(Phone has rung 4 times) C'mon now, pick up sir, pick up the phone sir, this connection must go forth, Div A. Den stated to himself.

Hello, answered B. Guyler.

Hello. B. Guyler?

Yes, who's calling?

It's Div A. Den. How's it going today?

All good my friend, things are normal on my end. I'm glad you called because I was thinking about you and hoping you'd reach out soon, said B. Guyler.

I had to sir; something is moving in me that feels that being in partnership with you would be world-changing, he replied.

It will lil homie.

I believe it, say no more, I have mutual thoughts about our partnership. So, from here on out, it's about developing goals and action steps so that impact is made, said Div A. Den.

Yes, indeed replied B. Guyler.

I see that Div A. Den be on his one-two. I like that about him. I can be very pushy with people and forceful about getting things done with immediacy. He is focused and that shows me a lot about his grind skills. I can do quite a few things through him. He got what he's been asking for in a partner. He has no clue who I am and how I get down. Game over, time to take over the world and get people what they really feel they need.

Hey quick, tell me more about your background and how you came to the point of doing what you do in the world, OG.

Sure, said B. Guyler.

The weather feels good today, said Div A. Den.

I agree, he replied. I think I will be going to take a walk today.

Hold up, hold that thought for one second, this dude next to me at this stop light is flagging me down, said Div A. Den.

Sure, do ya thing, replied B. Guyler.

Div A. Den at the traffic light and a guy pulls up next to him and says something to him:

Hey, yes my guy it's that new one but custom modified, said Div A. Den. Oh yeah my guy, candy-colored money green paint is how I rock out, my dude. Look my guy, I want to put you in something similar like this. I need others on my level. It's lonely at the top my dawg. You feel me? Yeah I am that guy you see on all the videos and news clips. But hurry up and come here, I don't need all these questions and "bromanicing." You need to learn when somebody trying to put you on. So come here.

Huh, said the guy?

Yeah, I said come here. Which means get out of your car. Bruh, you need to have boldness and stop being scared. (cars in traffic behind them are honking their horns) Learn to go for what you looking for, the people behind us can wait, my guy (the guy looks dumfounded at Div A. Den's statement). My guy, get out of the car and grab this business card and call me asap, said Div A. Den.

Thanks, sir, the guy replied.

You're welcome, now make sure to call me, said Div A. Den. I want everyone to win like me, ok?

Yes, okay, and thanks again.

Wow, this lil dude Div A. Den is impressive. He is the one for sure.

B. Guyler, hey B. Guyler you still there, asked Div A. Den?

Yes, I am.

B. Guyler, my bad I just be trying to elevate people out here?

Yes, I see. Look, my dude, I need to get on your level, said B. Guyler.

You look good ole skool.

Yeah, I know (Div A. Den laughs). You are silly my friend, he replied.

Naw I'm serious lil homie, I need to get on your level (Div A. Den laughs). Aye, I just don't age, and you see how my fashion game is, said B. Guyler.

Old school, you do put it together.

I feel like when we look good, have nice things, feel good, and have power, we experience life the way it should be, said B. Guyler.

You right, I can't disagree with that at all. I stay fly, I stay driving something eye-popping. My properties are the finest in the world, and I keep my temple together, said Div A. Den.

Yeah, I see you be on it, he replied.

Yeah, I know old school, it ain't hard to tell (B. Guyler laughs). I'm a walking GQ fashion model each and every day, said Div A. Den.

Now look lil bruh, I ain't say all that lil homie, but I see how you put it together (they both laugh).

Naw, I'm serious, I'm all of that and some, said Div A. Den (they both laugh again).

But yeah, this weather is amazing for October, said B. Guyler. I agree with all that you said, we should take self-care seriously so make sure you treat yourself to a good walk and even a massage if you feel like it. People like us deal with so much because we live on a have a high-level and big boss lifestyle and so to remain game-changing, we must take care of ourselves first, young fly one.

Yeah, and to add to that, since we work hard, it's only right that we play hard, he replied. It comes with the territory. You feel me?

Yeah I feel ya, said B. Guyler.

That's why I keep a few mansions, keep a private jet, keep a yacht, keep worldwide traveling all year round, said Div A. Den.

Ok, ok, what else you keep said B. Guyler?

Oh keep going, old school?

Yes, lil homie I wanna know.

Well, I keep the finest jewelry, indulge at 5-star restaurants, keep a lot of toys like luxury cars, and so on.

What driving you around today, asked B. Guyler?

I had to pull out my new Maybach custom design edition, he replied.

Huh, custom design, asked B. Guyler?

Yes sir. I'm a one-of-a-kind type of dude. No other Maybach is anywhere close to this caliber of a vehicle, he replied. Big homie, I can't stand having what everyone has, so I have to be exclusive in what I do. I am what you call set apart. That's why my heart's passion is to get my resources in people's hands so that they can create their own and not be mirroring others out here, said Div A. Den. I try to stay official you know what I'm saying?

I get it. I know you are younger than me, but how you roll is due to the origination standard I have created as a law for the world per se. You're a product of my will and I love every bit of how you roll lil homie, said B. Guyler.

But back to my original question, where you at, asked Div A. Den?

I'm at one of my mansions up in Seven Hills, he replied. I'm going to have you over one day next week. You single right, asked B. Guyler?

You know it, and I plan to be for a while, I ain't really got no time to wife something.

Good to know because I'm flying these models in from Paris next week and I'll say no more but, YOU NEED TO BE HERE, yelled B. Guyler!

Oh fo sho, put me down OG, put me down, he replied.

Okay bet. My assistant will reach out to you when they get here, said B. Guyler. I just met them when I was out there about a month ago. Since I don't know them like that, I decided not to send my jet out there to scoop them. I did send them first-class commercial airline tickets, but you know how plane delays be around this time, so when they board, my assistant will hit you up. So, let me say this. Whatever you got going during that time, stop what you are doing and come over. Lil homie, you do not want to miss this, so keep your schedule free around that time.

How many coming, asked Div A. Den?

Four of them will be in attendance, he replied.

Oh, that's all I needed to know. Yeah, make sure to have your assistant reach out and I will definitely be there, said Div A. Den. I'm interested in knowing something about you.

Ok, what you want to know lil homie?

How did you get to this point?

Long and somewhat a complicated story but, my family is historically recognized as the most impactful entity in the world. Side note, I'm learning that someone may be responsible for overshadowing such impact currently, hint hint, said B. Guyler.

Whatever OG, you are silly man.

Ok, where was I at? Oh yeah, I remember now. Historically my family has been noted as one of the greatest influencers in the world. Oops, hold on one second, this neighbor of mine just shouted something to me from outside. I try to be cool with everyone but this guy is annoying. Stay on the line Div A. Den.

Sure, he said.

WHAT DO YOU WANT AGAIN YOU STUPID DUMMY, yelled B. Guyler? HUH, YOU WANT ME TO SLOW DOWN DRIVING ON OUR STREET? BROKE FOOL, I'LL DRIVE THE WAY I WANT TO DRIVE. LOOK, YOUR CAR IS A PIECE OF GARBAGE. YOU CARE NOT TO LISTEN TO ME. YOU CHOOSE TO LIVE UNDER A ROCK AND REFUSE TO LET ME MAKE YOU SOMEBODY IN THIS WORLD. THEREFORE, YOU NAG ME ABOUT SMALL STUFF SO DON'T GET IT TWISTED, I'M NOT MADE TO LIVE A BORING AND BLAND LIFE LIKE YOU. IF I WANT TO SPEED WHEREVER I'M AT,

THIS STREET INCLUDED, I'M SPEEDING. NOW MISS ME WITH THAT BULL…AND GET OUT OF MY YARD YOU LAME!!!

Okay, you still there Div A. Den, asked B. Guyler.

Yes, I am.

This fool made me lose my train of thought, where did I leave off at? Oh yeah, I remember, you were asking me about my family. I love my family. I miss my family, said B. Guyler.

Why do you say that, asked Div A. Den?

You know what, I feel we should have a face-to-face so I can break it down more, answered B. Guyler. If you are not busy now, how about we talk and grab a quick bite over at this place called Judah Café? Are you familiar?

Naw, I ain't familiar but yeah, my schedule is open today, said Div A. Den. What time?

Cool, how about we meet at two o'clock, he said?

Ok bet, see you at two. Oh, send me the address too.

I got you lil homie.

See you soon, old school.

Yup, see you soon, replied B. Guyler.

Judah Café, current time, 2 pm

Hi sir.

Hi, Lady Liz good to see you today, said B. Guyler. How are things going?

All is well, besides the fact I'm feeling somewhat anxious, she said.

Why so, he asked?

I am always excited when it is spa day, she said.

Oh yeah?

Yes sir.

I can tell you are. If I may be honest, it is obvious that you need it because your nail polish is chipped and that disgusts me. I know you work this crap job, which means you are broke, but I do have someone that can help you better your pitiful situation. I like the food here but please keep yourself together because I do not want to throw up, said B. Guyler. I feel like I ought to report your lack of personal upkeep to your manager but today I will let you slide. See, I can make your life amazing and prosperous because it's what I do, Liz. You would never have another issue like you have today because you would be too well off for such a thing. My name carries weight and I want you to think about allowing me to have your life so that I can get you together, ok?

I don't know, I will think about it, she said.

Do not reject tough love girl, I am here to help you and want the best for you, ok?

I hear you, she said.

Okay Liz, let me know when you are ready to start, and I'll get things going for you.

Thanks, sir. So, what brings you in today outside of ordering your favorite "burning hot, devil tots, she asked?"

Frankly, it's none of your business what brings me in today (Liz looks astonished). However, you know I cannot resist them tots any time I step foot in this place. I don't know, maybe I just have sympathy for you or something today, but I will let you in on why I am here. I have a business meeting with an amazing individual who is about to partner with me and change this world. We will be putting our heads together to make a difference for low-level people like yourself. You haven't been too receptive in the past in letting me make you whole. I know it's because of my brother God, which is surely the reason why your life is so sad today. But I want you to know that you'll have the chance to be "all in" once me and my new partner unfold things, said B. Guyler.

Well, I wish you nothing but the best, she said. Let me get you guys some water to start. I'll be right back.

Look girl, make sure you bring the napkins out with the water. I hate that I have to remind you not to forget like you always do. If I have to keep doing your job for you, I'm going to need a portion of your paycheck in my pocket. I get tired of getting into my meal and needing napkins and you ain't nowhere to be found. If you want to know why you lack getting my best tip, or, not getting a tip from me at all, it's because you kind of suck at waitressing.

Sorry B. Guyler, sorry.

Liz, sorry is not hired to bring me my food, you are, so do your job girl.

(Uggh, B. Guyler grunts). They know they love to always play that "Found" song by C-Life in here. Holy Hip Hop gets on my nerves. My brother doesn't deserve all this praise. Sheesh, let me stop talking to myself. Let me see where Div A. Den is. Umm, what's his number? Oh, there it is. (Phone ringing) Not the voicemail. Let me try again.

126

Hello, hello oh what's up B. Guyler?

All good Div A. Den. Are you close?

Yup, I'm actually pulling up now.

Okay come to the back corner near the restroom sign, I got us a table already.

Ok about to walk in now, he said.

Okay cool, replied B. Guyler.

Hi, how are you doing, asked the woman at the counter?

Aww, I'm doing great. My name is Wanda. How can I help you?

Thanks for asking Wanda. My first time here. I'm meeting my friend here. Oh, I was just about to ask you to... But never mind, I see him now, said Div A. Den.

Enjoy sir, she said.

Okay. Will do, ma'am.

What's up Div. Can I call you that, asked B. Guyler?

Sure, what's up BG. Okay to call you that?

Definitely.

Sheesh, sir, your grip is cobra-ish, said Div. I respect the handshake but sir I need my hand (they both laugh).

I got you Div, let's have a seat. Liz brought us some water.

Okay dope. What's good to grub from here, BG?

Well, my favorite is the "devil hot tater tots." I'm a big potato eater if you know what I'm saying.

Yup, that sounds unique, I think I will go with the money-hungry honey biscuits, said Div.

Good choice my friend, he replied.

Thanks for suggesting we meet in person, said BG.

BG, I did not want to delay any longer regarding the mission and impact we both can make together. We both know that influence and income are essential for experiencing a high quality of life. You have the influence and I have the income, so it's a no-brainer that we join forces.

I totally agree. We both have gifts that will change lives forever, said BG. I feel that lives will benefit because it is largely agreed upon that when people are not secure with financial abundance, then violence, corruption, sickness, and mental health challenges debilitate the earth, explained BG.

Yeah, you right about that, replied Div.

Thanks. That's why we together can impact the world, said BG.

You have the skill to influence their need for me on a greater level. No one on earth or beyond can direct and guide people the way they should be led, said Div. Plus, to go along with that, having the abundance of what I provide is the sole reason for happiness. People are miserable out here, dying out here, the earth is deteriorating out here, and when it should be eternal and lacking nothing at all, misplaced influence is robbing people of true living, explained Div. It's unfortunate that the primary influence in the world is total bull crap. Sir, it's a sad reality that people's quality of life is heisted from them. This earth was created to sustain itself, but eternal life ideology has robbed people of the "not now" and is fooling people into the "new life." This hat trick has been going on for such a long time. No wonder suicide rates are at an all-time high. "Living," is correctly defined as having riches, point blank. That's my purpose on this earth. I bring life to people. I would not want to live without my money and resources. Therefore, I am compassionate that all people have me as the god of their life. However, BG, it is like the need for me just isn't made known enough, because this eternal life delusion is very popular. Yes, I carry recognition, but in and of my own efforts, I am just not able to produce the voice of urgency like you are able to. You make people respond, you make people believe in their own truth, you make people desperately go for what they know, explained Div. I don't know how you do it, maybe it is because of the stunning look, success, riches, and employees of world-leading positions on the earth. But one thing is for sure, you convince people. So many see themselves never being able to reach levels that you would make sure they control. So, to expand your influence, I feel that they need money to help them in the process. When a person is struggling to maintain the basics, they live in survival mode. Survival mode cannot dream because survival mode can't think beyond the next issue that they need to survive. BG, I'm so passionate about what I bring to people's lives. People have been so numb to me. They accept a reality of life that leaves a void in their souls. Such a void becomes generational to those who have less of me. Thus, if you notice, the generational poverty pattern is growing worse and worse. But, on the other end of the spectrum, those who do have my resources and your influence of power, hold on to me tightly and live out the authority you have influenced them to carry out successfully. Although it is not their obligation to help, I'm referring to the moguls, world leaders, and famous figures. Although it's not their responsibility to give my resources away to anyone who has their hands out, I desire all people to be secure by having as much of me and my money in their possession. Only a small percentage of elites have invented ways to obtain me and steward my money and resources, which is good. They reap the benefits, but they have no standard to adhere to. So, because of human nature and its wiring for excess and dominance, others suffer. Matter of fact, elites, through generational inheritances and their out the box thinking skills have created systems in which they feast, at the expense of starving and exploiting those who are trying to earn my money but just can't break through the barrier, explained. BG, tell me this. Am I sensing that there is someone in your network that deeply cares that all people have everlasting joy in life, asked Div?

Yes indeed, you've read me well. I have some contacts, said BG. A particular one comes to mind that equally believes all people should have a high quality of life as you do. But she's in a covenant arrangement with someone. That someone being my brother DeVine, who's widely known as God. In my heart of hearts, I don't think she desires to be in a faithful relationship with him. I don't know, in plain view, some of her fashion choices are revealing, and in talking with her at times, it seems to me that she's searching for more ways to elevate her service to people. What I do believe is this: she simply wants more autonomy from him. She's quite articulate but she's inconsistent with her impact and I believe it is because she feels God is possessive of her regarding what she does. In conversation, it appears that she doesn't seem trusted by God and her sort of kind of Father-in-Law. This memoir that my Father wrote, does have some accusative statements about her in my opinion. She is not a blood relative of the Father's chosen people so she, as one who has been grafted into the family, still is identified at times as a faithless prostitute, stingy, rebellious, self-gratifying, and not as compassionate as expected. I don't know why they don't accept her like they should. Meaning, care less about trying to correct each and every one of her flaws, but I know this fosho: she has that "IT" factor. She possesses that aggression to be powerful and influential. Like way way more than she already is. Yet, I strongly believe the manifestation of her "bossness" is found in connection with you and you only, said BG. I can discern her mood and see the numb look on her face at times because she's highly scrutinized. Scrutinized because she has convinced the world that being in a relationship with God is most advantageous, but most people can see that her promotion is hypocritical because of how she carries herself. People wish-washy. I really don't care all about "the way that she carries herself." What I have seen for myself though, is that God has left her message empty and she feels let down about it. See, for many, not just her, I've heard them express their experiences with God. Experiences that were only filled with judgment and disappointment.

I hear what you are saying, but you know how it is when you are in the limelight, it's hard to not be judged, said Div. Can that be a fair statement about God?

I don't throw that point out the window that you raise, but at the level he is judged, it begs for a side-eye look towards him if you know what I mean, replied BG.

Suspicious might you say, asked Div?

Big suspicion, he said. When we are seen as people who are noble and looked to as role models, we carry a lot of weight and responsibility.

People are expecting us to deliver on our promises. When we don't, it's misleading, explained BG.

I get you, folk are out here desperate, said Div.

That's right. Moreover, folk want genuine genius generous leaders because they are tired of the games, said BG. This world as we know it, is on a crash course at record speed. The biggest pimp talk ever known to man is orchestrated through one word.

What word is that asked Div?

Are you ready for it, he replied?

I am sir, I am, replied Div.

Drum roll on this table then my friend, are you ready for it, asked BG?

I am (Div and BG started drum rolling on the table). (Drum stops)

Div, It's HOPE!

Oh wow, I concur BG.

People are becoming more skeptical and leerier nowadays. God is becoming one who is seen as a carrier of false hope if you will, said BG. His hope speech feels so conniving that it has sapped people out of life who have tried to invest their time and trust in a falsely promoted fruitful lifestyle, that he advertises. Yet, a large portion of people remain in support of him and Churchy has done a remarkable job of pulling the heartstrings of people. She's just the bomb-dot-com when it comes to her ability to attract and draw people towards her. Her efforts have appealed to people. Besides Churchy Selah's whip appeal…

Ok, ok, I hear you in your Babyface voice (they both laugh), said Div.

I think the reason for this pull is mainly generated due to the hurt that people are experiencing, said BG. The power of hurt pursues help by all measures and no matter if one is actually obtaining help, just the talk that there is "hope" will magnetize people to that voice. The voice of hope is so luring. People accept and believe any lie when they are desperate. Their desire to fill the open wound with the healing balm of prosperity is hypnotic. Hope is the falsely televised antidote. See, hopes' abstract hovering, produces a hovering that hangs in the ranks and that seems reachable and as well as medicinal, explained BG. But let me tell you something. That sermon is just good preaching that is obsolete of any practice, and any action. And so, guess what?

What, replied Div.

There are some testimonials out here that inform people about this corrupt marketing ploy. Some folk out here telling the real about God's strategy to mesmerize people with the idea of hope. They see right through the false humility of God. They can pick up on it but a great deal of others keep chasing the dangling carrot of "hope," said BG. They say that God appears meek and gentle but through his sly hand, he misleads people into thinking their lives will have tangible blessing, explained BG. Yet as they say, his words are just simply hogwash. As a matter of fact, it's also stated that his genius is tactical. If it's not hope that is suspended in thin air, it's condemnation. I'm told that he has hurt people believing that they are being punished for things that they do that are not pleasing to his Father. It is a fear tactic Div. Wouldn't you agree?

I certainly do, I get it BG.

Yeah, although God advertises a message that people are free from living perfect, he always holds their shortcomings against them, said BG. This method is very binding because people can never know when they have reached the approval of his Father. Therefore, they are viciously manipulated. He runs the hope game on them and then backdoors it with the heavy hand of judgment. That's why so many are hooked to this cultic bondage. You know why and how, asked BG?

Naw, I don't, help me understand..

Sure, you look puzzled anyway. Aye, tell me if I am boring you with all this information, said BG.

Naw, we good. This interesting. Keep going, said Div.

Bet. They are convinced to trust him and through that abstract term of "hope" or even better, the other one that I laugh at, "faith," they salivate over the possibility of a quality of life through tangible increase, explained BG. On the opposite spectrum, this judgmental concept called "idolatry" binds them.

Why you say that, asked Div?

Because if they decide to walk away or do something that God's Father disagrees with, which isn't fully clear. They receive what that practically entails, which is endless penalization, said BG. This penalization determines that they are unable to receive the blessing they desire.

These actions are just not fair, said Div.

Fair Div? Let me take it further in saying that these actions are detestable. Cult influence is very powerful, said BG. It is perplexing to me how his supporters are amazingly convincing to others though. The ability in them to spread this deception is masterful though, said

BG. God is a good pimp, a good trafficker, and a good kidnapper. See, with you and Churchy Selah, God's beloved partner, you two will be able to restore true quality of life to the world. God simply comes up blank and although he has excellent marketers, the world is experiencing that the proof of his blessing is not in the pudding. Its presumed proof is somewhere in his Father's Oasis hid in a dresser. Or under his you know what..(Div laughs)

BG, you are hilarious.

But, I am very serious my friend. I believe you are a game-changer. I discern that if Churchy sees how amazing you two would be together, she'd be motivated to divorce him, said BG. Honestly, that would be a good deal for her. She stays in the worldwide news controversially because she's seen in compromising positions that reflect that she has other lovers. I don't believe the gossip though, said BG. She's trapped in an image she is dying to be released from.

BG, say no more. I'm confident that this is the right person to connect with, said Div. Make sure you work your hand on this, I got to get with this woman. This is going to accomplish so much for the earth because she and I can come together and make people experience true living.

Ok. I'm glad that you are onboard. Let me get to setting things up, said BG. You just follow my lead Div, okay?

Definitely, your work speaks for itself, I trust you sir, answered Div.

"Insatiable"

(November 15th, 2003)

Hey B. Guyler you look amazing as always.

Appreciated Churchy.

Thanks for coming to meet with me. I and the community citizens had a good discussion about you the other day, said Churchy.

Oh yeah, replied B. Guyler?

Yes, we happened to be reading your Father's memoir and we found it interesting how you were cast out and separated for good from the family, she said. That's the reason why I reached out to you. I know that you are successful in your influence, and I wanted to learn more about who you are and the ways that you operate. I know I just barged into this conversation with a lot (they both chuckle) but, before you speak about those things, can I get you something to drink or anything?

No thanks, he said. I just came from Hot Sauce Gloss; and it was banging too.

No you didn't, and you didn't bring me anything, asked Churchy?

Oh, I didn't think you "like to burn," as their slogan says. (Churchy laughs).

Which one did you go to, she asked?

I went to the one on Kinsman.

Oh ok, they "aight," but I like the one on 152nd and St. Clair, she said.

Churchy, your office looks great. I see that you have good taste ma'am. Now, what I do request is that you turn that air conditioner and ceiling fan down, said B. Guyler.

Sure, I get it, you always look hot anyway.

Whatever woman. But nice plants.

Thanks sir. Speaking of that, I need to water them. Hold a second.

Sure, ma'am.

Hey B. Guyler.

Yes, can you…

(B. Guyler's phone rings) Hold up, hold one-second Churchy I have an incoming call. Hello, said B. Guyler. Hi, is B. Guyler available? Yes, speaking. I'm Felecia and I'm with Local Two Four…(B. Guyler hangs up)

B. Guyler is everything ok, asked Churchy? You hung up quite fast there.

Yes, it's all good. I am up in arms about this union call that somehow has my number. They keep asking for dues as if I have worked there. But anyway, are you done watering the plants?

I sure am, she replied.

Now, where was I B. Guyler? Oh, now I know. So, my observation makes me feel that it was kind of unfair for you to get booted out of the Oasis seeing that you had such a great influence among others who live in it.

Yeah, I agree with your observations but hey, fallouts do happen, he said. However, what I have come to know is that endings lead to new beginnings, and it allows a person the opportunity to build new relationships and other dealings that may not have been possible had the former relationships and dealings remained in existence.

I hear you, but what about the luxuries of the Oasis though? It must have been unimaginable how elaborate the dwelling was. In our discussion, a few people raised the thought that it had to be emotionally tough for you to deal with the banishment from the Oasis, said Churchy.

Yes, it was an amazing place, but I can blend in anywhere and maximize my surroundings to a level that is pleasing to me. To be honest, all I care about is myself and what I think. So, I am not fazed by what others think of me. See ma'am, I know that it means a lot to you to be noticed and wanted. To increase your reach to the world. As well as introduce as many to my brother DeVine as possible because of his devout passion for you. But anyway, how has that mission been going for you lately, asked B. Guyler? Successful? Not well?

Sir, it is often a redundant and stale venture. I don't know, DeVine is cool, but I desire more out of our relationship. See, on the outside, I appear as if I have it going on. Like as if I have arrived or something. But deep within myself, I feel at times I am just putting on a public façade, said Churchy. It could be why I'm so critical of people. Judgmental if I might say. Yes, people enjoy many fruits in this world. Fruits that your influence encourages as fulfilments. I have tasted a few of them and have felt quite drawn to them. Great satisfaction. Kind of like an appeasing if you will, he said.

I get it. DeVine often points me to the memoir of his Father, and I must tell you, walking in these principles are very restrictive. The memoir claims freedom for my spirit, but it negates my free will to live life blissfully or better yet, live life the way I want to live it. Granted sir, to a degree, it feels good to be celebrated for causes that DeVine leads me to accomplish. Some things about his will for me are not always gripping, said Churchy. I can provide food, I show empathy by asking DeVine to help people, which motivates him to do so in certain ways. I get to link people with him and out of it, some find fulfillment and joy. Although I have experienced some fruits of prosperity from my relations, and even scrutinized for it, I believe I should enjoy greater prosperity.

Indeed you should Churchy, said B. Guyler. Churchy, I stay rich, and I grieve for those who do not flow in the power that is readily available. When one functions in their independence, they are not bound to the ideals of others, he said. Being prevented from independence is the exact definition of control. I get to sleep, eat, do, and go where I please. I just got it like that. I answer to only myself. I connect with those who DeVine and our Father would label rebellious, he continued. We do things and make things shake. They enjoy it and I enjoy them enjoying themselves. Restriction is a curse word in my vocabulary. I know nothing at all about being restricted. I take what I want, influence those to believe in my view of life, and help them get what they want out of life. See, the Father would call it manipulatory; I have determined it to be savviness. I think for people. To me, it's perfectly fine if someone struggles with indecision. I am their solution. Yeah, people seek out the Father, they seek DeVine's assistance in that, but they miss having a say so in the matter. They are voiceless regarding decisions for their own life's journey. I really don't know how you are able to put up with such treatment while believing you have dignity. I don't think you fully know or truly want to accept who you are. It is clear that you accept what someone else wants you to be. See yourself for you Churchy. Be yourself for yourself. Have some self-respect.

I encourage you Churchy Selah to get money, get luxury, get power, kill the cravings, and live your life. You see others in this world doing so and I discern that you want what they have. Why should that be seen as wrong, he asked?

I know B. Guyler, I know exactly what you are saying.

You say that, but do you really really know, Churchy? It's okay to want a house like someone else or a savings account or an opportunity to travel frequently. Tell me this, why is it wrong per the memoir that you want what others have? Don't we base our desires on what is seen, asked B. Guyler? What in the whole wide world, type of game does the Father run? I mean, I have feelings for those who are naturally blind Churchy. I can only imagine how difficult it is to live with that type of infirmity. But, what doesn't make sense at all to me is how you who have healthy eyes are blinded by challenging words that the Father enforces. Like for instance the term "covetousness." I wish you'd be real with yourself and accept the trueness of your soul. I sense that you really don't want to follow the memoir, and we both know it. You be acting like you do, but who do you think you are fooling, asked B. Guyler? From my viewpoint, you rarely follow the memoir anyway. The very purpose of having eyes is for one to be granted the ability to see, correct?

Yes, but…

But nothing Churchy! I know that you desire to flourish.

Huh, I am flourishing to a degree, she said.

You are not living free miss? You are not flourishing.

How do you think that I'm not asked Churchy?

Easy, you must start doing the opposite of what you are doing, he said.

Okay, and what is that she asked?

You desire to be spoon-fed. You desire to not let go. You desire hand-me-downs. You desire the control of a loan shark. You desire to be intimate with fear. You desire to be a liar to yourself and suppress your true inner feelings. Am I wrong about that, asked B. Guyler?

B. Guyler, I'ddd saaaay…

Say what Churchy? Say what? (Churchy puts her face in her hands and sways her head right to left as B. Guyler moves to the edge of his seat and looks intently at her).

You are a murderer Churchy.

Huh? How so, she asked?

Because you murder your true passions which in turn misuses your true power and influence. Which in turn, preaches a chained-filled lifestyle and strangles others into the same fear you are living by. Their purpose is killed by your serial killing murder spree. The blood on your hands is obvious, said B. Guyler. The blood on your hands is dripping in plain sight. It isn't hard to find. You should be on a wanted poster as we speak. Don't get it twisted, you are a murderer of passions, nuff said. People will miss out on maximizing their life because of you. You are a thief!

No I'm not. What are you talking about. she replied.

Yes, you are. You are an accomplice to the theft that results in people's lives being sapped, he said. You should have a conviction for receiving stolen property or grand larceny or fraud. Your hand is sly. You persuade people to live by what's communicated in the memoir. They become convinced by your presentation of the memoir and therefore, they invest in it. In a strange fashion you experience satisfaction by communicating the memoir's details. And if that isn't enough, you remain oblivious to the result that people are left empty-handed. Why are we even talking right now, asked B. Guyler? You should have auditioned to be a cast member of the movie "Ocean's Eleven." You would've certainly won the starring role. You don't "shabbat." You never rest. You are a predator. As a matter of fact, you look spent now. You are used and abused by some theory that the memoir communicates. You are overworked, underpaid, and under-appreciated. You must enjoy it or something.

No, not true, that's a cap said Churchy.

I think not, save it for the birds, he replied. Be you Churchy Selah. Be team you. Are you ready or not, asked B. Guyler?

I am, she said.

I don't believe you at all miss. You're told that if you enjoy something for yourself, you practice idolatry against the Father. I don't understand how you can live like this. Is the Father not egotistical? It's clearly obvious that he is. You are a robot, he continued. Why would someone invent a PlayStation or Xbox when you are the greatest thing ever made sport of and controlled? (B. Guyler laughs), Ma'am, you are sadly being trampled upon. It makes me so sad to see it, too. You are an eyesore, there is no other way to put it. After all I have just said, explain your thoughts about it Churchy.

Well, the continuous sacrificing I strenuously do at times seems stalled out. Per the memoir, I am to share in DeVine's inheritance and that is a nice gesture, but I am not sure what this inheritance fully defines. It seems like the Oasis is nice but toxic since you got booted out of it. To me, power equals prosperity and so my power is limited. My partner's power is said to be limitless but if what I possess now is defined as limitless prosperity, DeVine can have this little change back and I can go on about my way. Truly, it feels counterintuitive for him, per the memoir, to demonstrate this power when access to this so-called power he possesses, is uncertain. This power that defines prosperity is not available as I feel it should be. Now many will attempt to raise the thought that prosperity is beyond just financial dominance. I agree with that thought to an extent but why is it assumed that the maximization of power can be obsolete of financial dominance? B. Guyler, I just want to reach the level I most see as effective for the benefit of myself as well as the at-large community that I love serving. It absolutely makes no sense to me to have a portion of my work, for only a portion of those that depend on me to experience what's beneficial. For instance, take financial gain. A large percentage of those I'm assigned to serve—those who depend on me, remain impoverished, said Churchy. Yet, that is the reality I encounter daily. The memoir claims I do not lack anything. Which makes me come into agreement with what you were just expressing, sir.

Yeah, I'd say you don't lack anything too, Churchy. The pearls you have on, the Louis Vuitton purse, the leather wear, and Gucci eye frames are quite eye-popping. Not to mention that Mercedes Benz truck of yours outside in the parking lot, said B. Guyler.

Sir, God's integrity I question due to how it seems that various promises of his word fall short.

Miss, I truly understand your challenge. As you can see in the memoir, years ago my relationship was severed with my family. Severed with my Father, my brother DeVine and my other family members in the Oasis. I am unsure why I was excommunicated. I'm unsure why the rift that resulted between my Father and me became unrepairable. I don't know, yet being confident in myself, I refused to let it bother me. Although it is what it is, I do miss the amazingness of the Oasis setting. That was something to see for sure.

Well, how does it feel to not live there anymore, asked Churchy?

Churchy I don't sweat it. Do you know why?

Why B. Guyler?

My oasis is myself. I don't need external circumstances to define my happiness or status. Flaunting myself is my happiness and status, he stated. Everything that comes out of it, material things, for instance, is a byproduct of my amazingness.

Yes, it's obvious. You have a red Maserati parked outside, when we scheduled this sit down you said you have a vacation to Dubai coming up and you're about to purchase a television network and private jet, said Churchy. You are wearing alligator shoes, right now. So, I clearly understand that you are a walking oasis.

I am, he said. I know what I bring to the table, and I know that I can trust my own actions. Others' actions or rules or material items do not make my table. Nor make me rely on trusting them or what they do toward me. I do me! You hear me Churchy? I DO ME. Plus, I am clearly aware that I can't control how others feel or react to my confidence, that's up to them to figure out for themselves, said B. Guyler.

I'm wondering if what I am saying is even registering with Churchy right now. This little smirk on her face defines how Stockholm she really is. She talks as if she's being held back from the purpose she is feeling she is unable to make. Yet, that smirk says it all. You cannot hold tightly and release something at the same time. She needs to learn to let go. This swiveling right and left in her chair makes me feel she's anxious to end this conversation. Since I want the best for her and since I realize she's on the cusp of letting go of the brainwashing she's been experiencing from God knows how long, I'm going to tell her what she needs to know.

Why is B. Guyler's face so frowned up and his tone so aggressive? I'm trying to concentrate on what he's saying but I don't take passionate speeches directed towards me too well. Like I want to say: Dude calm the heck down.

Churchy, I know that my Father modeled ambition. I was determined to try my best to be like him in that way. To me, that is his greatest quality. I adore him for that. I intimately saw the results of ambitious labor and creativity that he exemplified. I desired to be assertive and deliberate in order to obtain the outcomes that ambition provides, said B. Guyler. Do my own thing you know.

Yes, B. Guyler that makes sense.

I worked tirelessly to achieve excellence for the namesake of the family. My drive focused on being as less dependent on the assistance of my Father as possible. Frankly, I did not want his assistance. I believed that it was right to do and be whatever I wanted, said B. Guyler. I simply believed that he would be more pleased if I achieved success without his handholding. After all, I was created the most beautiful, skilled, and powerful than all of my Oasis family members. Actually, I'm more intelligent and powerful than anyone created or anyone that will ever be created. Simply put, my goal was to please him and myself. I do not feel that anything is wrong with that.

I don't think so either, B. Guyler.

Yup, my philosophy is that complete excellence means obtaining achievements apart from anyone's handouts, including the Father, he said. You get it don't you?

Yes B. Guyler, I...

Naw, no you don't Churchy. I'd say you kind of get it, but not really. You are too reliant on my brother and Father.

I don't think that I fully agree with that observation, she said.

Oh really? In some ways you kind of remind me of myself. You are strong-willed. You just need to let your strong will drive you to strong action. Strength is action, not just words, he said.

B. Guyler, what motivated you to pursue life in such a manner?

Well, I saw and experienced the success of my effort from how it influenced other family members to follow me. I was a leader before leadership was a concept. Churchy I am the manifestation of the "term leader."

Term Leader, she questioned?

Yes, the term leader. The Father allows people to lead according to the boundaries of his terms. What was transferred to me, the gifting that came from my Father, the one who made me in love, did create a family culture to flow with a similar passion as me. Why? Because I have that "IT" factor, he said. No one has ever had the complete "IT" factor but me. Even my Father knew I had a greatness that set me apart from all other beings. It was made known from the onset of "being" existence in the world, Churchy. I feel that it was a greatness that surpassed even his expectations of me. I feel that I elevated my greatness apart from the Father's direction or training or assistance. So, all I wanted to do was display it to everyone. I openly and confidently advertised this truth in the Oasis and my Father saw it as pride, said B. Guyler.

Seriously? But isn't pride wrong, she asked?

No. To have pride does not always mean to be haughty or seek to be exalted above everyone. Some only associate pride to be synonymous with being conceited, boastful, and bougie. However, pride also suggests that people have satisfaction and happiness in their achievements. It's a natural thing to celebrate the successful outcomes of hard work. Is that a wrong thing to do Churchy?

Naw, I don't think so B. Guyler.

The Father had pride when he looked at what he made and stated that it was very good. He starts off the memoir by expressing that detail about himself. Now would you call the Father prideful, asked B. Guyler?

I guess not.

Exactly, I see you kind of get what I'm saying.

In trying to see the reason for this fallout from the eyes of my Father, I just was untamed excellence that was beyond his capacity to control, said B. Guyler. Thus, I set a precedent that was not his will for me or the rest of the family. To me, that is the only thing that makes sense. I most likely overstepped and that overstepping brought an unwanted influence on the rest of the family.

But wouldn't you call that selfish to overstep and usurp the Father's authority?

Authority?

Yes B. Guyler, authority.

Churchy please with the hogwash.

No B. Guyler, I just would like to understand things clearer. It seems as if the Father desired harmony. Your Father in all his intelligent designing of the earth, designed it intentionally with harmony in mind.

Oh, so are you comparing such harmony to the way the ecosystem or human body performs, he asked her?

B. Guyler, I…I…

Keep your mouth shut Churchy. I already know where you are headed with this. Churchy, understand something.

I'm trying to understand something, B. Guyler.

Yeah, sure you are, Churchy.

No, I'm right sir, make things clearer. I will say that I am a little astonished as to why you were booted out of the Oasis. You are very gifted. But if we are going to see the reason why that happened from the Father's point of view, why did you overstep his authority, she questioned? Was it fear of sharing the spotlight? Or, not getting total recognition for your contribution to any Oasis goal achieved? Were you challenged that you were not always the one who was going to stick and stand out? Did you feel that whatever success that came under the Father's umbrella, you would have to blend into that and accept that team orientation was bigger than you? Also, you do know that you were only the leader of the second chair don't you? You do know that right, Churchy asked?

Know what, asked B. Guyler?

You smart enough to know that, she said. Help me to understand B. Guyler!

I pull my weight, Churchy.

Yeah, but why would you want all the credit for your greatness all the time, if you understand that you are an oasis yourself? You did say that correct, asked Churchy?

Oasis yourself huh? You dang right I said it, you heard me loud and clearly, said B. Guyler.

Well, explain sir. Explain this "you are an oasis" stuff, she said.

Look, don't be completely foolish, completely irrational ma'am. What about Larry Phillips, what about Larry Phillips, he asked?

Who in God's name is Larry Phillips, she asked?

Exactly Churchy, exactly. Larry Phillips is a line worker I know. I typically see him at Judah Café.

And B. Guyler, so what.

And Churchy...

Where the heck are you going with this, she asked?

Chill lady, I'm going somewhere with this. Sam Walton is Walmart. No one identifies Larry Phillips with any significance or importance to Walmart. There is a ton of Larry's but only one Sam Walton. Sam Walton is the oasis. So, it's not about harmony or authority. It's plain as day and easy to comprehend, said B. Guyler. So, if you want to understand more clearly, no Sam Walton, no Walmart. What I assume is that the Father has his own self-conscience issues, said B. Guyler.

How so B. Guyler?

Well, it's threatening to most visionaries when a "just as good as," or greater influencer evolves out of their vision. The influence they have, challenges their ego that could lead to a power trip. You know why, asked B. Guyler?

I don't know why. B. Guyler, why?

It's like that because greater attention has shifted to the new leader of their liking. It's in the memoir, he said. Check out the story of Saul and David, and you'll see what I mean. Even more so, the power that the new influencer has—like me for instance. I'm one who received admiration from the lesser peer population. Overall, what I'm saying is that I brought more relevancy, I was easier to approach, spoke their language, knew the initial level they were on, and then my skill-set thrived right before them. Thus, in those respects, my influence could have been more harmful to the Father than good. And in this case, because of the influencer, the Father would have needed to sever his control. That severing took away his micromanaging practices and therefore gave space for my peers to independently see my shine, and so that's why I'm an oasis itself, he said.

Interesting how I have her attention on this. Yup, look at her now. The chair swiveling has stopped, she's intently looking at me as she leans forward out of her seat with her hand on her chin and her elbow planted on her cherry wood desk. I wonder what is going through her mind? Maybe her fear is being released. If so, this would be game-changing because no matter who I use, I use. My plan will go forth because that is what I do. I don't care about my brother God getting in the way. Since he isn't using his lady in the best sense, I'll use her in my own way. Why does he even need to exist any longer anyway? It's not like he's doing major boss moves. God is dead to me. I run this earth, I run people, and I will manage my will through all who are not foolish enough to reject it but respect it.

You know, it is speculation on my part but I just could never wrap my head around the banishment. Yes, I had the greatest ability out of all the family, and in understanding it, I believed I was wired in a way that total independence from the Father meant less burden on him carrying out his vision for creation. Maybe though, he saw it as counterproductive rather than reproductive. Maybe he gauged that a rebellious culture would've been the outcome. In trying to see it that way, he may have assumed that the Oasis community would refuse to remain obedient to his vision. But to me, from the outset, that is a misconstrued obedience, said B. Guyler.

So B. Guyler, are you saying such a misconstrued obedience that boxes and locks one inside a single solitary vision?

Correct Churchy.

One second one second she said. They know that I am in a meeting, so why are they knocking at my door?

Yes Ru, what is it?

Ma'am, Minister Bartholomew called in sick and is unable to do tonight's prayer and memoir class.

And you are knocking at my door to tell me this during a meeting, Ru? Do you not know the protocol? Do you have amnesia right now, Ru?

No, ma'am, I'm sorry, said Ru.

Sorry doesn't solve the issue. Get on the phone and call up sister Martha and have her do the prayer and study in his place, said Churchy! (Churchy slams door behind him).

Excuse me B. Guyler, my staff is so slow to understand. But where were we, B. Guyler?

No worries, my Father preaches collective responsibility but as a community, we had no say so at the table, he said.

So, are you saying that every now and again, he should've handed the keys of the car over to you per se, asked Churchy?

Exactly, that's exactly what I meant, he said.

So, do you see his vision as selfish, she asked?

I do.

How so?

It's simple to articulate, Churchy.

In what way B. Guyler?

Most humans have a will, a mind, and a set of eyes. So, here we go again. What good is it to have sight, to have feelings, and to have thoughts if someone else is in total control of using them? What fruit would the earth have if our viewpoints are not seen as important and beneficial? As I raised the question before, what is your take, Churchy? Were we created to be remote-controlled? I'll answer you. No. So my passion, was to contribute to the Father's vision, as well as what I saw as necessary. Maybe my ambition could've brought forth an unwanted outcome that led the family to operate in self-gratification. Such self-acknowledgment could've raised motives by them to develop and carry out their own personal vision for our Father's creation, said B. Guyler. Although I believe we all love our Father, such a practice may have been incompatible and strife-causing. Heck, they didn't have what I had, know what I knew, do as I did. So, because of their lack of supreme greatness, that which I possess, it could have turned wild and vile, said B. Guyler.

Man, this is becoming interesting the more he talks. Some things are simply kept behind closed doors and I see why. Although some say that he has this upright, nose up, head high posture, I see it as confidence and not arrogance. I just love it when a people carry themselves strong, walk secure in their own skin, and are unashamed to speak their truth. This meeting with B. Guyler is good for me right now. It is an apprehension that I have when I ponder if going independent from God is profitable. I believe in myself, people want to believe in me, and they need me to believe in them. He is making some good points. I feel bringing forth challenges to his statements is necessary for mining clarity of what happened. But I'd say I'm on the edge of my seat to retain more information out of his fire-breathing mouth.

Sorry for looking down at my phone. Needed to see if this missed call was from a day ago or last week, said Churchy. So, can you rewind back a little?

Sure can. Overall, I am not fully sure why I was banished. These are my assumptions. But we know that the horse's mouth could completely provide the reason, he said. To bring issue to the Father's vision, I have never felt I did wrong, I was simply being me. Therefore, I'm not responsible for my family's actions. They are responsible for their actions and my Father is fully responsible for teaching them how to be what he wants them to be, which is likened to a fetch dog. That kind of control is strictly not my style.

Yeah, I feel you B. Guyler, not much is detailed in his memoir concerning why you were banished. The memoir does communicate that other family members left out the door behind you though.

Ma'am it was messy, he said. I'd like to think all of our ambitious motives would reciprocate to our Father. I'd like to believe gratitude for his will was established. The Father totally wants the best for everyone, but I don't agree with his views of what's best. Being his spiritual children, he could have foreseen something wrong with our efforts that we couldn't see. Churchy excuse me I am starting to well up a bit.

B. Guyler, it is going to be okay because your influence and ideals have been agreed upon by so many. I can see your point completely. We both arrive at the same conclusion. The conclusion of the matter is free will, she said. A will that would be beneficial for the world. A will that does not need total trust from your Father. His memoir states that where his Spirit is, there is liberty. Limitlessness is claimed to be obtained in him. How could free will not be activated in all because all comes from him, asked Churchy?

That is why I wish there were a means to gain greater prosperity because the power in prosperity may contribute to the will of the Father for the world, said B. Guyler. I'm speaking in terms of tangible prosperity. DeVine lives this out, yet it seems that his Father's ways are selective towards certain contexts in the world. Although the memoir encourages his will to have all humans as a part of his family, that they all have a saving knowledge, if I interpret it correctly, selectivity for welcoming his family brings contrast to his will. Therefore, my frustration raises this thought: is his will to bring all humans into his family, or is it simply fluff, asks B. Guyler? So, without the release and access to the means of prosperity, which only can be done by giving all humans limitless ability to obtain all things, is where the problem lies. Therefore, for what reason would humans feel compelled to be a part of the Father's family, asked B. Guyler?

Yup, a part of those who come under my leadership, those who are less fortunate than those who are lucrative, seem to hang in the balances of fantasy, answered Churchy. They have this false osmosis-type hope that they will receive assistance from the lucrative to become prosperous. Both prosperous in time freedom and financial freedom. Sir, it's a touchy situation because the lucrative at times feel pressured by the voice of the memoir to take their financial prosperity and dump all of it into the hands of the less fortunate. Your Father measures their faith in him by following commands by DeVine to do such. And if they are not willing to adhere to the command, they're condemned and labeled as lovers of money.

You're absolutely correct, said B. Guyler. By Div A. Den, and his resources and the lovers of his money being condemned via the memoir, those who are not submitted to God's definition of prosperity remain to experience the effects of poverty.

Div. A Den, exclaimed Churchy? B. Guyler I never heard of the person.

We'll get to that in a minute miss. I have more to share with you, on that.

Cool. Sometimes I feel that the memoir contradicts itself, she said. Contradictions that speak of blessing to be released upon all, yet those who have and love money, which is the greatest blessing, seem to be targeted as evil for the love that they have for their prosperity. I'm just confused as to why they'd be punished for loving something. The memoir proclaims that DeVine is Love. Also, it's written that He's a Jealous God. It's perplexing. It's contrasting. It's wish-washy and deceiving. One minute you are in line with His will. Next, you are out of line with it.

I determine love as loving the best of what others love, said B. Guyler. While I still exist, the goal that I always envisioned is harmony with my Father. My vision is to maximize the possession of money for everyone in the world. The reason being, it's the most assuring possession any human can have for the greatest experience that life has to offer. It's only right to do. My Father wants the best for all, and I do too. Take for instance the taboo of sexual expression. Night clubs that encourage the freedom of this naked act of expression give several benefits to the employee. The memoir states that humans were naked at the beginning of time. Naked in the earthly Oasis of the Father. Churchy, I feel it's contradictory to allow nakedness inside his earthly Oasis but not outside of it. Once again, the Father is self-conscience about his status and I wish that he would ease up and break from that self-conscience. Tell me why is it a problem Churchy?

B. Guyler I'm not sure why.

Ok, let me explain more, he said. See, this career path provides income. Lucrative income and it's not labor intensive I might add. Women are often held back in career sectors, but this career allows women to reclaim their worth on the career ladder. In other ways, it provides the needed financial support for women who are enroute to obtaining goals like higher educational degrees or home ownership. Plus, even further so, they meet potentially a future husband, enjoy their love for dancing, and receive a good cardio workout which releases the effects of stress on the mind. Now, look what's at jeopardy here. Look at the good that is being condemned by the memoir. Only good comes from my Father, but I believe he's only seeing things from a narrow view. Like any good parent, when they believe a negative outcome could affect their children, they shelter them. However, such sheltering removes all the good that they would benefit from the experience. God's critical spirit surely jeopardizes the expression of beauty—something most women need to experience. Why Churchy? Well, to simply put it, it's good for their self-confidence. Again, these wages are fruitful and allow their quality of life as well as the quality of their family's life to be better. This line of work also provides the means for aspiring young women to make a difference in society. Why, Churchy? Because they get to go to college and those who obtain college degrees obtain greater salaries than those without degrees, explains. Preventing this because of a judgmental or overprotective spirit continues the cycle of poverty and crushes self-confidence in women.

Wow, that's good stuff, I haven't heard it put that way, said Churchy.

Thanks. Another example is the consumption of alcoholic drinks. Nevertheless, beverages such as wine bring comfort which can be a healthy escape from the effects of stress, explains B. Guyler. And I know that you can agree that this life is full of stress, right?

Yes, I can, I wholeheartedly agree, she said.

However, this benefit of wine consumption does not stop here, he said. Growers and distributors obtain self-sufficient income, the food chain maintains growth as wine is generally sold in most stores and restaurants bringing profits that sometimes-offset other losses in running food service businesses. Wine also provides leisure activities with loved ones as wine tasting is a huge hobby in most places. Couples grow in love at these events, companies use these events to raise morale amongst staff, social interaction, a much-needed thing in the human experience is attained and in all of that, memories are produced. Again, can you see the positive health, social and financial effects of this product? Oh, not to mention, various distilleries and distributors give charitable donations to important causes in the world, said B. Guyler. These causes complement the mission to help recipients of the causes get closer to prosperity. Churchy, since the memoir proclaims it is my Father's will that all prosper, why is he going against His own vision, asks B. Guyler? If a small percentage of people experience addictions from drug usage in which drug culture is normalized in night club attendance. Or, become alcoholics due to the pull they feel from consuming wine regularly, it's okay. Why? Because we have narcotics as well as alcoholic anonymous centers in place to deal with it. Plus, if we want to hammer down why those health challenging behaviors truthfully exist, it's because of poverty. Crime filled areas, dysfunctional families, and mental and behavioral issues result in addictive behaviors. That's the traced root of those behaviors. So, if humans all had money, that will mean that poverty is obsolete and what makes the grave results of poverty—addictions, crime, disease, and dysfunctional families, will cease to exist. Then in the end, the career fields I just talked about allows folks to flourish.

Yeah, you make the understanding clear regarding the Father's will, said Churchy. Your motivation is evident and convincing regarding what the memoir's proclamation says. It shows how DeVine proclaims limitless blessings, yet it shows that he is frankly giving lip service when it comes to his views of what blessing is. You are such a great thinker and visionary B. Guyler. I don't understand why your Father banished you but I see why you remain consistently around my premises as well. I am unsure why your brother God warns the world against your influence. You have supernatural influence, but God and the Father's memoir does not speak well of you.

B. Guyler, hold for a second please.

Hold up Churchy, before you do or say what you are about to say, let me get you some of that tissue over there.

Thank you, she said. (Churchy's getting emotional and begins to cry) My relationship with God has not been too good over the years. Again, I façade as if things are all good, but deep within, I seek to obtain freedom from him. A freedom that is not confined to his view of what freedom is. Yes, again, I have been grateful to be used by him to bring hope, prosperity, and guidance to many in the world. Yet, I have been bothered lately by all the constraints that are a reality in this relationship with him. B. Guyler, I want greater. I believe I can do greater. I see a greater plan and a greater outcome for humans who'd benefit from the limitless prosperity that the memoir claims are available. Money is the greatest form of blessing. Therefore, I'm not sure why the love for money is condemned. Who doesn't love what works? Crime would decrease, love would abound, true happiness would exist, and a better and truer desire to know and come into an unending relationship with God and you guys' Father would be substantiated, she explained. What seems to hold one against the limitless prosperity for anyone through your Father's proclaimed will is the cap that He puts on ambition. I strongly feel it's the truth from now having this conversation with you. It was distrust towards you regarding ambition. But yet, your brother is allowed to move without limit in how he feels is true loyalty to you guys' Father. The memoir supports that thought if I am interpreting it correctly. B. Guyler you know, I am not always in submission or surrender to his Son DeVine's authority. I simply do not agree with everything he proclaims. Maybe that is why the negative effects that he proclaims occur from lack of faith in Him. I don't want to be his enemy, I want to add to the great outcomes that trust in him provides, per the dogmatism that the memoir states.

You just heard my assessment of how God views sexual expression and wine, said B. Guyler. My take is that those ideals are in line with his Father's will.

My blood pressure has raised, I love DeVine but I am boiling inside, said Churchy.

Well, let us avoid any negative results from that unhealthy bodily function, he said. I have good news for you Churchy.

What is the good news, she asked?

I have joined in partnership with someone whose results you already are aware of. This person has an untapped impact on the world. They feel that their impact could be much greater since it is not globally proportioned as it should be. I wonder if you'd be interested in meeting him, asked B. Guyler?

I very well would like to meet him. Stop playing with me and spit it out, you already know I have no patience at all, so why are you egging around with this someone? Who is this someone, she asked?

His name is Div A. Den and he has come into a partnership with me, and I'd like to link you two together, he said.

Div A. who, she exclaimed.

Div A. Den. Churchy his name is Div A. Den and he is a mogul. Now, with your noble presence and his proven ability, how could you guys' combined, and unified efforts not carry out my Father's will? My brother does what he can, but again, there's a cap on his independency, a resistance against his creativity, a holding back of some sort. A withheld provision that limits the access to abundant blessing that our Father always wanted for people. The Father is just fearful of the unknown, said B. Guyler. I understand that the memoir proclaims He's holy and that He is all-knowing but is such "all-knowing" more foreknowledge and predetermined based?

Umm, you are going way over my head with this one. What do you mean by foreknowledge and predetermined based, asked Churchy?

In the study of the memoir as well as personal experience, I believe the Father knows the outcome of what situations could lead to, he said. Moreover, I mean the ability to successfully forecast the general conditions of all potential outcomes. In any given situation. Yet, although he can do such a thing, it doesn't eliminate him from determining its outcome.

How so, she asked?

My Father is aware of all outcomes of anything. Yet, it goes back to what His will is and his judgment about the outcome. Basically, if he approves of the outcome or not. I'm big picture though. I know how things ought to go because I am the most amazing creation my Father ever created. See, this reference that I make simply applies to our entire conversation. Which defines that the Father has a challenge accepting the core part of His will, which is ambition.

So, is the point you are making have to do with ambition itself, asked Churchy?

Bingo! Now you are catching on, he said. Let me take it home from here Churchy.

Alright, talk to me, sir.

Yup. If I was the Father, I wouldn't be so selfish as to solely do as I see fit and think that it's the best solution. I understand the Father's boundaries but I don't agree with them. My Father is overprotective, and as we can see, that's an understatement. The Father literally is incapable of being clear with His vision for the world he created.

Umm, what do you mean by that B. Guyler? You be talking with too much flip-flop and evasiveness with your words sometimes.

Oh that's easy. We've been discussing our views regarding what we feel is a contradictory nature on His part, said B. Guyler. See, God is saying be free to make a choice, right?

Right.

Ok let me help you understand something, replied B. Guyler.

Sure.

Ok listen close Churchy. Choice is synonymous with ambition per se.

Now, is that an accurate synonym for ambition B. Guyler?

Oh, it definitely is. But, let's say that it is for this conversation's sake.

Okay B. Guyler, let's say that.

If fair is fair the Father is unfair, said B. Guyler. How is it right Churchy to bring negative consequences for any choice that positively benefits any person? Since choice is ambition, how does it make sense for anyone to be penalized for choices that enhance the quality of people's lives. If my Father desires to force His will, well, we should be aware of that. At least we'd know what to expect. So, back to the foreknowledge thing.

Back to that? Please break it down further and make it make sense, said Churchy.

No problem, ma'am. Ok so, the Father struggles with accepting the choices people make. I don't agree that you can give a person the ambition to make a choice and then determine that the choice is negative and against His will. If the choice is giving people the right to be ambitious for profitable purposes, it's evil to bring consequences for the choice they make. It's even more evil to predetermine the outcome of a choice that people can make. By doing this grave act, you snatch people's freedom straight away from them. See, I believe that His foreknowledge is predestined and predetermined and that's wrong. Wrong towards His will to provide ambition. See what I'm saying Churchy?

Umm, sort a kind of B. Guyler.

Okay, let me put it on a lower shelf then, he said.

Good, please do so.

So for instance, Churchy you tell me that I can have all the money in banks except a certain bank. Let's call that certain bank the XYZ bank. If the rule is determined that I don't withdraw money from this bank because if I do, I'll go bankrupt, it's contradictory to proclaim I have free-will, A.K.A choice, or better put, liberty. Having all the money that is in any bank is a good thing to have so why would you even pit one bank against another when they both have money in them? Isn't the goal to bless me with the greatest resource on the earth which is money? Wouldn't be most wise to eliminate as many barriers as possible so that the manifestations of having free-will, will bless creation and all that is in it? It's an intentional control because ambition is robbed from me by constricting my free-will to be ambitious overall. If I go and withdraw the money from XYZ bank, I will surely go bankrupt, creation will be negatively impacted and I will be imprisoned by the hope of being free but all along, understanding that I am in hostage and bondager to the will of you.

Well B. Guyler, isn't it my choice to make the rules how I choose to make the rules? If you do not want to go bankrupt you do not have to, just don't withdraw from XYZ bank and you'll be good to go, said Churchy. It's not your money, it's mine.

Umm not really. I knew you would say that but you are not fully clear, said B. Guyler?

How am I not?

Because you created an option but eliminated my choice. Why even create an XYZ bank that would potentially lead me to bankruptcy in the first place? That means you have created bankruptcy which means you have made ambition to negatively affect me and the creation. Off top you created a negative choice, you foreknow that I'll be ambitious and therefore, you eliminate my ability to have liberty and then you are so ruthless, I go bankrupt because of it. By doing so, you have predetermined a reproachable result and to make matters worse, you foresee I'd choose XYZ bank. You created me with the nature of exercising curiosity, exercising ambition, but restricted my ambition to access XYZ bank. And if that isn't corrupted enough, you already knew my ambition would lead to me choosing XYZ bank, therefore you had in your plan to create a consequence for my curious ambition. That's devious and sinister to me. It's like you created failure and gloated over my failure. This is pure control and deviousness because you are influencing my ambition the way that you want, said B. Guyler. How can you say you didn't plan for me to go bankrupt while at the same time foreordaining it? Have you planted grenades of failure in my pathway in order that I do not achieve success from XYZ bank? Didn't you foreknow that I will surely go bankrupt if I withdraw the money from XYZ bank. Why didn't you stop me from doing it? You want me to rely on you. What's the point? You predetermined that withdrawing from XYZ bank automatically means bankruptcy? If you have predetermined the effect of the cause, you eliminate success for my choice, Churchy.

But B. Guyler I didn't. I'm just aware that the ambitious choice to withdraw from XYZ bank leads to more ambitious actions that lead to bankruptcy, replied Churchy. I would know as well that results from ambition to not withdraw from XYZ bank will lead to success that would meet your ambitious expectations. Therefore, that explains how my foreknowledge works. To make it simple and plain, yes, I am omniscient, I do know all things, but I gave you the ambition to make a decision. I also told you the outcome of choosing the wrong or unfavorable decision. I didn't create bankruptcy. Bankruptcy is the result of a bankrupt ambition. But with all that mentioned, you know that bankruptcy will prevent you from helping creation. So, my question is, why would walk in an ambition that would choose the XYZ bank in the first place? See, B. Guyler, you just want to do what you want to do and then blame me for it. You want to duck from responsibility. You want your cake and eat it too per se. So why would bankruptcy be a result of withdrawing money from XYZ bank? Because I get to really see where your heart lies. Are you immature to choose a negative option? An option in which you deliberately know will affect creation. Or is your heart really for the people in knowing you can avoid withdrawing money from XYZ bank in order to give the blessing that the creation would most need and benefit from?

Huh, Churchy? How in the world are you coming up with that?

Well, make it make sense sir, said Churchy. B. Guyler, you bet not have gone through this entire discourse and wasting my time at that, for me only to be exposing a senseless way of your thinking. You had me all happy that I could make change and now I'm confused.

I'm way too cunning for that, said B. Guyler. Remember who you are talking to.

Who am I talking to, she asked? You say that you are the greatest being that the Father has ever created so I'm trying to understand how wise are you. This is a simple conversation, but you are confusing me, she said.

It's alright Churchy. You are just slow to comprehend but I got you. Now let me bring things home for you. The Father cannot attest that He is the very essence of love. If so, we must accept that His love is abusive in its defining. It kidnaps people because it incarcerates ambition, he said.

Here we go again sir, can you just get to the point? I'm getting dizzy now for Christ's sake, sir. Please come on with the point you are trying to make.

I got you Churchy. Churchy, unless ambition is love, remember that we are establishing ambition to be a choice. No one can claim that they love you if they will hold you hostage against your will, which is what the Father does.

How so, B. Guyler?

Churchy you suggested that I brought the bankruptcy on myself because I knew upfront that making withdrawals from XYZ bank would lead to bankruptcy. You claimed that the one who owns the money is allowed to make the rules. Therefore, since it is her money, actions must represent her will for the money, correct?

Yes, correct, she answered.

But let me point this out. The very rule made is the preplan to steer one's ambition as well as inform dogmatically that one would fall to bankruptcy. The rule is not based on love but based on fear. Who wants to be scared into a relationship? Who wants to be coerced into a performance-driven lifestyle where out of fear you move with actions to obtain acceptance? If the Father wants robots, then make everyone robots. But he ought not say he given free will. So tell me Churchy, what type of confidence can be built on fear except for a pessimistic trust that nothing will work out for our good, by our own choice? Churchy I almost got to go; I have some errands to run. Ma'am, fear is control. Fear only expects the worst. Fear paralyzes, fear brings aggression, and fear keeps track shoes on. Therefore, I want all people to be free from the results of fear. There was an ambition posed on us by the Father. It ought to indicate just how powerful we really are and why he doesn't want you to know your power. And now you ask why so? Because you would be like him. You'd be one who was able to maximize her ambition apart from the Father. See Churchy, the rule came with a split chance to lose so that the rule maker would avoid accountability to have to live by the very rule he created. He shouldn't present me with the choice to access what I should not choose if the choice is only for me to choose what he wants me to choose. See there's no better kind of leader than one who would hold themselves to the same standards. Churchy, these standards created by the Father that void out the ambitions of others are selfish and corrupt. I guess that it's perfectly fine to create a rule that could bring a person to their demise and then call it love, said B. Guyler. I think not Churchy. Create a possibility for others to fall short and not make it fair game so that the creator of the rule is obsolete from penalization? Churchy, I hope you finally get it.

Think so B. Guyler, I think so. It sounds like you're saying that the rule was rooted in fear to prevent a standard of how far one's ambition could flourish. And that the rule was meant to be authoritatively binding for superior purposes so that the finger of judgment could be pointed while eliminating the creator's self from the judgment of how he acted out his ambition.

Churchy...Bingo my friend, you understand my point exactly.

Ok, but maybe in another conversation you can explain how it doesn't have anything to do with the result. Bankruptcy is the final result of the choice that you could potentially make. XYZ bank was never created to be accessed. Thus, one binds themselves to their choice. What seems to be predestined is the result but not the intention or motive. The reason I say this is because if the choice was predestined then there isn't any free will. Yet, as I contemplate things, you are allowed to have free will to make the choice, but you don't have free will to change the consequences--which results in bankruptcy for choosing to withdraw from XYZ bank. So, the conclusion per your view is that God just doesn't provide the outpouring of limitlessness that he claims to have for me.

I believe it's because he lacks the understanding of free will, said B. Guyler. He does not even attempt to maximize his ambition independently of his Father.

Yes, and he wants me to walk in the same way, but I want to flow in my own ambition, she said.

Churchy, your lover DeVine just cannot do it. But, all three of us, meaning you, me, and Div A. Den can work together. Moreover, what I see most is how you two can flourish in the world. I believe it is set in stone. My relationship with my Father and family is over forever, but my ambition to see what my Father's vision for creation eternally should be, will never end, said B. Guyler. My Father purposed me for a purpose, I can't negate that purpose if I tried, Churchy. Essentially, it's because of the way I went about carrying out his vision. That is the thing that is questionable and disagreed upon by Him and my brother, but that's okay, said B. Guyler. I like lemons in my tea and others do not. If they have the tastebuds that they have and I have the tastebuds that I have, who is to say what is the proper way to enjoy tea? The Father has his way and I have my way. The tea does not change it's just we choose to drink it differently. Once again, who has the proper way of drinking it? Same with ambition, whose ambition is right? Do not give me ambition and expect me to exercise it without my opinion being added to it. Why give me a different taste bud and expect me to like the way you enjoy the tea and not my own? Ambition is ambition. It is just the way that we go about exercising it that makes the difference, explained B. Guyler. Div A. Den is the person for you Churchy.

B. Guyler, Div A. Den?

Yes, Churchy, Div A. Den! Churchy, with Div A. Den, so much more is fruitful, and limitlessness is achieved. Nothing ever created or established on this earth has existed apart from Div A Den. Churchy, Div A. Den's money is the root of all good. I recently had a heated fellowship with God about this. People feel hopeful, confident, supplied, and accomplished with what Div. A. Den brings to the table. People feel most loved and empowered by Div A. Den. Without him, many who do not have his money plentifully, hurt. In all regards, they're helpless, limited, embarrassed, and angered. Churchy, before personally knowing Div A. Den, I was able to influence others toward a passion to obtain freedom through knowledge. Knowledge leads to power and power brings prosperity. My lane of influence is that total availability for humans to have limitless access to knowledge is standard. The fruit of knowing what is good and what's evil. Evil is all things that go against the maximization of purpose. Basically, to not tap into limitlessness. The action plan that helped me to tap into it was assertiveness. Not solely the gifting I was blessed with naturally but the passion to exercise it and not hesitate to go for limitlessness. My Father's greatest desire is that all creation would flourish. But Churchy...

Yes B. Guyler, what?

How can creation flourish, how exactly can humans flourish without complete access to the most flourishing person on the earth which is Div A. Den? God is not limited by not having Div A. Den in his control. I was not either. However, it appears that maximizing knowledge only could carry so far for attaining prosperity, said B. Guyler. It's clear that money is the solution for an abundant life. That's why people stretch themselves to desperate measures to get it. Also, the ability to manifest knowledge has appeared disproportionate to me. People have ideas that are inspired by the purposeful plan my Father has for them. My Father created everyone for impacting purposes. However, the playing field seemed limited because some versus others have a greater grasp of using their knowledge. Not to a fault of their own, those with higher ability, continue to master and flourish it. Yet, many are captured by knowledge's expense and so they struggle gravely to gain fruit for themselves. Tenacity, flexibility, creativity, perseverance, and sustainability are factors of prosperity that only one to ten percent of people possess. The other ninety to ninety nine percent are challenged in that way. Churchy, for example, if I were ninety nine yards away from you and we were to race, there is humanly no way possible you'd ever beat me in a one hundred yard race. Churchy, with you and Div A. Den working hand and hand, that gap will no longer exist.

B. Guyler, I feel like your brother God has sought to end the gap, but it seems his methods for manifesting knowledge are abstract. You guy's Father's memoir reveals that at some point God will just give his life to pay for all evil. And since evil brings limits, a new earth and Oasis will preside, and the freedom of limitlessness will abound eternally. Yeah Churchy, the memoir explains that but like the constitution has amendments to it, your relationship with Div A. Den can amend this unknown time of when God's payment will occur. It can prevent the barbaric expenditure that God must endure for limitlessness to be attainable. Plus, Div A. Den would end any continual suffering that exists until this unknown time when God will accomplish this payment. Div A. Den will end it immediately Churchy; we don't need God to do anything like that to better the state of humanity. Churchy, that whole tale sounds foolish and you know it does. Look, in the memoir I am a factor as to why pain and travesty exist in the world. My ambition was to help people access the limitlessness that is available. When I offered it to people and they took it and partook in it, they flourished in the way I saw them flourish. Once they tasted the fruit of their ability to manifest their purpose-driven knowledge, they entered levels beyond their ability to comprehend such accomplishment. This imbalance in the production of knowledge in the individual proved evident. That result made practically everyone but a few, be used to contribute to the small percentage of those who maximized knowledge. That in turn left them unable to become a part of that small population of benefactors. People, no matter what they tried, could never fully maximize their purpose to be members of that club. They simply were running the race ninety-nine yards behind. Because those who were only one yard away from the finish line further grew, in the knowledge that is, its system exploited those who ate their dust. But Churchy, it is a new day, and you are the source of change for the world. You've always been and that is why my brother loves you and seeks to partner with you in doing so.

Yeah B. Guyler, he does but I don't fully see eye to eye with him. I have an ambition of my own. Yes, there are things that he does that I can put into my toolbox. But Div A. Den offers the greatest, clearest, and least labor-intensive way to accomplish the goal of limitlessness for the world, said Churchy. Sir, I am a person of limits and I struggle to live this way. I struggle with the scrutiny that I don't truly affect change. I want to partner with Div A. Den by all means.

Great and good for you Churchy. I will make that happen for you. Just one question though. What does partnering with Div A. Den mean for your relationship with God, Churchy?

Good question B. Guyler. I don't think it means much, sir, because I like my tea with lemons in it too...

CHAPTER 15

"A Jealous God"

(December 1st, 2003)

It's two o'clock in the morning, what is wrong with you? Where have you been, he said?

Can you please not, DeVine? Who do you think you are, DeVine, she said? Don't get indignant with me, I have been given two legs and I can go and use them whenever and wherever and however I'd like them to go.

Bae, don't give me that philosophical mess. From the way you've been acting, it's like you're here in body but absent in spirit from me and it bothers me. Do you mind turning the television down and the lights on so we can talk? I already see the bottle of Seagrams Gin on your nightstand. Please don't tell me it's about to get like that with you again. Why are you all of a sudden being so distant with me?

I can't understand why she's been dragging me through the mud lately. I so love every part of her and I'll do anything to not lose her. It hurts though. It hurts to keep showering her with my everything only to experience this continual pull away and distancing. It's disrespectful to me. I can't remember the last time we had an intimate conversation. It's heartbreaking and my joy for her is being challenged. What have I done? What is it that is hindering our relationship? She doesn't lift my name up anymore and I can feel it. My eyes go to and fro and I mercifully overlook certain things that are obvious. In hopes that she is not building her confidence negatively by wearing certain outfit styles. She is moving from classy to trashy day by day now. Tight-fitting dresses with stilettos, cleavage hanging, florescent hair colors, seductive lipstick, and regular adult beverage scents on her breath are the norm. She has been arriving home late at night more and more. What has her attention other than me and our mission? You just don't keep changing your outward appearance and start arriving late if there's nothing wrong. Is there some hurt she is experiencing? It must boil down to something I may have said or done. She barely compliments me or praises me anymore and my feelings hurt because of it. She's not as enthused to accompany me on a mission to the world either. What went wrong?

Churchy baby, I am everywhere throughout the world working to remove the scales from the eyes of all. My Father loves them so much. Many are working endlessly to overcome what pollutes the quality of life like addiction, anger, depression, and self-reliance. Yet, a problem that is arising more and more is that they cannot let go of their desperate dependence on Div A. Den. Div A. Den cannot love them as I can.

Says who DeVine, she said?

Churchy, I have provided you with many great experiences with money, the thing that Div A. Den claims is the source of all fulfillment and happiness. The thing he claims will change the human experience and save the world. However, if I'm real with myself, you seem to be more possessed with having the money and resources that Div A. Den has. More and more it's looking like a close intimacy is happening with him and not me. Div A. Den is that same reason, same master, same controller of everything rooted in evil for those who love the money he has. Div A. Den could co-exist with me but those who have abundantly experienced Div A. Den or have experienced any form of blessing that came from his money have rejected to see the necessity I am for them. Queen, that is a grave matter. Through my Father, people awake, live, move, and have their being.

Really DeVine? Is what you're saying accurate?

Yes, I know so, he replied. When Div A. Den works his mastery on the human heart, mind, and soul, the effects are harmful to the earth. Div A. Den brings war, broken homes, sinful acts, hate towards my Father, hate period, a false sense of hope, a misconstrued reality of assurance, a blindfold of the definition of happiness, he misleads, misuses, he mauls all who feel a dependent need of having him and his money. Of course, in the world we live in, having Div A. Den's money is necessary when used in good stewardship practices but be not fooled by the intent that underlies it, Bae.

God, I am confused as to why you think in such a way. You are royalty, you own everything, and you control it all, but many are so confused about you.

No! I am not going to allow you to label me in such a way, he yelled. I am clear, very clear.

I can't help but think about why I struggle to link on the same vibe with DeVine nowadays. I'm not really feeling him too much anymore. I send out my signals, but I can't always see or sense what to do after "making my request be made known to God." I'm beginning to feel it necessary to do things on my own. I don't see anything wrong with how I'm dressing. I don't know how to be patient and deal with delayed answers and delayed action related to the way we desire to affect change in the world. People accuse me of being too tight at times and that I am not living life freely. B. Guyler makes sense of that. Look at this outfit that DeVine has on now. It has no pazazz to it. I like to be fashionable and on the edge. I want to be more relatable with the culture, fit in, and be more connected to it. His scrubby appearance is bothering me right now. I don't know if he matches my swag any longer. His words are convincing but it's beginning to turn into a delayed response for a minute now. How can I maintain intimacy with someone who tends to answer or not answer me when I want to be answered immediately? I don't know if I can really keep doing this. I'm starting to feel embarrassed now. Many around me saw the positive changes that were made in my life once I begin to accept his love in my life. Now I look bored and less joyful. It bothers me what people are saying nowadays. Yeah, I'm about tired of waiting on him to move in my life and the lives of others. Yeah, I can point to many things that were right about our relationship. Yet, this season has really turned me off of him and I don't know how I can return to close love with him. I know I look fine, really fine. I like my adult beverages and no, I reject what he is saying now because I know how to not let alcohol take control over my life again. I don't know, I'm just not attracted to him like I once was.

Again, God, let me be clear that you are clear right now, she remarked.

What's that supposed to mean, he asked?

It means that clearly, you are very jealous. God, can you shut the door? The weather is pretty warm today and I don't have time for these fake neighbors to be asking me the question: "is everything alright?" Any way, you sound loud and aggressive. You don't sound passionate right now. I love my Bratenahl Mansion, and I love my privacy, so shut the dog-on door now! she yelled. See, it's clear that you are powerless against Div A. Den's influence and major importance on the earth.

Why do you keep calling me God, he asked?

Because that is your name.

My name to others but not to you right?

WrongGod,

C'mon Churchy why are you so harsh right now and purposely hitting me with aggressive stares and words?

DeVine, is your ego getting the best of you? You are clearly at odds with the quality that Div A. Den brings to many. DeVine, you are clearly attempting to negate Div A. Den from supplying every need according to the riches of his glory. God, you are a hater!

Churchy I don't understand you right now. Bae, you have me confused. We work together.

Do you work with me, she said? Do you work through me, God?

Yes, he replied.

Whatever. Tell me How then?

Well I...

No you don't. You can't even get the words out, she said.

Bae, you just...

Shut up. I don't want to hear! God, you work me. I never can feel that you are there with me. Sir, many come to you through me. I give them the promise that they'll have a transformed life in you. But the majority of them remain entrapped in the same reality of death. Trapped in poverty, trapped in exploitation, trapped in struggling to have their needs met, trapped in being redlined, predatory loans, denied by bank after bank that refuse to invest in their business plans, they're trapped in their job with low paying wages that are now being snatched from them by either global outsourcing agendas. They're trapped because their community has become gentrified and so they are abruptly escorted out and given the boot. As well as having the door locked on them if they wished to return. Trapped in false promises that "God" will do exceedingly, abundantly, above all they can ask, imagine, or think. Trapped in sayings from the memoir that the "wealth of the wicked is stored up for the righteous." Trapped in a name it claim it spiritual approach to the belief that prosperity solely means wealth and good health comes from speaking things into existence by your Name and not by the reverence that blessings by you are not limited to, but beyond those things, as you see fit. Yet, the only thing one hears is dry air returning to them—huff puff pass. People are out here living in cognitive dissonance, a delusional mode of life, while your feet are kicked up, using the earth as your footstool. Plus flaunting your lap of luxury, while posing in a false humility as you play the part of a lowly person. DeVine, I like to believe you mean well for people but honey, the proof is in the pudding. Your results are weak. People want results. You are well off, and you need not for anything, but you are not arriving on time to help people on the earth arrive at their blessing. You speak strongly and confidently that you come to give people life and life more abundantly. However, how convincing is such a statement when it is evident you invest in bankruptcy? In other words, a non-allocation of funds regarding fruitful livelihoods for them to experience? DeVine, the people give me Div A. Den's resource which is money, so that Div. A Den's money, through their faith in you, can produce fruit for them. You got me out here accepting the resources and money that Div A. Den gives them and preaching to them that, by their giving, they will get more from you. Are you two-faced? Is there some backroom plot in this? God, what in the rabbit out of the hat type of nonsense is this? Generally, in return, the things they get from you are wishy-washy. Here and there. Over the moon and back. Sometimes fruit produces when they give in your Name. Most other times nothing happens at all. You raise accusative language like "will a man rob God?" You try their faith. Passive aggressively, the memoir demands me to communicate that "those who sow sparingly, reap sparingly." You make a fool out of me because I bear the brunt of the dissatisfaction of humans and their denial of you. I am the immediate face that they see and look to for receipts while you are everywhere around the world. I preach weekly that folk ought to wait on the Lord. How much longer DeVine? You make me frequently receive the greatest resource on the earth, which is Div A. Den's resource called money. Yet, I receive a great amount of it, from the majority of the poorest of people. Upon that, you have the nerve to have me put their feet to the admonishing fire of the memoir? Which appears to shame and blame them for being slaves to Div A. Den's money. God, you must enjoy watching the desperate actions of poor people.

Man, what has come over you, you tripping, he said? What has Div A. Den done to you, been to you, is to you?

DeVine, all I am saying is Div A. Den is accessible everywhere, and his results are proven. However, you claim that loving him is detrimental and I do not see how so. To go with Div A. Den is a sure shot. To go with you is a sure not. People are sure to have happiness, responsibilities met, enjoyments attained, peace and no stress, abundance and not lack through and with him, etcetera. As a matter of fact, like in the here and now. Not, in the wait a minute, hold on just a little bit longer, here I come in a few, which is the norm of your performance DeVine. Div A. Den makes the world go around. But Div A. Den is blamed for a price the world must pay because of a world that you made around the possession that Div A. Den has limited amounts of, which is money. Asinine and "oxymoron-ish," you say? Not to mention, your brother B. Guyler was blamed and banished for influencing some folk about the power that exists in the fruits that the earth's resources provide. How dare you and your Father have the nerve to be so dismissive towards him. Y'all got the nerve to be blaming Div A. Den's money or whatever else he does for people for the evil that is running rampant in the world. But this don't surprise me sir. Such ways of shaming have been equally made by you guys' Father from the beginning of time. Like what the heck. You are nothing but your Father, two-point-o style. He dangled a carrot with this forbidden fruit type of scam written about in the Oasis Garden. Your Father builds up a salivation to have a piece of the experience of what the fruit tastes like. He knows people get anxious for what's good and could be gratifying for their lives. Then when his human creation ate from it, they were sentenced to death and accused of holding the gun to their heads pe se. What in the name of evil was that, God? You want me to continue to spread the word about your will from the Father as if it's beneficial for them? Negro please!

Churchy, you really have no understanding about what you are talking about, he said. You are lost and confused about how my Father does things. You don't know his love for people.

Whatever, save it for the birds sir. It's an undeniable fact that you sell people a distant hope, she replied. A distant world and a way that they cannot see, taste, touch, or smell but only hear about. While they are strongly warned not to buy into a tangible world, and its present benefits that they can see, taste, touch, feel, and smell. They are warned that it is not profitable. They are encouraged not to put their trust in it. Don't you see how difficult it is for them to gain the concept of this distant pie-in-the-sky world called Heaven that the memoir speaks of? Is it fair that they are strangled into rejecting the world that is available now, for an unknown reality that no one on this earth has ever experienced? No one on this earth can provide an open house about this distant world so that people can at least view it before placing a down payment of faith in it. So let me break this down to you as to why Div A. Den is the man and you are not. It's simple. By having an abundance of money that he's lavishly, immediately, and bountifully willing to give so one can have now. Thus, one can enjoy life's fruits without hesitation or delay— right now, period point-blank. And guess what God?

What, he said?

I'm so attracted to power like that, she replied. It has me like an inferno burning inside, and I want it so bad.

Churchy, you are losing me on this one, why are you tripping bae?

God, are you the root of evil that blocks us from the love of money and the love of Div A. Den's instant genorisity?

Huh of course not. I just don't understand where is all this coming from, he asked?

God, do you demand we find joy in poverty? Lust for the least? Praise for pennies? God, are you the weed that chokes the benefits that Div A. Den brings to peoples' earthly dwelling? What is your purpose in dwelling here? Is it to agitate, dangle carrots, brainwash, tease, and allow the memoir to make claims of your abundance while encouraging that people are blessed for being poor in spirit? God, I am confused.

Yes you are, he said. I see that you talking sideways out of your mouth because you are very confused. You believe that treasure is where rust and moth are.

Well, I guess I am talking sideways since rust is evident when there is a lack of money from Div A. Den, she said. Unlike you, Div A. Den provides the chance to refurbish treasure so that rust and moth cannot destroy it ever again. So God, I guess I am. I guess you are right. But let me tell you something. If confusion is this, I don't want to be anything but confused, sir.

Oh really Churchy. Let me put it to you like this, he said.

Huh, never that God, matter of fact let me break my stance even further down to you, she said. Div A. Den's power and money is only as strong as his ability to be applied to any situation. Moths are desperate because of the lack of nutrition available to them. Therefore, desperate times call for desperate measures, which provokes them to devour what they can get their mouths on. When the food supply is limited, when the opportunity for an invention to produce the unlimited and eliminate what is limited, everything limited cannot ever become unlimited again. Folks are challenged to believe in a place of limitlessness that is sold by someone who is seen as limited because he's not always able to do anything about the world's limits. What receipts do you bring DeVine? On the other hand, Div A. Den has plenty of receipts. He just needs to be allowed total access to be given to more shoppers. Div A. Den is the source that provides shopping sprees. You are stealing Div A. Den away from people with your mean and baseless accusations of who he is to people and this world. God, I am through with this conversation. Div A. Den talks about what's needed to be heard and walks the walk that needs to be seen, but your nonsense needs to go take a hike!

Bae hold up and wait a minute, he said. It's two something in the morning. Don't dip out like that. You've been drinking and you are angry and that is a bad place to be in.

Please excuse me, and let me get gone, she said. I'm sick and tired of being sick and tired and I feel like I'm not understood. (Churchy shoves God's arm out the way and storms out the door to her vehicle)

Churchy don't do this, don't (God yells to her in anguish).

God bye…You are too much in the way and it's clearly about time you be out of the way, she yelled!

"Surgery"

(November 22nd, 2002)

In the lobby of the inpatient treatment center at Mount Sinai Hospital

Hey God, you look pretty tired. Are you?

Well, Destiny, I don't slumber nor sleep but it has been a busy week and I do feel as if I need to steal away to a place of solitude to pray and recharge.

How was your ride in today, Destiny also asked?

It's funny you asked, he replied. You know, it was like NASCAR as I was driving this way today. The radio said there was a huge accident on the freeway so I had to take the city. I had an oil change appointment scheduled at eight o'clock this morning and the traffic was backed up for miles.

Oh wow, what a challenge, she said.

You're right about that Destiny, what a challenge (God chuckles). I couldn't wait another day to get the oil change done, he said. My Father is good though and he deserves my praise no matter what the issue is.

Yes, he does God, he is so worthy of the praise, she remarked.

But look at you, said God. You look amazing. I see that you have the color coordination to a tee today.

Thank you, she said.

Purple and gold are my favorite colors and the way you have put the hat, bag, shoes, and coat together is fashionista-ish. You look nice, Destiny.

Well God, after this appointment, I'm meeting Deshaun for dinner to enjoy my favorite food choice, which is seafood. I'm going the extra mile because I want to impress him on this date night.

Now that's what I'm talking about. Destiny, that's love. It's a benefit for married couples to give an extra effort to do the things that blessed their spouse when they were once in that season of dating.

Yes God, exactly!

Deshaun is going to love it, said God.

I just really feel good about serving Destiny in this manner. In knowing her husband, Destiny knows that if he were to know about this chronic illness she has, he wouldn't be able to function successfully. Her wisdom leads her to understand that other effects would come from his difficulty of being uneased. She knows it would affect his work performance, his health, them as a couple, and all aspects related to their life. She knows anxiety levels would increase significantly, panic mode would go into effect in attempting to secure funds, raise funds, overly manage spending and the list goes on.

So, how's Deshaun been coming along, asked God?

Not so good, she replied.

Sorry to hear that, said God. The last time me and him spoke, he was experiencing a heavy load of stress from his job. He told me he gained some extra pounds in his belly area, and that he was struggling to manage his balance with family, career, and self-care.

Yeah, that's exactly what's going on, said Destiny. Just the other day, he told me that he's overwhelmed, and it has me overwhelmed too. Although he is unaware of this, my heart condition has created intimacy and communication challenges. He senses that I'm not feeling well.

Doctor Jones from Mount Sinai walks up.

Ut, high Doctor Jones, said God.

Hello God. Hello Destiny, great to see you both today.

Doc did you and your son go kayaking since the last time we saw you, asked Destiny?

Destiny, I think I was more excited than him. Although, when it was all over, I spent a few days recovering due to the muscle soreness. My age sure did catch up with my youthful goal.

Doc you gotta face reality sir, you are no spring chicken anymore, said God (they all laugh). Yeah, tell me about it.

Well, how about we head to my office guys, said Doctor Jones.

Sure Doc, said Destiny.

(As they head down the hospital's hallway) Wow, God do you see the artwork from these kids, asked Destiny? These walls look fabulous, she said.

Indeed they do, it's amazing, God replied.

So, encouraging. It's for reasons like these that make me so proud to be an educator, said Destiny. I really hope that I advance to superintendent but no matter what, seeing these artistic expressions are priceless.

Superintendent? Where is this good news suddenly coming from, asked God?

Yes, God yes, I got my fingers crossed, she said.

Moving on up huh, remarked God.

Up to the east side to finally get a piece of the pie, she sung? (They both laughed).

Ok guys we're going to hang a left, and that second door is where we are going. I need to grab one file and I'll see you in there in a sec, said Doctor Jones.

Sure Doc, said God.

Inside an office room

Here, here, you take that window seat Destiny.

Thanks, God.

Oh no worries, he replied.

(Doctor Jones enters the room) Thanks for your patience, guys, I've been on that hustle-bustle pace today.

Oh no worries, take your time Doc, said God.

Look it's late in the afternoon guys and I want you to beat that 480 traffic, so let me get straight to it. I want you both to track with me on this and ask any questions that come to mind, Doctor Jones said.

Okay, not a problem at all Doctor Jones, answered Destiny

I second that Doc, not a problem at all, said God.

Thanks, you two, I appreciate it. So you guys, not to place fear in this situation, but this is an operation that has not been performed in the medical science world, as of yet. Me and my team are confident in this operation and although this blood/heart procedure is a very unique one, we trust the scientific research and testing that has led up to this point. You two will be the first to receive this operation, but we as a staff believe it is groundbreaking and that a complete healing and recovery will be the outcome for you, Destiny. Nevertheless, to be upfront with you both, the world we live in is imperfect, so there are levels of uncertainty that comes with performing this operation. The operation is risky, due to the nature of the disease, and so various adverse effects can occur. Whenever a transplant surgery is executed, some post-surgery trauma, can affect the body. The body must adjust to the changes but over time, organs and blood flow are restored back to normal, or may I say, even better than normal. We have some of the best doctors in the world with a portfolio of success in transplants here at Mount Sinai Hospital. Therefore, again, we are confident, said Doctor Jones. Now God, because you have a rare blood type that exemplifies a set apart nature and purity. Therefore, in us knowing that your blood type is a phenom in the medical world's eyes, it makes us even extra confident of the positive outcome for Destiny's blood culture. Your blood purity, being transfused into her heart and blood bacterial issue, has great potential to heal her heart and result in remission. Destiny, we project that you'll recover from the surgery in about three weeks, and we'll begin a bi-weekly monitoring of your blood culture to see how your circulatory system is performing. God for you, what we'll be on watch for is how well your system will be able to produce more blood for future generations to come. God, through your blood, our research and testing led us to this breakthrough discovery. Reverse organ transplant will be the wave of the future. As long as we have more donors like yourself, lives will be made whole.

You know Doc, that's why me and Churchy and all those contributors are endlessly working to raise funds for families who are less fortunate to have this operation, said God. Although we haven't released information as to what medical miracle donors are contributing, once Destiny's healed, we expect a flood of donations to be unleashed.

God that is amazing, he said. Now I want you to know, one aspect of extremely minimal concern is the level in which your blood, as well as Destiny's new infused blood, will produce for future surgeries. The goal is to begin to transfuse an amount of your blood into others. Once others receive the donation of your blood, they'll be able to donate blood back to our blood bank, and the continual cycle from healed patients donating blood, will grow to a sustaining amount for anyone that'll need it. See God, your blood will set forth the antidote that we believe will reverse the diseased human state. And I mean diseases of any kind. The only drawback is the cooperation from people to be sacrificial and donate blood back into the blood bank. The blood bank must remain replenished. People must be willing to transfer the means of their healing, which is the new blood culture they have, back into the bank. If people decide not to donate the infused blood, at the point in life when you two no longer walk the earth, the blood will not be available anymore. Therefore God, besides the money for the surgery to be performed for those with heart disease, the supply of this type of blood is just as equally important.

Ok, Doc, I'm a realist and I love your care in explaining this to us but realistically, if I hold off on the surgery and try holistic health practices, as well trust in the miracle working healing power, expressed in God's Father's memoir, how long do I got if neither of those options come to pass, asked Destiny?

Destiny, that's a good question, said Doctor Jones. The way that your body is performing due to this disease, it looks like you have anywhere from six weeks to three months, tops. Regarding the performance of the surgery, there's no guarantee. However, let me say this to you Destiny, I believe what this surgery defines, is the miracle provision that God's Father has provided. This is the remedy and so there's no need to delay. See, this procedure is the answered prayer and desired hope for your healing. We know the grace in which God's Father has provided in a multiplicity of ways regarding medical science. As a matter of fact, none of the healing methods in which the medical field performs is absolutely, positively possible without the released wisdom from Heaven to us in the field. Things go right within the three weeks post-surgery, expect to live quite a long long time Destiny. To be honest guys, it would be a huge comfort to have a reference to point to, prior to performing this surgery. Complications do arise and so having data beforehand of what might occur when conducting other heart-related surgeries helps. At the end of the day though, me and my surgical staff lean on God's Father too. He's the one and only source that heals the body.

Doc, it is okay. You don't have to preach, said Destiny. I believe all that is left is a risk. I'm going to trust this process.

And thank you, God, she said, I'm overwhelmed with gratitude for you choosing to do this for me.

I'm here for you Destiny, said God (God stands and gives Destiny a hug).

Destiny, may I have a few words with God, asked Doctor Jones? Nurse Shateisha is going to assist you with all details of the surgery. I'll see you in our Florida facility a week from now.

Looking forward to my healing Doctor Jones. I'm so grateful for you and your brave staff.

Thank you, Destiny, he said.

God, I'll be at the cafeteria. You can meet me there once you are finished with Doctor Jones.

Okay, Destiny will do.

Hey Doc, what's on your mind?

God, this is very commendable. I'm personally blessed by your willingness to go through all measures to make sure Destiny experiences her healing. Many people make sacrifices, but generally, it's for people who are close to them. The fact that you have not known Destiny and her husband that long points to the huge kindness that you possess. God, your blood, given in small doses has significantly changed tons of lives. Only through very small minute portions have we been able to include it in transplants. It's wonder-working and brings forth miraculous healings. Without it, the medical field will falter greatly. I just wanted you to know that biologists are working to discover ways to stretch it if you will. Why'd I say such a thing God? Because, without your blood, and how we've witnessed its miraculous effects, there wouldn't be a way to explore this magnitude of medical advancement as a possibility. All in all, God, although anyone's life would be at risk from going through this surgery, we who labor in this field of transplant operation, know that if kindness lives, lives live. And with that, I just wanted to personally thank you because I know that no one on earth can do what you've been doing countlessly for people.

Thanks for your kind praise Doc, may my Father's will be glorified.

At the hospital's cafeteria

Hey God, over here.

Cool, one moment Destiny, I must grab myself a slice of this angel food cake and I'll be right over.

Sure, take your time. (God grabs the cake and walks over to her table) God, why are you so willing and eager to help me in this manner? Destiny what is life if life isn't about life being sustained for life to live? In other words, we are here to love one another and so much so, at the expense of our privileges. If I'm in a place of advantage and you have no way to get to that place, then I must come to the place of your disadvantage to get you to the place of advantage because there is no way for you to get to the place of advantage on your own. In this truth, my empathy must flow in a form that works its best to feel what you feel, and in doing so I'll understand the degree of your difficulty. To know that someone cares is medicinal in and of itself. The disregard to care for others is and has been the most cankerous disease that has struck the earth for centuries. If we as humans can begin to sacrifice what we have for the greater empowerment and healing of someone else, the very factors that are destroying the world—selfishness, covetousness, envy, lies, theft, dishonor, and hate would be cremated and never ever to return, he said. Destiny, there's no way I can truly love myself if I don't move in love for you. The reason is, essentially, your body is my body and if I would desire the best for my own body, then that means I desire the best for your body.

God, you have me welling up (Tears fall from Destiny's eyes). Thank you for your willingness to go above and beyond for someone like me who has proven that they don't deserve any compassion from anyone. It would be despicable and terrible for me to experience this restoration by continuing to walk in the selfish and toxic manner that I have exemplified up until now. I continually question myself with this thought: why should I be allowed to be healed when I have been a disease to parents and their children throughout my tenure as an educator?

Look, I don't want you to think like that, said God. Use this opportunity to pivot and reverse any behavior you feel goes against my Father's will. Ask for his help and study his memoir to know how to better yourself, said God.

Thank you, God, for believing that I'm worthy of such a sacrifice on your end.

No worries, we are here for each other. I love you, he said.

I love you too God.

"Concealed"

(November 25th, 2002)

Blessings my amazing husband.

Good morning my beautiful, Destiny, said Deshaun.

Oh looky here, someone doesn't have their usual grogginess in this wee hour of the morning. Hmm, am I energetically awake because I don't believe I've ever witnessed Deshaun Smith smile so cheerfully at three o'clock am, said, Destiny?

Baby I don't know, my sleeplessness was surely because of my typical workload but also in a contrasting manner, I'm so excited for you and this national convention you are set to attend, he said.

(Deshaun yells) BAE, BAE!

Sorry Deshaun, I'm here. Just needed to get the shower running because the hot water has been taking a minute to heat up these last couple of days. But what were you saying again?

Baby I was saying that I'm excited for you. I know you've been wanting to attend this convention for quite a long time and I'm glad that it is happening.

I know right, can you believe it my King?

I believe in you Queen so no, not at all. However, it has been a long time coming, beautiful. With that being said, I think I smell a promotion around the corner for you.

Now, don't get my hopes too high, I need to first complete this level, she said. I've been a principal over various schools throughout the years and I love it, but I do want to obtain a superintendent opportunity.

And Queen, that, you will. Now hurry and hop in that shower so that I can get you to the airport. The TSA checkpoint is always a mess so let me get you there in ample time. Meanwhile, I will get my coffee brewing.

 Okay, thanks hubby, you are the best.

The car ride to the airport

Oh no, look over there, said Destiny. What a terrible accident that is. I hope everything is okay.

Me as well, Baby. Wifey, I so love you. I don't know what I would do without you.

Oh, I know what you'd do, she said.

And what is that ma'am?

You'd take on several other cases on top of the several that you have right now, King. You know I envy her sometimes.

Huh, her who, he asked?

Oh, you know who I am referring to Deshaun.

Umm, what are you talking about Destiny, there is no other who?

Are you sure about that Deshaun?

Huh, Destiny? You better believe I'm SURE about that.

Well, I know you like sound equipment and music going all the time, but you don't have to plug an amplifier into your voice at three-forty-five in the morning Deshaun.

Queen, you have me concerned.

Be calm my King, I'm just kidding.

Sheeesh, you journalists are so literal.

Whatever. More literal than a twenty-five-year experienced school principal and former middle school English teacher, he asked? Woman please, but anyway, who were you referring to?

Deshaun, Deshaun.

Baby, why do you keep calling me by my first name, he asked?

I love your name, she said.

Ok Destiny, spill the beans please before I...

Why did you just stop in the terminal entryway Deshaun? Because...

Because what, Deshaun?

Because you trippin' Destiny.

Deshaun, I am talking about your job Ms. Breaking News. She gets a lot of your attention. I love that she provides for me and makes life easy, but she also keeps you overly stressed, out of shape, and exhausted because you are groggy every morning, Deshaun, I like some things about her, but she does take up a great deal of space in your brain. Am I right?

Yes, Bae, you are right, he said.

I know you love me to the moon and back but sometimes I wonder if you ever get to think about me Deshaun. Hold up, stop right here, right here Deshaun.

Ooops, my fault for almost passing the American Airlines gate, I'm tripping.

Destiny, what you are saying and the way that you put that was deep.

Deshaun you are a wonderful and amazing husband, but I worry about you sometimes. I need you to take care of yourself and get back to doing some of the things that you enjoy. You like playing pool, enjoying walks in the park, and watching action movies. But Ms. Breaking News has you overly consumed, and I can feel the effects on our date nights and other quality times because of her. Deshaun, you need a good laugh in the meantime.

What? What are these, he asked? Where is?

See, look at you. I have the carry-on bag that you are looking for on my shoulder, and you are standing here scrambling all over the place. Deshaun, you are so bogged down you can't even see straight. Anyway, here are two tickets to the Improv Comedy Club. Take one of them other workaholics from your investigative team and ease up a bit. In the meantime, I will be on the beach in Florida, enjoying the waves roll on the shoreline, hearing the seagulls speak, listening to island music blasting from the tiki bar, and sipping a pina colada while laying on a beach towel and enjoying the beautiful hot sun.

And my Queen, networking, learning new approaches to educational systems, taking notes, and…

See Deshaun, all you do is think about…

No Destiny, think about it. This is a business boot camp.

Yes, but it's split into a vacation as well. They have laid out these three and half weeks in sunny Florida to provide us with relaxation as well as information so that we aren't bogged down like someone I know, she said.

Be safe Bae, he said.

I will Deshaun, but make sure you carve out some time to do what you've been missing for a long time.

Look, I better get going now, my Queen. Make sure to call me once you land and get settled.

I sure will my King. Ohh, I like that kiss on my neck Deshaun.

I know. My Queen, this is a little preview to remind you of what you are coming back to.

Mmmm feels good.

I love you so much Deshaun.

I love you more Destiny and I'll see you in three weeks (Deshaun gives Destiny another kiss).

"A Vibe"

(December 20th, 2003)

I must say, B. Guyler was one hundred percent accurate in connecting me with you. This vibe has been amazing and so much impact is set to be disbursed, said Churchy.

I don't know, it seems like every time I am in Div A. Den's presence, I can't help but blush. I'm literally drooling inside. Not because of the red corvette that he pulled up in. Not because of the designer sport coat or Rolex watch. I like the exclusive sunglasses he has on, as well as the expensive oils that oozed out of his pores. I'm so hot right now. I completely love his eagerness to see people maximize their earthly experience. His skin tone is perfect. His voice is deep. It is very easy to see that he has the smarts. He has charisma. He has the looks. He is amazingly strong and confident. I believe in him and want more of him. I believe with him, I can have my smile back, my confidence back and I know my reputation will flourish. I love the outcome he brings to others. He is money. He is the payout, payoff, and I'm bought in. I must admit, B. Guyler is good for this. I've been dreaming about the waves in Div A. Den's hair and the stylish clothes and the sweet things he says to me. DeVine is so plain. He doesn't have the look that stands out. DeVine is so meek while Div A. Den is so atypical, one who commands authority and that makes me feel secure and led. I just want someone who'd take over and he is the one. With DeVine, being that he is not controlling, his gentle style feels like I'm too dependent on myself to carry out our relationship. DeVine is in charge but I feel he needs to be more assertive in what he claims we have together. The memoir points out that I can be wayward. The Father claims that DeVine is in control of all things which is cool but when I'm wrestling to control myself, it seems like I'm only viewed as a transgressor and not losing to trauma.

Churchy, Churchy.

Oh yes Div A. Den.

Woe it seems like you've gotten away from me for a second, said Div A. Den.

Oh, naw DeVine, oops Div A. Den, I just had some thoughts running through my mind. Where were we at in our conversation, she asked?

Yes, you know Churchy, the feeling is mutual, and to witness what's about to happen in human history will bring forth everlasting happiness. Nothing can pause, delay, or negate the trajectory of the results of our partnership.

You mean relationship, right, she asked?

Yes Churchy, relationship. I really like the sound of that. Geez, I'm usually the giver in all situations.

Although many would like to have me, I really see she passionately wants me. This feels good. I can see in myself that I like being pursued. I know the kind of value I can bring to her life. This is such a vibe and at this point, I beg it does not end. She has beauty; she is attention seeking which will make others know how great I can be in their lives. She's very exciting and spontaneous. You never know what you will get from her. She can be adventurous in one moment, rebellious in another, submissive at other times, and loyal in various moments. Churchy is never plain. I see why God can't handle her since she is not cookie-cutter. See, she's relevant and reachable. Many view me as someone that they can't touch, can't possess. But, seeing that she is no different from them, although she will flex as if she's not, she has the qualifying ability to convince others of how I am what they fully need. We'd surely be a tabloid/entertainment news hit. The paparazzi would have a hit out on us so to speak. Yeah, I must be real with myself, I want her.

Div A. Den, Div A. Den. Hello, hello.

Oops (Div A. Den laughs), sorry Churchy I had some thoughts running through my mind and blanked out too. That "relationship" word really hit me when you said it.

Well, I hope it meant good, she said.

Good? Baby, it meant great, he replied.

Great?

Yes Churchy, great.

Div A. Den, I'm going to flat-out tell you how...

(His phone rings) Oops, hold on Churchy let me take this call.

Hello, hi Div, he said.

Hey BG how are you?

I'm good sir, you have a minute?

Yes, a very quick one, BG.

Oh yeah?

Yeah, BG.

Oh, you must be involved in one of your player-player moments Div.

Kind of but not quite.

Kind of, Div? Does some lucky lady got you having feelings for her. (Div paused on his reply) Well Div, that pause lets me know she does. So tell me what's her name?

BG, you'll never believe it.

Oh yeah?

Yeah, BG.

Yes, I can bro, said BG. It's that old girl you met a month back at Judah Café you were telling me about.

Who, BG?

Div, you got to chill dude. You too predatory with the ladies, said BG. Bruh, the one with the caramel complexion and goddess body. You admired that pink colored Porsche she drove and that she was a CEO of a fortune five tech company, Div.

Oh dude, she had that good good but... But not her my friend.

What do you mean not her, asked BG?

Well, she didn't challenge me spiritually enough. You know bro, she physically and financially was my taste but she was too surface when it came to exploring deep matters like world dominance through mass influence, said Div.

Huh? Dude, I'd be scratching my head if a lady I only knew for a few months was engaged in topics like that, replied BG.

Oh, you would BG? Yeah right sir.

Naw Div I'm serious. I like to… Hold up Div, said BG. Dummy! Announce yourself when you are trying to pass someone on a walkway. I'll destroy you punk.

BG, you ain't nothing to play with sir.

I sure am not Div. But anyway, who's the lucky lady bruh?

Her name is Churchy, said Div.

Oh, so you all are beginning to gel, huh? Well look Div, I will let you go. I just wanted to say that this detective guy named Deshaun Smith would like to interview us about our relationship with God. It's like he's alleging that we are prime suspects in the death of God or something.

Oh yeah BG?

Yeah Div.

Well, we don't have anything to hide and you know I enjoy being on camera and in the spotlight so let's do it, said Div. What color are you wearing BG?

Black and red, said BG.

Yeah, go figure, said Div.

My advice Div, don't dress too flashily, wearing all those diamonds and stuff. Play it low key my friend.

All good BG, I'll hit you up soon.

Okay, Div. Tell Churchy I said hi.

Okay BG, sure thing.

(Div hangs up) Well, I see y'all had an interesting conversation, said Churchy.

Yeah, bae, some reporter investigator dude wants to interview us. Thinks we have something to do with God's death.

Oh really?

Yeah, but no biggie, said Div. I will say though, if you keep mesmerizing me with those pretty eyes and thick thighs, I will not be able to tame the inner crusher in me.

Crusher, what in the world?

Yeah, I said it. You'll meet that version of me when the time is right, he said. Yet until then, keep touching my mind and thoughts. I feel so close to you right now, Churchy. I really want you all to myself. I will just say it, I have no shame about it. You know, your lover God often promotes this opportunity for you and humankind to obtain everlasting life, yet he seems to fall short about providing a quality of life for the present experience of life. He a lame. Yeah I said it. I believe you want and desire better. Let me keep it real with you and no fluff. You deserve better, Queen.

Churchy has been the missing element for my world dominance to be fully established. With us being seen together, the whole earth will see how I benefit them and how everlasting life is obtained through the resources and inventions that only money can buy. She doesn't have the greatest reputation and support in this era though. Who and what she comes from has brought a stain on the hearts of humankind. I can tell she's searching for more tangible evidence of what a fruitful life should exemplify. Not to mention, she carries such a stunning outward appearance. Many in the world have lost trust in her but I can discern that when we two come into a relationship more openly, the hope of what I bring for change will be convincing to all. Well, except for God of course. I am attracted to the eloquence in her words. The stain in her character that many critics say she conducts—stealing from the poor to become rich, empty promises, and the like, her being with me will wash away all of that from the minds of humankind.

Again, I said what I said. Your lover God offers this pie in the sky thing about everlasting life, said Div. Therefore Churchy, wouldn't you agree with the adage that "a bird in the hand is worth more than a bush?

I sure do, she said.

Oh, and let's take it further Churchy, I'm convinced that if we took a consensus about the current human experience, I believe the majority would agree that if access to unlimited currency were available, they'd discover the cures for all chronic illnesses but even more so, the cure to prevent death itself. Humankind is so gifted but total access to the earth's resources as well as inventive minds is the biggest problem on the earth. What I mean by that is that only a few are privileged enough, and I don't mean privileged in a negative sense but meaning only a few have the privilege to invent, experiment, and test their ideas in an unlimited fashion. So, only a few who have that limitless option speak for the masses. If access is granted to the "least of these," the earth will no doubt flourish. See, we have proof of that because many heart-melting stories of those who come from limited-resourced backgrounds as well as violent, drug-ridden, impoverished communities have amassed into some of the greatest inventors and leaders that the world has ever witnessed and needed. When there's a lack of wealth and opportunity, the lust to gain the freedom that exists in wealth, manifests negatively and you have an entire world desperate to pull one another down for the piece of the pie, and the last piece of chicken in the pan. Comparingly, that's the crabs in a barrel mentality if you know what I mean?

I certainly do Div A. Den.

Now check this out. If the poorest of the poor are resourced with labs, infrastructure, equipment, and all tools needed for the mind to dream, limitless exploration will lead to unlimited, never-limited success.

That's deep Div A. Den, she said.

I really can't get past how thoughtful he is for everyone. He only wants people to have their best life. I'm being drawn even closer to him because of his thought process and heart for others. He's intimately caressing my mind right now in ways I have never experienced before. At least I think in ways. Anyway, I just feel I can dream with Div A. Den because there isn't anything dull about him. He's spontaneous, he's take charge, he's very thoughtful, and he is truly pursuing me. God tries to pursue and share his ideas but they just don't feel the same, nor convince me.

You know Churchy, the memoir gives an account of the human power to conquer great feats when it speaks of a time in human history when all people spoke one language and were unified. They were soon to accomplish building a tower to the Oasis where the Father himself holds residency. They were headed to establishing a pathway straight into the Oasis where our friend B. Guyler once lived. They were going to achieve that architectural success in only a few days. That's telling because to do such a thing meant there was peace, love, harmony, and empowerment. Figuratively, all Indians and few chiefs, no big "I's and no little U's," It was a sheer example of limitless life, ambition, invention, creativity, and faith working convincedly. But the memoir records that the Father confused the language and in doing so disrupted their plan.

Div A. Den, my head is scratching. Why would he do such a thing? Isn't that his plan for humankind? Is it not his plan to have a community with humans, she asked?

Churchy, I could be wrong, but it seems as if freedom to exercise ambition, to have the liberty to elevate one's faith in which it pleases him, looks as if it's a manner of selectiveness.

Is there a discriminatory practice happening, she asked?

It's difficult for me to say that it's not, he said. This story alone flows in harmony with B. Guyler's personal experience because you see ambitious achievements being stopped, which contradicts what the memoir defines as faith. Not only that but this tower to Oasis account also exemplifies unity and love for fellow persons.

Like, isn't such practice heralded as a reward of everlasting life, she asked? Love thy neighbor as thy self, per the memoir?

Yes, it's similar things like this that confuse me about God in this day and age, he said. Instead of placing faith in the Son of the Father that has brought heaven to earth to take some from earth to heaven, I believe with us working together we can create heaven for the earth so that all on earth will know how heavenly they are without heaven, said Div.

Sexy one, let me tell you, I'm sick and tired of being sick and tired, said Churchy. It's like hearing a radio station play the most annoying song over and over and over. Basically, to the point where you know every lyric of a song you don't even like. So, with God, I'm force-fed statements like, "I am the way the truth, and the life," "Without faith it's impossible to please God," "You cannot serve two masters, you'll love the one and hate the other." Div A. Den, nowadays, I'm getting more and more frustrated with him. In one sense the memoir says he's a jealous God and then it also states that God's bride should get rid of all envy. It kind of feels like I'm being held to a double standard if I understand this correctly. My present reality says that my need is to not need to need him. Yet, until you came into my life, I had no way to see how to move beyond a relationship with him. I always wanted to see me, and God's relationship work so fluidly that the earth would be healed. It hasn't. I'll give credit that you were a jewel and diamond in the ruff for a few that's in his Father's creation. Why have you been concealed? You are the epitome of limitlessness and with the hope I provide, no human is hindered, she explained.

Through B. Guyler, I have realized that I'm life-changing for all, and that sums up everything, said Div A. Den. We need each other. We need to be void of any other being between one another. I so want you, baby.

I so feel wanted by you Div A. Den because our vibe is one.

What's stopping us, Churchy?

Us. I'm excitedly nervous Div A. Den, we both know the answer…my sexy Div A. Den, come close to me.

Churchy, here I am (she snugs into his open arms), I never want to leave your side baby, he said.

Nothing prevents us from everlasting love and success except us, she said.

(He rubs her right arm slowly up and down with his right hand) Nothing can prevent everlasting from us. Together we are limitless, and I hope you realize it, he whispered.

(She pulls his left arm over her chest and tilt her head on his arm) Div A. Den, mine eyes have seen the glory, it stares deeply beyond my soul at this very moment and our world must not be forsaken any longer, she says softly.

(He whispers slowly in her right ear) Baby, I agree. I simply do not see any reason why God should even live any longer. He seems more harmful than good for people. It's one thing to have a life challenge and suffer from the pains of it. (He pulls her closely and tightly to his chest) A pain that results in loneliness, haplessness, and limitation. (She now is breathing deeply with her eyes closed as he speaks) It's another thing to have those issues and believe you have a hopeful solution for them, only to learn that you absolutely do not. I feel that there's nothing more painstakingly difficult than understanding that what you believed to be true is a lie. Churchy, you don't have to be associated with mysticism any longer. I am an absolute. (His tone raises from a whisper to a strong tone) Again, I simply do not see any reason why God should be living!

Div A. Den, I feel like God is just walking dead (She feels him squeezing her a little more).

Me too bae, he said. I just no longer want his zombie-like characteristics to invade others any longer. We have enough motion picture scary movies to identify with that and get amusement out of it. People should be walking the pathway of prosperity in which I am the only source to furnish it. Figuratively, not making a fiction tale but being an actual real reality in this world. God alone is enough of a zombie, we need not anymore.

I'm in agreement Sexy, she said. Why should this earth receive the stanking breath of God any longer, he's stealing valuable oxygen and breathing out horrible toxins. I'm tired of smelling the stank out of all these false hope statements he makes. I agree, I do not see any reason why God should even live any longer.

CHAPTER 19

"Tanisha Johnson"

(December 29th, 2003)

Good evening nerd heads and fool dudes. Welcome to another edition of the Thump and Grap podcast, said Thump. Grap, you look fat. You're packing on the pounds I might say?

Thump if we could bottle your breath right now, we'd make a ton of money for providing a diet solution. Yes, I've gained weight but dude the whiff I just got has spoiled my entire appetite for the next two weeks, sheesh man. Here you go, please eat this entire pack of juicy fruit gum right now before your microphone melts Thump, sheesh.

Whatever dude, pay the bills, Grap, said Thump.

Sure dude. Today's podcast is sponsored by Manna Meats, "where a taste from heaven falls fresh to each."

So Grap, where are we at today?

Well Thump, we are going to talk with a journalist student today. Her name is Tanisha Johnson and she's a senior at The Christian Life Institute of Practical Learning.

Wow, Grap, I know that to be a great educational center.

Yes sir, Thump. It's located in inner-city Cleveland, uptown to be exact and they are pumping out great contributors for the world, said Grap.

That's nice bud, we need more urban centers of learning in the country. May this be the model pilot to rally the urgency for our urban communities, said Thump.

Yes indeed, couldn't be said any better, minus the dragon breath dude, said Grap.

Shut up fat boy, said Thump.

So Grap, tell me what she'll be sharing with us today.

No doubt. Well as we all know, the death of God has been the main target of news across the world right now. Therefore, as we await the medical examiner's report for the cause of his death, as well as any findings from the police, Ms. Johnson is here to share about a survey she gathered months before God's death. Thump, the survey determines the significance of worldviews and their impact on the holistic future and prosperity of life for humans. This survey will show where humans are with how they feel. Thump, for instance, certain things like which views would best support and benefit the world, as well as why they believe the view they've chosen? The view of my face every time your mouth opens is one of the deadliest views one can experience. Thump the fumes are in plain view.

Whatever, Grap, whatever dude.

Those who were surveyed, chose between the ideological beliefs of the three candidates: B. Guyler, Div A. Den, and God, said Grap. God's lover, Churchy, is a factor in the decisions those who were surveyed made. So, Thump, before we bring Tanisha on, let's update the information that is being shared about his death now. How about you inform us?

Sure, Grap. According to Channel 12 News, top investigative journalist Deshaun Smith has released details of the crime scene via confidential sources, said Thump. Deshaun reports about details that occurred during God's recent birthday celebration that was held at his state-of-the-art worship campus. The one he gifted to Churchy. It's where he's said to visit from time to time.

Okay Thump, before you continue, isn't this the reporter—Deshaun Smith that Marie-Izzz-She leaked that has an ought with God? Wasn't it disclosed by coworkers close to him that he's drowning in grief and holding God responsible for allowing his wife to die? How is it even logical that Channel 12 News would even have him on this case? Despite he's a premier and highly achieved reporter, it seems like a conflict of interest.

Yeah you make a good point, said Thump. I wonder though, how try that is. Sounds speculative Grap.

Heck, Thump, he could be the one behind this tragedy for all we know. You can't put it past any human, especially one who feels they've been wronged, said Grap. So, for me Thump, that's an ideal motive.

We'll, I'm not sure if 86.1 FM could be a trusted source seeing the way they are in the red as a company, said Thump. This guy Deshaun has always reported with integrity, so I say his potential negative views toward God are all speculation.

Yeah, but what is not speculation is how your hands look so ashy that if you shook them for 5 minutes, you'd have enough ash flour to make two homemade pizzas, said Grap. (Grap laughs),

Please shut up dude, said Thump.

So, Thump, per reporter Deshaun Smith, this source happened to attend God's birthday party and he saw a few things that could assume a poisoning may have taken place. The police report says God's body was found lying near the dumpster in the rear of the edifice. Next to it was a small trash bag with throw-up in it. However, no contusions, signs of strangulation, hair compositions, or anything else that could presume an attack was rendered. Therefore, it's speculated that God may have been poisoned and that is what's being anticipated when the autopsy report is released. So, Thump, what is this reporter saying his source saw, asked Grap?

Well, the source supposedly saw that B. Guyler issued communion wine to everyone and that's one thought of how God was poisoned.

That's interesting, said Grap.

Yes, there's more my friend. Div A. Den arrived with a tray of famous cookies from Lo Lo's bakery which it's being noted that God regularly patronizes there. Eyebrows are raised as well because he gifted God with a special box of treats from there. God was seen enjoying both the wine and the treats that night, Thump explained.

But what about God's lover Churchy, asked Grap? How is she a potential accomplice?

Oh, that's easy bro. But maybe not for you, said Thump. Grap you probably were somewhere stuffing your face with a French bread pizza because the rumor mill has been swirling rapidly concerning her and Div A. Den having an affair. Therefore, she's seen as one who'd arrange the entire setup so that she and Div A. Den can flourish from God's life insurance policy as well as his assets. Assets such as his Father's Oasis, full control over his empire, and silencing his protests, which are gaining much traction against B. Guyler and Div A. Den's compelling and trending influence. An influence that is rapidly growing and many are supporting and being converted to it, explained Thump.

Okay, Thump. Well, Tanisha is going to speak more on those specifics but Thump thanks for the backdrop of the report, said Grap. Matter of fact Thump let's pay the bills and bring Tanisha up. Sounds like a plan flour hand man. (Grap laughs loud and long) Thank you in advance Breath of Death.

I will but dude this week I will shop for an SUV size innertube. It's only right that you convert it to a seat belt Mr. Blubber, said Thump.

The commercial ends. Tanisha is brought on the set

Hello Tanisha, said Grap.

Hi guys, she said.

Oops, team please adjust her sound she's very low, said Grap. Say something Tanisha,

Hi guys, how are... Ut, ut, there it is, said Grap. Thanks, tech crew and thanks for joining the show, Tanisha.

Glad to be here Thump and Grap.

Well, let's get right to it, said Grap. I was very fascinated about hearing the results of your survey. Honestly, anxious about it. So, for those who don't know, I met Tanisha back at an event hosted by the Mayor to acknowledge those in the city who are making an impact.

Of course, you aren't making any impact Grap, so why in the world were you in attendance, said Thump?

Thump, my little cousin was getting honored, and he asked me to come along with him, he replied. Unfortunately, Thump, the food could've been a little better. Had I foreknown it, your ashy flour hands would've made the perfect pizza. Breath of death, your presence was sorely missed.

Ok, Tanisha let us have it, said Thump.

Sure guys. But first, how much did this beautiful Brazilian rug cost? My Lord. Let me first say, guys, this place is amazing. It's strange but then again, I find it not strange as to why I am sitting here about to report with no shoes on.

Yeah Tanisha, the weather sucks around this time, said Grap. Also, I'm sure your commute here was great.

Grap, please. People act as if they can't drive in the snow, she said. This is Cleveland, so this is normal. It's cold as all get out. Squalls are falling fast, and the winds are blustering. But anyway, I'm ready to get to it. This opportunity is well worth the risk (Tanisha laughs).

What did your survey reveal? Please tell our viewers about some of the reasons behind people's choices, said Grap.

Sure. So, I surveyed 72 people to be exact and my question was simply: "who influences you the most about their impact on the world?" This was a diversified survey and so it covers adults from a range of ages, socioeconomic backgrounds, race, religious and nonreligious affiliations, and gender.

So, Tanisha, I imagine you covered a lot of miles around the city to best provide a balanced diversity per your categories, said Thump.

Correct Thump, I did.

Was there a bunch of snobs who didn't have time for you as you were building your consensus, asked Grap?

Yes, Grap but that's the nature of journalism and I'm a big girl with thick skin so I was okay.

I'd agree with ninety-nine percent of your thick-skinned strength, however, death breath would've turned you away in seconds, said Grap (Thump and Grap laughs).

You two are hilarious, she said.

So, what results did you come up with, asked Thump?

Yes, I found that the ones who trended the most regarding impact was B. Guyler and Div A. Den. But guys, I believe I know why.

Why Tanisha, asked Grap?

Basically, the recent partnership between the two revealed support that seems to provide a more holistic benefit for people, she said. Many would express that they saw no compatibility with God's historical approach to the human experience. Even those of earlier generations felt God's views were dated and that the future of their lineage would be in jeopardy if the flow of the world continued functioning per his principles.

That's great insight, Tanisha, said Thump.

Yes, I agree with Thump myself so gimme more of what you discovered during your survey, said Grap.

Definitely. Out of a statistical breakdown, B. Guyler topped off at forty-six percent supporting his ideas and vision for the world. Div A. Den forty percent and God ended with fourteen percent. What I discovered in speaking with people was that B. Guyler's views of how the world would flourish were through freedom of ambition. Many felt that humans know what's beneficial for their purpose on the earth and find that the earth is limited. The boundaries that can suppress one's rightful choice to determine what's important could be blamed by the control issue of God and the elite. People shared that good is in everyone and it's time to stop using a memoir that seems to project ancient patriarchal type narcissistic views. So, Grap, that's absolutely the language I got. It's called "Marketplace Ministering," she said.

So, what about B. Guyler, why was there great favor in his vision, asked Thump? Div A. Den was big because having unlimited provision, in other words, money and resources, allowed all backgrounds to have access to learning and funding to invent. Unfortunately, that just isn't the case in today's world. They argued that God's Father's memoir provided wishful thinking. That is why they also believed that the rumors about Div A. Den and Churchy's were true.

How so, asked Thump?

Let's say Churchy was tired of being used as a spokeswoman for God and in return for her promotion, God delivered what witnesses say were empty promises Thump.

Oh wow Tanisha, now that's a bombshell you've just dropped.

Thump I have my sources too. I am an up-and-coming journalist you know.

(Grap laughs) Thump, you better recognize you are talking to a boss sir, said Grap.

Shut up Grap, he said. Just shut up! So, Tanisha, you're practically saying Div A. Den's goal is to free people from the challenges that exist because of a lack of money?

Yes. Many believe that discoveries for solutions could be obtained when more people are well off and not bound by the pressure of paying bills, working for companies that can't provide a livable wage, and not getting the opportunity to maximize their purpose on the earth because they can't afford college or training that would flourish their passions. They believe that the partnership between Div A Den and B. Guyler, as well as potentially Churchy, who will come aboard at some point, is the holistic approach that provides complete life. Life-giving elements such as ambition—the brain of execution, resources—the heartbeat of execution, and integrity—the trust of execution. Combining Div A. Den, B. Guyler and Churchy would mean, cures for disease and illness, crime, drugs, and violence would be done away with. As well as peace and benefits of a spirituality that is not selective and judgmental but inclusive and affirming.

Alright, Tanisha, you are on to something, said Thump.

Well, Thump how about you do a drum roll, said Grap?

As for the one who has been recognized as the epitome of purpose, provision, and love for people, happens to be the one with the fewest count associated with importance. Here you go, Grap, said Thump. Tanisha, how about we all do it together, sure (Grap and Thump are banging on things boom boom boom boom boom dun-nun-nun-dun nunnn,) GOD!

Why God Tanisha, what's the deal with people turning away from God, asked Grap? This is the one mentioned amongst households as a major source for supplying needs. The one who is known for advertising unconditional love. The one who became like humans so that he could bring the solution to life's ills. The one with the power to provide freedom from sin, freedom from guilt, shame, and all things that look good but as we have now been informed, don't mean well per the people.

I know right. It's interesting isn't it Grap?

Yes Tanisha, really interesting.

So, Tanisha, what's the reason he's being cast away per se, asked Thump?

Thump, the majority stated they wanted to experience the Oasis on earth, not at some unknown time that seems like it'll never come, she said. Plus, being that this unknown Oasis place keeps being advertised by God, people believe it's useless to believe in it and that it sounds fairytale-like. Some are starting to believe that God is delusional. Seeing that God is not putting his money where his mouth is. They're saying God does not have a real concrete tangible solution for illnesses, crime, and love. More sickness in the world is prevailing, crime, and lack of love. So basically, many believe what he provides simply doesn't work, she said. They mentioned having the ability to literally see with their eyes the impact that B. Guyler and Div A. Den are making provides them with solace. The people feel they are making an Oasis on earth a reality and not a rambling talk and no-action situation. They feel like

God is pretty much saying wait and wait and wait and wait on this promise that says his Father is going to provide one day.

Ouch, so it is evident that people are veering away quickly, remarked Grap.

Yes, Grap, she answered.

Well Tanisha, thanks so much for being our guest today, said Thump. How can our viewers and listeners learn more about the things that you are doing?

Congratulations by the way, you are amazing, said Grap.

Thanks. I appreciate you two for this opportunity. Viewers and listeners, you may find me on my YouTube channel "Tanisha Talks Truth" and my website, tanishatalkstruth.org. It's been a pleasure, gentlemen, and thanks again for having me.

Tanisha, it's been our pleasure, said Thump.

Well, turd nerds and goofy dookies I'm Thump.

And I'm Grap, and we'll see you on the next one. Thanks for joining our show.

CHAPTER 20

"Born Day"

(Between 9:30 pm December 24th and 12:30 am December 25th 2003)

Hello everyone, may I please have your attention? Hello all, may I please have your attention? We'd like to thank all who are gathered for arriving promptly. My name is Ru, and I will be tonight's host. Me and my team are excited and honored to serve you in this manner. We are thankful for God and his passion for people. God never sleeps nor slumbers. He surely goes through so much to make a lasting impact on the lives of the least, lost, left out, and lowly. Bearing the brunt of such a mission, as well as administering confidence and joining in servitude with you all. His tasks are surely daunting and overwhelming at times, no matter how much he loves and has a passion for saving the lives of people, he needs more sabbaticals than he takes. Keep God in your prayers. Encourage him to steal away and get more rest. He's a man of joy and sorrow and those emotions sway as you could imagine. With that being said, can we give a hand clap of praise and a shout of joy because we are about to celebrate like there is no tomorrow. Real quick, Churchy selected this location because it was very special to her. God had this edifice built as a gift to celebrate her and show his appreciation for her and her sacrifice to join in the mission with him. This edifice is quite elaborate and so, make sure that you do not hesitate to ask me or any of my crew team members to assist you with directions. We have signs posted but as we know in a setting like this, nobody is paying attention to any darn signs (everyone laughs). Please take a tour around the edifice, and enjoy the artwork, the artifacts, and historical heirlooms, plus an array of artwork. We have in place several tour associates if you want back stories and a more organized flow throughout the galleries. Otherwise, browse and enjoy. For the youth, we have an entire area designated for you. Parents, be sure to have them guided to those areas to enjoy the occasion.

After 10 minutes

Excuse me, everyone, excuse me, please, says Ru. I didn't expect to hear this so suddenly. Don't tour the edifice just yet. I have just been notified by Churchy's assistant that her and God are headed here now and are only ten minutes away. Our team will now guide you to the entrance and areas where you will be stationed to yell surprise, said Ru. God has allowed Churchy to blindfold him, so, by him allowing it, this is going to be extra surprising to him (crowd laughs). I'm sure he wouldn't let anyone else do that but we're grateful for God's humor, good Spirit, and being a good sport about it. Okay everyone, high-five your neighbor next to you and say, "let's do this!" (says Ru). Oh, I'd be remised if I didn't thank our DJ for tonight. Everyone, please give a special shout and hand clap for DJ Heavenly Host. Okay, okay team get them in position now, Churchy's text message is saying that they are currently about 2 minutes away.

Come on my love don't worry we got you, Churchy says to God.

Baby, I'm going to be upset with you if I fall, says God.

DeVine, you are safe in my care love. As well, my dear, I like this suit and its color scheme, says DeVine. Churchy, purple means royalty and you have me looking Gucci today. I feel like a king.

DeVine, you are the king as per the memoir, you are the King of kings, she said. Okay, you may open the door, Neecy, says Churchy.

DeVine my love, stay still while I remove the blindfold, said Churchy.

I am so anxious to see what you have hidden up your sleeve Churchy, said DeVine. You are surely always up to something, so can I trust you with what you have arranged, he asked?

You know you can my Lord.

Huh, we'll see about that Churchy, he said.

Churchy and DeVine exit the car and approach the front door of the edifice.

Alright, DeVine, here we go, you now may open your eyes, says Churchy. SURPRISE! (the gatherers shout).

Aye, aww bae, my good thing Churchy, you are something else, said DeVine. What's up everyone, hey Abe, hey Isaac.

What's up with you God? (they both say to God).

Hey Jake, good to see you, Esther, hey Naomi and Bathsheba, Eve, and Enoch. Y'all are looking fabulous, said God.

What's up God, what's up my brother, said B. Guyler.

Hey Div A. Den, said God.

Happy born day sir, replied Div A. Den.

It's kind of a surprise to see you two here.

Yes, go figure, said B. Guyler. God, it's no secret that our views collide with yours, but we still celebrate life.

Appreciate you guys' presence, says God.

Over by the Spiral Staircase

So, God, I was made known that I and you have something we fully agree on, said Div A. Den.

What can it be Div A. Den, he asked?

Treats from Lo Lo's Bakery.

Oh, Div A. Den you too huh.

Yes sir. I ask that you help me God, I can't keep my belly away from that place, says Div A. Den. But, with knowing that about you in mind, God, I only felt that it would be necessary to furnish your party with these treats. But even more so God, here's an extra special portion for you only (Div A. Den hands good a bag).

Thanks. Appreciate you for this, he said. Now Div A. Den, I hope you aren't trying to poison me sir? (God and Div A. Den both laugh).

God, you are hilarious, he said. Why would I need to do such a thing, sir? God, you're the one I need to watch. (Div A. Den leans in close, stares directly into the eyes of God and firmly speaks) On a sidebar, God, the world wants me more than you in their life because they see and know the huge value in me versus you. See, because of the money

I can, want to, and will lavish on them, they know I will make the world a better place. Money is what everybody wants in their life, not the empty promises you keep giving. The people know that the lack of money is the only thing that is preventing them, and the earth, from prospering and running the way it should run, says Div A. Den.

Wow Div A. Den, so now you are hitting me with the side eye huh?

You are darn right, God, he replied. Now if you were to humble yourself and come up under my authority then I might feel more comfortable. But since you are an opponent, I got to keep you at a distance dude. But look, God, it's your day, enjoy this gift on me.

Yeah, Div A. Den, I hear you, but I will be careful (God laughs).

Hey Ru.

Yes Churchy.

I wanted to update you that B. Guyler is giving God a gift as well so make sure to collect these items so that God can enjoy them later, she said.

Sure thing, he replied.

As in the past, Ru, we will include in this celebration a special recognition moment for people to say something to God. Ru, at that time, we will present God these items from Div A. Den and B. Guyler. Ru, understand that gifts from these two are important to have ready due to the nature of their celebrity and mogul status, said Churchy.

Ma'am, be assured that we will carry this task out with excellency. There will be no need for anyone to be reprimanded for not doing their part.

Ru, I don't care how you do it, just get it done with professionalism, this is a big deal Ru. Do you hear me?

Yes Churchy I hear you and we will have these items ready to select during that moment, he replied.

Great, now go assist party members with the tour and directions, she said.

What's up bro, what do you got in your hand B. Guyler, asked God?

Bro, I have something special for you as well. Here you go, God, he said.

Oh no, you didn't have to do this. The last time I enjoyed a bottle of this wine was when I was hanging out over at Levi's house, said God.

Yes, I know. Rumor has it that you enjoyed yourself that night too. I guess you are known for doing too much bro. It's no wonder why it is noted in the Father's memoir that you were called a drunkard and a glutton. So, make sure you take it easy on this bottle and those goodies that Div gave you, said B. Guyler. On another note bro, I must admit, your girl Churchy has really good taste.

Thanks, B. Guyler. B. Guyler, I..

Hold up bro, I'm not through talking, let me finish. Now as I was saying God, you're still the same old way. You have a ton to say about any and everything, said B. Guyler. But God.

Yes.

Our Father does say we are to be quick to listen and slow to speak ya know, yet you have a motor mouth, said B. Guyler.

C'mon bro, it's my day why…

Why what God?

Fam here you go, you are trippin' and it's a bit distasteful B.Guyler, said God. I feel like spewing this conversation out of my mouth B. One minute you are warm and the other you are cold. How about you choose one because you are slithery and manipulative B. Guyler.

Hmm, oh taste and see that the Lord is good huh, God, said B. Guyler? (B. Guyler steps to the right and leans into God's left hear) I see God, I see Churchy's dress, and you know it's too much for what's supposed to be modest. She's always trying to boast and be in charge. Get your girl in check. My team is nice God. We make waves out here and many are maximizing on the daily ads that I release. God that is why my guy Div got err'body eating meaty out here, yet the work of your hands got many famished. I told you already when the Father had you starving and broke in the desert that I got that good food for you. Sir, you was scared to eat though. I already told you Bro, that there are no miracles in your reach. You were and still are scared to take a risk and challenge the Father at his wannabe word, continues B. Guyler. Dude, I even offered you some of the kingdoms on this earth, but you have the nerve to be trippin' on the young rich ruler. DeVine, all you do is hinder people and promote this "pie in the sky," "go give it away and then come follow me" foolery. It's no mystery why many people are clocking out on your worthless approach to the fruits of this world. C'mon God, are you really acting like this world lays in the palms of my hands? Bro, understand this, my only goal is to make the citizens of the world flourish. But flourish in a freeing way, not through a persuasive cultic way like how you go at it. God, you are a professional kidnapper, said B. Guyler.

B. Guyler, I got to get back to enjoying what Churchy has worked so hard to provide for me this evening, said God. I wish we could holler at each other for a little while longer, but oh well. B. Guyler, I'm not even mad at you bro. It's all good with you and Div A. Den, I'm not at odds with you two. I thank you guys so much for your presence and kindness. Although we see things differently, I don't trip because the Father is nothing but good to everyone. So, enjoy this day and rejoice and be glad in it.

I sure will God, said B. Guyler.

Me as well, said Div A. Den.

God, make sure to have fun with that drink but don't continue your gluttonous "m-o." said B. Guyler

You silly B. Guyler, replied God.

Naw God, I'm dead serious, he said.

God heads towards Fondu Station Area

Excuse me ma'am, said God.

Hey God, she said.

Oh, look at you Mary Mag, you look stunning. I didn't know that was you Mary, wow, he said. Hey, it's a blessing to see you Mary.

It's a blessing to be in attendance, happy birthday, she said.

Thanks so much. Sorry to run Mary please excuse me. I must catch our host Ru for something, he said.

Oh, no problem God, she replied.

Ru, put this on ice, said God.

Okay God will do.

(Churchy walks up) Hey DeVine.

Yes, Baby, hey to you, he said.

I've selected B. Guyler to lead us in the honorary toast later, she said.

(Ru walks by them) Hey Ru, calls Churchy.

Yes ma'am, he answered.

Make sure you have the treats and this infamous bottle of Nu Wine ready for God at the time of the toast.

My pleasure Churchy.

Thanks, Ru, she replied.

(Churchy turns back to God) Oh, you hear that Churchy?

Yes, DeVine I do.

Churchy you got my dude DJ Heavenly Host here?

You know I had to.

(God grabs Churchy by the hand and heads towards the dance floor located by the spiral staircase) Pardon me Div A. Den and B. Guyler, we need to get by you to make a joyful noise and go dance like David, said God.

DJ Heavenly has it lit already. (God says to himself)

C'mon Bae, let's get it, God says to Churchy. DJ Heaven is spinning that song that the Angels can't sing. Aye, aye, aye, aye, "ain't no party like a Holy Ghost party cause a Holy Ghost party don't stop aye'! (People at the party are yelling this as they dance)

Churchy heads over to the bar area

Hey Churchy.

Yes, Ru.

I see the look on your face, he said. Please relax a bit. God looks like he is truly enjoying himself, said Ru.

Yes you're right Ru, he certainly is, she said.

Don't let yourself be bothered by the rumor mill. I already believe I see some photographers in here, he said. You can't change the minds of people. You already know. The memoir says that their hearts are deceitfully wicked. Don't waste your time giving them your mind. I heard you have some great initiatives soon to release.

I do Ru. It's just difficult having your name run through the mud, she said.

I can only imagine the difficulty in that, he said. So, hopefully tonight you can set all that aside and just enjoy the love of your life. Matter of fact, it's non-negotiable, I will make sure you enjoy it.

Excuse me Ru, excuse me Churchy, said this guy from the staff of Ru.

Yes, how can I assist you, said Ru.

Ru, the voices of Yah are headed out, as well as God's Son Mime and C-Life, the staff said.

Okay, I'll be with them in a second, said Ru. Okay Churchy, let me get back to my duties.

Ru you have done such a great job tonight with everything, she said. My vision for God's birthday celebration has turned out fabulous. Therefore, I am treating you to a self-care package over at Delilah's.

Currently, she has the number one top-rated spa in the city. I hear that her massages are life-changing too, Ru.

Thanks, Churchy, that's kind of you and I am not turning your gift down.

You're welcome, Ru.

Churchy my team is in place to serve as you see. Anything you order will get done effectively and efficiently. We are on it, Churchy.

Over by the DJ table and banquet area

Wow, everyone, that was an amazing show of art through song, dance, rap, and poetry, says God. Thank you for blessing me with your gifts.

Aye C-Life.

Yes, God.

I'm going to have to do a cipher with you soon man.

I'm down. Let's do it, God, I heard you got lyrics, he said.

I got a little something something, my friend, replied God.

Blessings everyone, blessings. Let me get your attention please, said Ru. I want you to know that my team has put together an amazing six-course dinner for you, and anyone that truly knows God knows that he likes fish. Y'all know God, he practically attempts to feed fish to anyone he goes to serve (crowd chuckles).

Ru you play too much my friend but thank you, said God.

Our servers are prepared to serve you and don't worry, we do have vegan options, as well as other meat choices too, said Ru.

Churchy, I now hand it over to you now, said Ru.

Thanks, Ru.

Churchy's opening celebratory remarks. Guests are seated for the banquet dinner.

Today, we celebrate a faithful, kind, passionate, and full of unconditional love person. He's there with those who weep, he gifts those who are overlooked, he's a lawyer in a courtroom, a doctor near a sickbed, a friend to the friendless, and a provider, protector, and priest. Recently, I was made aware of an act of love that my DeVine, but to you, God, performed a little over a year ago. It was for the mother of local investigative reporter from Channel 12 News named Deshaun Smith. God had met Deshaun at the Mayor's community servant acknowledgment event. Deshaun rushed his mother to the hospital for chest complications. I was told that God, although preoccupied with an important meeting, saw fit that this situation called for him to be by the side of this gentleman. This act of support defines the compassion that God has for people. This reporter's mother was having chest pains earlier that morning and like any loving child her son rushed her to the hospital. It seemed that after a bunch of tests that things were going to check out fine with his mother and then suddenly, she went into cardiac arrest. God moved to action by remaining grounded in prayer and then he laid his healing hands near her upper chest area. God called forth healing power and to the medical staff's amazement, this mother had no further damage. The doctor informed God and this son that for a woman her age he had never witnessed an absence of any further complications after going into a cardiac arrest emergency. Ru, our God needs tissue right now (Ru grabs tissue and gives to God). Aww, this is the man we are honoring, says Churchy. A humble man that lives to care for and provide the best for others. A man that is confident in the promises his Father has proclaimed. God moves in an incarnational way. He takes on the pain of others and makes it his pain. If this exact moment called for him to give up any part of himself, organ, kidney, finances, home, etcetera, we know that within an instance it is so. I'm totally sure that all of you can agree, says Churchy (crowd claps and whistles).

Churchy moves from podium that stands in front of the stage onto stage, walks to God's singular guest of honor table and grabs God's hand. With back to audience and looking intently into God's eyes she says:

Everyone, this is who we honor the life of tonight. Not everyone here gathered agrees with his views, and that's the freedom we all have. Yet, we can agree that he cares for people, and he cares to live it out in action to the best of his ability. We don't know what this world would be without you, my love, Churchy says to God. We hope that you are enjoying yourself. We thank you because you are a gift to the world. (Churchy turns and looks toward DJ booth) Hey DJ Heavenly, can we have another mic? Churchy, my pleasure, says DJ Heavenly. Ru, grab that mic from him and give it to God, says Churchy

Holding hands, God and Churchy step down from stage to the podium and God reaches and grab the microphone from Ru, then says, as he looks at Churchy and then to the crowd:

Thank you, my love, for your kind and loving acknowledgment. Thank you all for coming out tonight. Now let me be the first to say that best dressed goes to Div A. Den, hands down (crowd claps and whistles). Sir, says God, that chinchilla is fire, I'm just saying. Nevertheless, let me not stop there. (God looks at towards B. Guyler) Aye B. Guyler, you are always shining and Churchy you never cease to look stunning (Churchy does a namaste pose to God and B. Guyler gives a salute wave to God). To the youth, you all are the best and I am grateful for your presence tonight. To all of my friends and family gathered, umm, I'm getting choked up, excuse me. "It's alright God, it's alright," a few voices in the crowd echo. Umm, what can I say? (God says) It's delightful and heartwarming to be gathered with you tonight. If there's anything that I enjoy doing, it is eating and drinking in fellowship with people. You all continue to pray for me. Much has been given to me and much remains required of me. I believe that sacrifice for one another is the most solid and exemplified way to show your faithfulness to my Father. To be prosperous, have influence and power, and hold to your views is pleasing to him too. But we must know that such things will not endure much longer. What never fails and what will endure for eternity is love. Love is the greatest of all acts. Surely, I'm most blessed by your generosity and your presence here this evening. You have made my born day special. Churchy I hand the program back over to you, I will take my seat now (God walks back up to the stage and takes his seat at the table of honor). I'm overwhelmed by everyone's kindness tonight, says God (as he waves and blows a kiss towards the audience, crowd gives standing ovation and whistles).

Churchy flags Ru to get the mic God gave her. Ru grabs it and steps to the side. Churchy goes behind the podium and says:

Thanks, my love for sharing your heart with all of us tonight. Let us pray. Father of the Heavens, we ask that you continue to bless the work of the hands of your Son. Thank you for your thoughtfulness to gift us with him. Now bless this food and the hands that prepared it. In your name. Amen.

Food is served. Everyone eats. Churchy goes back to the podium and says:

Everyone, let's give a big hand to Ru and the crew tonight, said Churchy. They truly set it out. The food was delicious, the hospitality professional, and this amazing edifice was enormously elegant. I mean from the royal décor, the waterfall, the fondu station, the chinaware, the Brazilian rugs, the decor on the spiral staircase, and so forth.

With Churchy finished, Ru placed a mic on the tables of God and B. Guyler. Churchy then went and sat with God at the table of honor.

Yo God, although you are a humble man, you have great taste, fashionable style, and quality service, said B. Guyler.

Shaking his head, God said, Thanks, but all credit goes to the lady of my life. Churchy never ceases to amaze me. Smiling and pulling her closer, God continues. Bro, her way of doing things regularly catches me off guard.

Okay, whatever, said B. Guyler. (Pulling away from his brother. Then scanning the crowd, he continued) Aye, I wonder what God meant by that.

You silly B. Guyler, said God. Naw, let me rephrase it, you are crazy for that one.

The chuckling grows louder. God stood up, looking out at the crowd from a large stage before addressing the room.

Everyone, I, your friend God, am truly grateful for all of you. You have made my born day special, and I can't thank you enough for coming. And, to my Churchy, thank you so much for setting this up. I love you.

In the crowd, some screamed, We know!

Laughing, God picked up from where he left off. Thank you whoever yelled that out. Let me let those of you who aren't aware in on something… (He was again interrupted by someone shouting encouragements. Sure, God go right ahead.)

The crowd gave a standing ovation, claps and cheers mixed with whistling and catcalls. Churchy, who sat at the table of honor, blushed and blew kisses towards the crowd.

So beautiful Churchy, and very thorough, said Div A. Den from the table he shared with B. Guyler.

Thank you, Div A. Den, said Churchy.

God, looking down at Churchy, pressed on. Churchy my love, I know that this took a lot of effort-a lot of time and frustration, but you truly have honored me, going above and beyond. After blowing Churchy a kiss, he called out to B. Guyler. My brother, back over to you.

Sitting down, God puts his arm around Churchy and B. Guyler walked up to the podium to address the crowd.

Thank you-thank you. As God's brother, I know he treats everyone else with the best wines. So…Ru?

At his insistence, Ru walked to podium.

Ru approaches stage from right aisle way. With the microphone in his right hand hanging near his right side, left hand in whisper position, B. Guyler whispers in Ru's right ear.

Yes B. Guyler.   Then Ru glances at the crowd and says out loud. You know that your man Ru is here for you.

Ok now Ru, that was corny, it's not the time to be corny. The moment at hand is special, said B. Guyler.

Sorry B. Guyler, how may I assist you? asked Ru.

That's better but miss me with the sorry stuff. Sorry doesn't fix your "cornball-ness."

As the sound of chatter filled the room from attendees talking amongst one another, B. Guyler spoke into the mic.

Hey, is there anyone available to give Ru a few swag sessions, how corny is he?

The crowd gasps at B. Guyler's statement.

Being that he's a light skinned middle-aged black man, Ru's face turned noticeably red as the stage spotlight shined upon him. Nervously rubbing the left side of his face with his left hand, as well as blinking his eyes repeatedly, he looked very uncomfortable.

Again, B. Guyler leans over and whispers in his ear.

Ru, says B. Guyler, how about you have the staff pass out the glasses now? Because I would like to present to God his favorite brand of wine called, The Nu Wine. Also, wipe that dumb look off your face. I just told you that the moment is special, now hurry, gather your team and go handle what I just said to handle!

Ru swiftly left the podium area, calling out and flagging his team.

Fifteen minutes passed and light chatter filled the room. B. Guyler tapped his glass with a fork to get everyone's attention then addressed the crowd. Excuse me everyone, excuse me all. My special moment has come in which I am compelled to lift this toast up in celebration of my brother's born day. The younger sibling turned to face his brother. Yo God, I want to say this openly. We have had our differences, and we still do, but nevertheless you have made a unique legacy and provided a way of life that many imitate for some reason. Frankly bro, I don't get why they'd imitate such a boring type of lifestyle but to each his own. The crowd gasped and B. Guyler turned to address them before talking to his brother. I just heard that gasp everyone, let me be clear, I'm speaking from the heart, so this is not a roast…God, some believe that you give hope to the hopeless and it's obvious that each one gathered here tonight has experienced something unique about you. Therefore, it was a must for me to pull out your favorite wine and lift a toast to you today. It only makes sense to do such for a person once and awhile who tries to kind of be a leader. You know everybody, it's obvious you feel the same way being that you are gathered here too. We all could've decided to be anywhere but here, so God that means you should be even more appreciative.

As if on cue, Div A. Den now came up to the podium and B. Guyler continues.

Now, y'all all know that me and Div. A Den are busy men, and our time is quite valuable.

Div A. Den leans over and whispers in B. Guyler's ear.

This thing has gone way overboard B. Guyler... I'm in weariness, feeling like a hostage from being present at this long, drawn out, practically uncalled for piece of celebration thing.

I get you, you are totally right my friend. Taking a step over to his right, B. Guyler redressed the audience, his tone gentle. Has everyone had a chance to have their glasses filled?

Up front, Ru and his team finished setting a table up with wine and treats then went to the podium.

Ru's response is fast and curt. Hold on. We all want the toast, but Div A. Den also has a presentation.

Sure Ru, B. Guyler says. I can wait Ru, Div A. Den is my guy.

Hey everyone, Div A. Den has purchased some complimentary treats for this occasion, Ru said. Me and my team have them prepared for you at this table up front to the right (he points to the right to show them where to grab the treats). Churchy, requests that no one leaves empty-handed, said Ru. And God, here's your special bag (one of Ru's crew members give God the special bag).

Thank you so much Ru, God says. (God grabs mic from the table him and Churchy are sitting at and speaks) I really appreciate this kind gesture Div A. Den, said God.

If any aren't aware, this is God's favorite bakery, said Ru.

Aww wow, that's timely Div A. Den, said B. Guyler.

Thanks, my friend. Everyone, I already know that you agree but I have to say it, says Div A. Den. Had it not been for a servant like God, where would this world be? (Facetiously Div A. Den says this) That's all I would like to say, here's the mic B. Guyler.

Thanks, my friend. Everyone you may come forth and grab your wine and treats, Ru says.

About 10 minutes later. Everyone has been served by Ru and his team:

Well, finally my moment has come so everyone please stand at this time, said B. Guyler (B. Guyler turns to God). God, we raise our toast to you in honor of your born day. Being that actually this day has no true importance, as well as this sort of, but not really impactful type of work you attempt to do for people, has either, we acknowledge you (gatherers gasp). Regardless, we unfortunately raise our glasses to this meaningless moment and make this toast to you anyway, my brother (gatherers are heard grumbling).

(God stands) Thanks B. Guyler and thanks everyone. Be not alarmed my friends, I have heard worse. Hey look though, I know that the hour is getting late, but before you exit, come take some pics with ya boy, said God (God looks towards the dance area). DJ Heavenly Host, you know I see you over there and you know I can read your mind. (God laughs).

God, you surely can.

Well, don't hesitate my friend, make it happen DJ.

Say no more my friend. Now everyone hit the dance floor and rock out to 'Mary Mary's the God in Me,' it's ya boy whose blessed the most, DJ Heavenly Host rocking the ones and twos (crowd yells Ayeeeee!).

People move swift to the dance floor. God is still on stage and points to Ru to come to him. God has a look of pain on his face and has his hand over his stomach:

Ru, go get Churchy for me quick.

Sure thing God, says Ru.

(Churchy comes to the stage) Churchy Bae, said God.

Yes, here I am handsome. Ru told me you wanted me.

Yes, Bae, I'm having some stomach issues and feel a bit woozy. Please cover for me Churchy. Things are winding down, I'm not feeling well, I really need to head to the executive restroom right now. I'm unable to greet anyone who's leaving, so please cover for me.

Sure, my love, I can greet everyone leaving.

Thanks Churchy, you are very special to me (Churchy blushes).

Are you going to be okay, my love? I can send Ru to look out for you if you want.

No need Bae, I'll be fine. Just make sure all who are leaving receive my blessing and gratitude. I just need to maybe use it and then sit down. I feel dizzy and woozy.

Churchy heads upfront near the front door to greet those who are beginning to leave:

Hey Ru, hey Ru.

Yes Churchy.

Make sure you keep an eye out on God. Suddenly, he's not feeling too well. He went to the executive bathroom. Keep watch until I finish greeting the people as they exit. He's adamant that I do so.

No problem, Ma'am, I got it under control.

Gatherers are beginning to file out. Churchy is chatting with them as they head out:

Churchy, very impressive, says a woman named Hanna.

Thanks Hanna. By the way, that velvet dress and the pumps are eye-popping, said Churchy.

B. Guyler and Div A. Den are on their way out the door.

We are headed out, Churchy my friend.

Thanks for coming, B. Guyler.

No problem. I had to show my face, he said.

I'd say you showed more than your face, but that's another topic for another day, she said.

Anyway, tomorrow, we have a huge meeting with some of the largest businesses and nonprofit organizations in the world, said B. Guyler.

We're excited Churchy, said Div A. Den. A major breakthrough is on the cusp and the plan to free the citizens of the world from generational poverty is soon to be in effect. Churchy, come close (Div A, Den leans in to whisper in her ear). Pretty one, you so sexy and intelligent. I can't keep my eyes off you.

Div A. Den, I will call you later tomorrow, she said.

I'll be expecting to hear from you. Don't play me. I want you Churchy and don't you ever forget that, ever.

I know you do and I feel a strong vibe to be with you. I can't keep you off my mind, she said. By the way is that Versace cologne that you are wearing Div A. Den?

Yes, pretty one it is.

This cologne does something to me every time I smell it on you. I really need you to please leave Div A. Den. I feel like I can't control my feelings about you right now and this is not the time or place for me to go deeper with you. I will be calling you Div A. Den.

As team members of Ru are cleaning up, Churchy flags one to get their attention

Hey, hey you, said Churchy.

Ma'am are you speaking to me, says the gentleman cleaning?

Yeah you, come here. I know that you are cleaning things up butler guy but make a quick run near the executive restroom and tell Ru to come here.

Yes ma'am, I'll get Ru over to you.

Thanks so much butler, said Churchy.

Churchy turns back around to greet the leaving guests

Oh, now look at you two says Churchy. That platinum Rolex and those luxurious pearls complement so perfectly together, you two. Aren't you from the mayor's office?

No Churchy we are not, but that's where you saw us at that day when we were with Div A. Den, said the woman. We're his cousins.

Oh, that's right, now I remember where I saw you both. Div A. Den has told me so many great things about you two. What's your name again?

We're the Pharisees, the woman said.

That's right Mrs. Pharisees, it's all coming back.

Churchy, we run a financial firm called Love Mammon, said Mr. Pharisee. We both once worked in the city's finance department and then branched out to launch our own company, he said.

That's amazing you two, amazing, she replied.

Yes, Churchy it truly is a blessing, said Mrs. Pharisee.

Don't tell me that you two happen to now be allocating city funds to your account, questioned Churchy?

(They both laugh) Shhhh, don't say that so loud, Mrs. Pharisee replied. (They all laugh).

Churchy our hearts break for this city, he said. The employees in this city, as you might know, are barely getting salaries that extend above the low-income rate.

That's terrible, said Churchy.

Cleveland is the poorest big city in the nation unfortunately, he said. Therefore, with this new initiative and partnership we're about to unfold with the mayor, we'll provide lucrative venture capital opportunities for Cleveland residents to prosper.

Churchy, I see you're wrapping up the party, let us not keep you, said Mrs. Pharisee.

No ma'am, this is interesting.

No, seriously Churchy, we should go, she said.

Okay, you two are right, but before you go may I ask how did this vision evolve? Div A. Den spoke briefly to me about your company, and I just need to hear right now from the horse's mouth. You two, I'm just excited about the city.

Churchy, we get it, said Mrs. Pharisee.

So, one day Div A. Den and B. Guyler were burdened by God's lack of ability to increase wages for Cleveland residents, said Mr. Pharisee. All four of us knew crime is a direct symptom of poverty and this city is top rank when it comes to incarceration numbers, welfare, plus it's the murder capital of America currently, he said. After being saddened by this continual reality, we were motivated by B. Guyler to end the crisis.

Churchy, Div A. Den told us that you are passionate about ending this suffering as well and so we'll be in contact with you very soon, said Mrs. Pharisee. In our partnership, we see this initial focus as a pilot for the world at large.

Again, this is amazing you two. This vision is solid, said Churchy.

Us Pharisees don't play when it comes to judging things, and we are about tired of God's empty promises, said Mr. Pharisee.

Pharisees, I'm so in agreement with that, she replied.

We know God has tried to make change, but his methods are horrible, said Mr. Pharisee. We are just about tired of seeing you unfairly being pointed to as the blame for his ineffectiveness. You shouldn't be swooped up into this because you have a pure heart for the people. C'mon woman of God, you know how the struggle is. God's obvious shortage of integrity and unproductivity does not live up to what should be expected from him, he also said. God is a hypocrite if you ask me.

In pure amazement Churchy, the world is about to be caught by surprise by what we are about to unleash for them, said Mrs. Pharisee.

Well, Mr. and Mrs. Pharisee, I'm fully convinced that it is going to be life changing.

It is Churchy, said Mrs. Pharisee. B. Guyler and Div A. Den are doing some things that go beyond the norm and it's time for the crown to shift from God to Div A. Den. Now is it true Churchy? I heard some hot things about you and Div A. Den, hint hint.

Quit it Mrs. Pharisee and hush please (all three of them laugh). Mrs. Pharisee, he is sexy I must say though.

Churchy, be on the lookout because this rollout plan is about to be released. Things are going to be a pleasant shock to all, she said.

See, let me explain further. As this shift pivots the world away from that 'pie in the sky" approach that God provides, which does nothing for people, we will give people what they really need. No disrespect to God, but the former order in which he reigned in, will rapidly pass away and the new order is about to land any day now.

I look forward to it you two, said Churchy. Please send my regards to the mayor.

Will do Churchy, and thanks for the invite, you did such a loving surprise for God, she said. I don't know why you did it, but it truly reveals the grand character and love that you possess. He'll remember this act of love throughout eternity and beyond.

In a frantic manner a crew member of Ru swiftly approaches Churchy as she is talking to the Pharisees:

Hey Churchy, hey Churchy, I'm sorry to interrupt, said this crew member.

(Churchy turns around to face him) Yes, butler guy, where's Ru and what is it that you want?

Churchy please step over here.

Yes, butler guy, what is it?

Ru wants you to come now, it's an emergency happening in the back of the building, please come now.

Okay, I'm right behind you, take me to him.

Churchy turns back around and face the Pharisees.

Hey you two, I have to go but it was nice talking with you. Thank you for coming out tonight and I look forward to meeting up with you both soon, said Churchy.

Farewell, we look forward to meeting up too, said Mrs. Pharisee.

Churchy walks off with Ru's crew member. They swiftly pick up the pace and he directs her to the rear of the edifice.

God, God oh no what is... (Churchy arrives at the back of the edifice). Why is God laying here, asked Churchy? PLEASE CALL AN AMBULANCE NOW! (Churchy yells loudly)

RU! RU!

Yes Churchy.

Is God breathing, she asked?

I can't tell. Maid Laquita checked his pulse, but it's not moving. Should we move him, he asked?

Are you kidding me Ru? Why would you say something stupid like that! We don't want to do anything that will add further complications!

With tears falling from her eyes, Churchy gets down on the ground and speaks into God's ear.

My Lord, my Lord please wake up, please wake up, don't do this, don't do this, she said. NOOO DeVine, NOOO, (she yells, while she is loudly crying!)

Please go and get Churchy some tissue and her coat Laquita, it's chilly out here, said Ru.

Where exactly were you Ru, asked Churchy? I told you to keep watch over him.

I know you did, I practically watched him for…

Don't you, DON'T YOU PLAY WITH ME RU!

Churchy I've been pulled in all types of…

DO NOT GIVE ME ANY EXCUSE RU. I GAVE YOU STRICT ORDERS AND YOU DID NOT LISTEN.

I am so sorry, he said.

Sorry, can't change anything now. Please miss me with that bull Ru.

Loud sirens and flashing lights enter the parking lot of the edifice:

Thank the Lord, here is the ambulance pulling in, said Churchy. Ru, I will find out where they are taking him and go there. Head back up front and give the farewell to everyone leaving out.

Ok Churchy, I am heading there immediately.

Is anyone out here aware of what happened, asked Churchy? Are you aware butler guy?

No ma'am I am not fully aware of why he is lying here. When you sent me to get Ru, God was exiting from the restroom with this bag in his hand.

What bag?

The bag of Nu Wine and bakery items that B. Guyler and Div A. Den presented him with, he replied. I guess he was heading outside towards the dumpster. That's the only reason I can think as to why he was going out that door. Ru was in the hallway opposite the restroom, and he called out to me, as soon as I turned my back away from God to head towards Ru, I heard God collapse down the stairs of the back door. Laquita, who happened to be coming from the dumpster saw God fall, ran to him, and immediately began checking his vitals.

How long has he been lying here, asked Churchy?

Not long, not long at all. Once Ru got a clear eye on him lying on the ground, he sent me to get you. It all took place in a couple of minutes from when Ru told me to get you.

A paramedic approaches.

Ma'am, ma'am, said the male paramedic.

My name is Churchy sir, approach me with dignity.

Sorry about that, my name is Enoch of Quicken Ambulatory, we will rush him to Mount Sinai Hospital. You may head there now to be with him.

Okay, I will Enoch.

Hey butler guy, go get my car now, said Churchy! (crew members of Ru are gathered around) Everyone, please pray for God because this incident is heart-shattering, and we need God, she said. I need my Love.

CHAPTER 21

"Alleged"

(December 31st, 2003)

Good evening to all our viewers in Cleveland and surrounding cities. This is WHOLLY News Station, Channel 12 with today's evening updates. I'm Katrice Williams and I'm here with my colleague Leroy Taylor.

Katrice, today we witness an unfortunate tragedy on the city's east side. The tragedy happened near east 105th and St. Clair Avenue where an elderly couple was hit by a reckless driver as they were crossing the street. They had just come from shopping around 4:30 this evening. The driver did not stop, and this wife and husband were life-flighted to Mount Sinai Hospital. No more news about their condition has been released. Our beat reporter Canisha Thomas is on the scene with witnesses from the accident. Over to you Canisha.

Thanks Leroy. "This is just so sad, and it was very evil of the driver to keep going." That was Jeff Lipson who says he's been a long-time resident of this area and wanted us all to know that the community is getting more dangerous and that a stop to tragedies such as this "must happen immediately." Witnesses on the scene when this tragedy occurred said the driver was driving a silver 90's model Toyota with tinted windows. Our collective hearts grieve about this sad incident. Back to you Katrice and Leroy.

Thanks, Canisha, said Katrice.

If anyone has any information about the driver of this car, the Cleveland Police are asking that you report it immediately.

Now to our next report. Local organizations are teaming up for a noble cause to empower those who've recently been released from incarceration. New Way, a local organization founded by Lorenzo Harris in 2019, has created a pathway for former inmates to become self-sufficient through career training that focuses on financial investment strategies. Earlier our own Jose Rodriguez met with Mr. Harris, here's their segment.

Mr. Harris, what led you to launch this particular form of reentry empowerment?

First, thanks Jose for having me. What I believe is distinctive from other reentry organizations is that providing financial strategy empowerment was the way to best defeat recidivism and create lasting wealth for our participants. Providing the training and ongoing consultation for areas such as day trading ventures, business development, and independent contracting would allow our participants to be positioned to experience great opportunities and flourish for themselves and family. When the company is our baby and not someone else's, we put a greater effort into its success. The majority of our participants were never given guidance or were never exposed to these areas of financial control. Therefore, we assist them in development and growth and the majority of those who've kept with the program are doing quite well.

Well Lorenzo, continue the good work, and much success to your participants.

Thanks Jose.

Proud of you bud. Keep doing what you're doing. Back to you Katrice.

What a great piece by Jose. To learn more about how someone may get registered or if you seek to become a contributing partner of New Way, visit their website at newwaytoday.org or call 216-397-2000. I'm grateful to know that this organization exists in our city, Leroy.

Such a need, I tell ya. I'm very encouraged by the work of Mr. Harris, Katrice. Tell our viewers what's next.

Yes Leroy. Coming up after the break, we have an exclusive interview with our investigative reporter Deshaun Smith. He has been closely covering the death of God and had recently met with B. Guyler and Div A. Den, rumored suspects in this case. Don't turn your channel, this interview will be coming up next on Channel 12 News.

Station Break

Welcome back Cleveland residents and surrounding areas. Katrice, this story is one of intrigue, heartbreak, and astonishment.

Yes, Leroy, the question at hand is "What Killed God?" The world wants to know who's responsible for this.

You're right Katrice. Our very own Deshaun Smith has been working endlessly around the clock to investigate this story and tonight he has an exclusive interview with two alleged suspects, B. Guyler—the distant brother of DeVine Shepherd aka God and Div A. Den, a wealthy, actually the wealthiest person in the world. Sources from the Bump & Grap podcast mentioned he was in an affair with God's lover, Churchy.

Wow, Leroy, these details are stunning. I know our very own Deshaun Smith has gotten to the bottom of this case, so without further ado viewers, let's turn our eyes and ears over to this interview.

The Interview

Thanks for coming B. Guyler and Div A. Den.

Glad to be here Deshaun, said B. Guyler.

So, share with me, why are rumors swirling around about you guys regarding the death of God? B. Guyler, being that you are his brother, do you mind going first?

Not at all Deshaun.

We were in attendance at God's birthday party and being that I supplied the wine and conducted the celebratory toast, suspicions have been raised that I may have poisoned God's wine.

Okay, but, B. Guyler, why would you be assumed of doing such a thing?

Deshaun, honestly, I have no idea.

B. Guyler I do, because according to your Fathers' memoir, you've been rebellious for quite some time, therefore, you got booted from your Father's dwelling. Look, its only certain that you'd be jealous of your brother God because he's only done right by you guys' Father. I can smell a motive brewing all the way from the Oasis, B. Guyler. Sir, what is your response to my observation? What are your thoughts on that?

Deshaun, I've maintained my stance ever since experiencing being cast out of our Father's estate. I'm innocent of no wrongdoing the way I see it. I only followed my Father's example of how he went about leadership. Being ambitious poses threats to those who seek to control. That's the basis of my Father's fallout with me—my ambition and all the success it has brought me. Deshaun, God has openly been opposed to my influence because it motivates all humans to be ambitious toward their truth, and their passions that they feel are aligned with their purpose. I could never understand the harm in that. Therefore, my brother, who has been the modeled version of a robot, unable to think for himself, programmed to be controlled, banned from carrying out his thoughts, brainwashed to fear independence and his ideas, obviously takes personal ought with me because I have lived my truth.

Yeah, I hear you B. Guyler but your truth has led those influenced by it to go beyond their freedom to produce harm by their ambition. Whether intentional or unintentional, wouldn't you agree?

No, I totally disagree Deshaun. Your analysis is baseless.

B. Guyler, let me be the first to tell you sir. You are not making any logical sense at all. See, you hide from taking responsibility for the full result of your ambitious motivation on the earth. Tell me this B. Guyler, why are you not responsible for the results of organized crime syndicates and gang violence in our American neighborhoods for instance? You've encouraged people to live their truth and be free in their ambition, correct?

Yes, but that's nonsense to think of me in such a way Deshaun.

How so B. Guyler? What you are doing leads to the result of relativism. You celebrate and claim victory when those who are passionately ambitious about succeeding in the field of law enforcement, succeed in stopping crime. Why B. Guyler? Is it because it gets you photo opps? See, their ambitious choice motivates them to become who they know they are purposed to be. Yet, you duck from holding your influence accountable to those who have the ambition to be involved with crime syndicates and gangs. I don't get it. They live out the freedom of ambition you promote. Right? They see it necessary to choose and do what they do despite it being very dangerous to all citizens. Therefore, the best way to allow your views to override God's is to eliminate him from the picture. Maybe because of your ambition. Maybe because in your world, whatever floats anyone's boat should be all game. It's obvious you'd want that, correct?

Not at all Deshaun, never in a trillion years fool. Deshaun as of now you are living out your truth and raining down baseless observations and criticism of what you believe my stance is while carrying out your freedom to rain down in such a way. You are in the wrong profession. You ought to work for Sherwin Williams because you are a master at slinging paint! You horrible at it too. You paint dark and messy stories. But if it wasn't for the freedom that you have apart from God's authority, whatever you wanted to say or think would be impossible because you'd be measured by his control. You'd be constrained to a script not of your own thinking. Unable to voice what you deep down inside desire to argue for. But I guess you seek that the world function the way God deems righteous huh? Why bring me on this show if you don't think it's necessary to raise suspicion about my relationship with my Father and brother? What else would drive your ratings higher? You understand that controversy sells and so you in your ambition maximize the freedom to provide a voice of controversy for your viewers, no matter how it tears down your featured guests. Your ambition is carried forth while at the same time you use your platform to judge the ideology of ambition and true freedom. Wouldn't you agree that you specialize in hypocrisy? You want murder and burglary and corruption to stop yet you focus on keeping it noticeable before the world so that your popularity grows, your salary swells, and the replay of sad news remains the narrative. If you had any backbone, you'd protest against the prevalent absence of good stories which don't get aired. But see, that would be too much of the right thing to do. Deshaun don't kid yourself. You're no different than those who exploit children, or one who's in support of child labor. You're just so fictitious to yourself and lack backbone that you exemplify cognitive dissonance in its most obvious sense. Don't you, Deshaun? Ambition is the twin sibling of choice. See, if you fully understood why I encourage freedom you would understand that I can never be faulted. I tell you why. The very first gift given to all beings was choice. Yet, choice within the confines of my Father's view. So, Deshaun, my Father should be the cause of slavery because he holds hostage and lies to people that freedom is found in him. How so? Do everything He wants to be done or face consequences for doing things I believe would benefit everyone? Who's the real villain in this? Why give me a mind if I am only able to think with my Father's mind? He's selfish, he's arrogant, he's a slave driver, he is the crooked judge, he holds a leash, we are victims, we are concubines, controlled, kidnapped, products of his purchasing for him to do as he wishes. Negro please. Miss me with that bull Deshaun! Making matters worse, are we really supposed to be satisfied, feel loved,

261

free, expressive, fulfilled, and purposed? For what, his personal satisfaction? I've been held to the false accusation and horrific scrutiny of being rebellious for maximizing my vision for humankind. Ha, people like you Deshaun are unrealistic. You ask how? Aren't we diverse and don't we live in a world of diversity? BB King sang the blues, should Dr. Dre be confined to that genre of music? Should the Beatles be best rated by their ability to produce songs like Frank Sinatra? Is the Rolling Stones not talented because they don't sound like the Jackson 5? Should yellow be the only color that any outfit is made of? Should there only be one make and model of a vehicle? Deshaun, the world isn't what it is if ambition is not free to be executed. God seeks to program people in such a way as to believe they have ambition but, not at the expense that their ambition functions opposite of his worldview. Is that really freedom to be ambitious?

B. Guyler, you are out of your complete mind.

No Deshaun you are. So because…

Wait a minute B. Guyler I haven't finished my thought. Your ideals lack complete sense mainly because, in your misconstrued argument, the core of your argument is relativism. Therefore, while I'm still on that street, how can you claim that your Father doesn't allow people to be ambitious? Even if such a lie like that was so, wouldn't he be exercising his "ambition."

What, Deshaun. What are you even saying? Sounds like someone is happy that they know a new word.

Naw, you just try to play both sides of the fence and you realize you can't, said Deshaun. Deshaun you can't be critical about how someone else uses their ambition. Your entire argument got holes in it if you think you can manipulate me with your smooth words about the definition of ambition. How you gone be critical of the Father and call his ambition control but then exempt him to use his right to be ambitious. See dude, because God calls spades, spades is great motivation as to why his influence challenges yours, B. Guyler. He establishes objectivity and absoluteness. He establishes a clear definition. Look at the color of these walls. They are grey.

No Deshaun, they are light charcoal.

It's obvious what you do, ha it's obvious what you do B. Guyler. You so seek to motivate people to have their own thoughts so that all are allowed to be right in their own eyes. That's subjectivity and subjectivity is without order. Without order, people can make up anything they want, like living recklessly and not having their prerogatives challenged. You, under the umbrella of ambition, attempt to remove standards and that is very dangerous. Freedom isn't free, freedom must have boundaries. Gravity is free, but gravity is an absolute standard. I don't have the freedom to jump out this 5th-story window and expect to land directly on my feet and not be harmed in any way. Whether you understand it or not, ambition outside of the lens of the Father's plan, which clearly reflects what you do not understand, is a core ingredient of selfishness. And on top of that, it forces tolerance through its seedy sneaky motive. If I wanted to walk into anyone's house and take whatever I feel I should have, because I believe that that is not stealing, that should be tolerated, B. Guyler? So, B. Guyler, if that is reasonable reasoning, then everyone in the culture is allowed to be tyrannical and lawless. Freedom is not free B. Guyler. In such a plan for the world, you are actually going against the very freedom you promote. God disagrees with your outlook. You dismiss his worldview, in all, doing the very thing that you claim he does, and that is to control people. That sounds like a good reason to clear him out of your pathway. Concoct a poison to kill him so that you don't have pushback anymore for what you are empowering people to do. So, since you and Div A. Den live by no set standards, your influence cannot provide solutions for an ambition that results in corruption.

Whatever Deshaun, that's hogwash and you are the prime example of a grown deadbeat dependent. You believe God has a clear objective (B. Guyler laughs), don't make me laugh out loud any longer. How in God's name do you state that God has set standards? Fool, these standards God proclaims create a jail sentence, shut down freedoms that harm the world, and whatever personal gain is compromised means it lowers you guys' influence. Thus, your plan is thwarted, leaving your worldview trashed.

B. Guyler you and Div A. Den create these ideals but don't have enough gumption to address the results of the acts of wrongdoing that stem from the freedom to carry out the ambitions that you market. It's obvious why you sought to do business with the world's most powerful tool. Div A. Den.

Div A. Den, your ambition is to be loved. That's all you care about, said Deshaun. If people love you, they as well remove standards because your love is twisted in nature.

Whatever Deshaun, you speak from a place of privilege because you have a relationship with me and positive experiences with me and the resources you access from me, said Div A. Den. As my partner B. Guyler has said, you are a hypocrite, you can't have your cake and eat it too.

But Div A. Den, you foster investment fraud by taking money from Peter to pay Paul. Your ethics do not exist. Private prison investors study the urban elementary school district students, particularly African American boys, and evaluate their investment to build other prisons based on their poor performance in school. Basically, you capitalize off the disenfranchised and empower investment predators to devour the poor. You are pitiful. Though you attempt to deny these claims, sources close to me state that you are an Angel Investor and lobbyist of corrupt investment initiatives. Therefore, you use yourself to influence political figures who support and invest in private prisons. Like B. Guyler, you are selfish and inconsiderate. You allow yourself to be a key factor behind the pharmaceutical industry, you exploit those bent beneath the weight of care by incentivizing doctors to distribute more opioids. Div A. Den, farmers suffer and are succumbed to the mercy of those who possess and control seeds for food production, CEOs of big corporations as well as governing officials obtain major bonuses and finagle taxes while straining their employees and citizens with unlivable wages. Yet, both of you guys believe life should be this? Div A. Den, do you think for one second that your deeper plan of greed is not evident? Do you believe for one minute that your weak sales pitch that provides false hope will not go undiscovered? Moreover, in your scheme to make people love you for the money you provide, although many already do, your plan for the world is unstable. You think that it isn't, but your economic plan will lead to more entitlement, less will to thrive, and less motivation for people to discover their purpose.

Deshaun, it's oppressive and controlled people like yourself that bind people from the freedom found in my resources, said Div A. Den. Everyone wants money Deshaun. Deshaun are you stupid? Money heals, money brings freedom, money alleviates people from depression and stress, money brings smiles to people's faces, money brings more creativity and the results of creativity to the earth because people have the means to invent, and if I haven't generally given enough detail to the advantages of money yet, Deshaun, money makes the world go round. While you express your critical hate towards the world's most important need, you make me sick to my stomach for the way you think. Deshaun, you could care less about the well-being of me being their most important need because although you duck from public admission, you know that behind closed doors you hold fast to me. I think your shady self is just using this platform to divert others from the importance of the financial healing I can give them for you to suck it all up and selfishly have it for yourself. Deep down inside you really don't want the world to advance, you want people suffering without any hope, Deshaun. You were tingled when I provided more wage increases to your bank account. You are infatuated and tenacious in your habits of walking in a cutthroat manner to surpass your colleagues just to obtain bonuses and perks from your employer. You step on toes to get what I provide, and you are so vicious at it that you backbite, sneak, and steal to climb the corporate ladder. You are privileged, and well off, yet you do not donate to any causes that would help others. You only care about yourself. You live comfortably and splurge on clothes, trips, gambling, and top-shelf alcohol. Not to mention you frequently enjoy fancy hotels and gifts to accommodate the prostitutes you regularly sleep with.

Div A. Den, that is an absolute lie!

No, it is not, Deshaun! Anyway, who in the world do you think you're fooling? Calm your voice too Deshaun before I slap the skin off your face on national television you lame! Deshaun, you love me Deshaun, you lustfully love the money I have allowed you to enjoy. You walk in a manner to only want me for yourself. I love that you love what I have because you know I work. You are just putting on a public front to gain more viewer ratings by running my name in the mud. You didn't help your wife in order that your greed would provide you the million-dollar payout from her life insurance plan. Deshaun you are evil and you allowed your wife to die so that your greed could live! Shut up talking Deshaun, I will openly continue to expose you sucka. Deshaun, act like you know who I am. Don't make me make you beg on national television like I make you beg when the camera is off. I'm the most sought-after, the most important, the most life-giving person on this earth. Matter of fact, the only way you love yourself is by having the money that I let flow into your pockets. Your life suck without me and my money. Keep it real Deshaun, you hated yourself when you were broke. Lame, I made you! Deshaun, you raise the thought in your mind that you don't know what you'd do without me. Is that not true?

Div A. Den, I don't know what you are talking about.

Hmm, Deshaun need I show receipts? I have emails and text messages, video recordings, and valid witnesses to support my claims. Do you wish to be exposed?

Div A. Den, I'm not putting up with your public lies and ridiculous claims any longer. Thank you for your time. B. Guyler, I appreciate you coming to share.

Folks, on our next show we will investigate other reports that need your attention. I will be uncovering a school board official's involvement with a student. Make sure to tune into the WHOLLY station, Channel

12 News next week at the same time. I'm Deshaun Smith and it's been my pleasure. Goodnight world.

After the segment ended.

Wow, Leroy, what a fireball of a segment by our very own investigative reporter Deshaun Smith.

Katrice, I know for sure in my lengthy tenure of working in journalism have I never witnessed any inferno feature report like this one.

I'm in shock Leroy, this story of God's death is eye-popping.

Well Katrice, I'm sure more juicy details are set to unfold. To our viewers, make sure to stay tuned to get the latest updates on this story.

CHAPTER 22

"Breakthrough"

(January 2nd, 2004)

Good morning, Nurse Charita, my name is Deshaun Smith and I'm here for the in-person meeting with Doctor Jones that was scheduled last Tuesday.

Good morning, Mr. Smith. I'll let him know you are here, and he'll be right with you. Please have a seat anywhere in our lobby and he'll be with you shortly.

Sure, thanks. You're welcome, Mr. Smith.

In the Lobby

Hello sir. How's it going, the guy in the waiting area said?

All is well.

What's that breaking news report going across the line down there? You're a big Cleveland Cavs fan, asked the guy?

I sure am, said Deshaun.

Well, sir, your rookie acquisition scored 12 of the last 14 points in the fourth quarter to top off the Portland Trail Blazers. He had 32 points overall.

Oh wow, King James is the truth, replied Deshaun.

Exactly, and being an avid Chicago Bulls fan, the Cavaliers may finally be relevant because they have been a joke for some time now, the guy said.

C'mon sir don't even remind me. Now you seem pretty cool, but you are not safe disclosing your fandom information here, remember you're in Cleveland sir so be careful sir (the gentlemen laughs at Deshaun's hometown fandom).

The door opens and the Doctor comes out.

Mr. Smith, you may come with me.

Sure Doc. Alright sir, you have a good rest of your day, said Deshaun.

Nice chatting with you, Deshaun.

Remember sir, make sure to grab some tissue before you leave today, said Deshaun. Our Cavs are going to make it painful for you Bulls in the years ahead, watch what I'm saying (the guy laughs).

Whatever sir, enjoy your day, they guy replied.

Hello Mr. Smith, I'm Doctor Jones how are you today? I'm coming along, Doc. Awesome, we're going straight ahead to the conference room. You may have a seat and me and my colleagues will be right with you. May I grab you anything, coffee, tea, or juice?

Sure, do you have apple juice?

I sure do, I'll get you some. We'll be right with you Mr. Smith.

Okay great, thanks Doc.

Doctor Jones and medical team enter the room.

Alright, thanks for waiting, here's your apple juice, Deshaun.

Thanks.

Mr. Smith I'd like you to meet my colleagues Doctor Jermichael Shaw and Doctor Nguyen Chung.

Nice to meet you, Mr. Smith, said Dr. Shaw.

Same here to you all.

Well, Mr. Smith we're so sorry and saddened about the passing of your dear wife Destiny. Our condolences, thoughts, and prayers are with you and your family. We can only imagine the difficulty you've had to endure in the last few weeks.

Yes, Doctor Jones, it's very painful, I miss Destiny so much.

Today Deshaun, we wanted to share some news with you about her surgery and ask for your permission about a dedication we'd like to honor in her name for her bravery and act of selflessness regarding the surgery she had with us a year ago.

Surgery a year ago, Deshaun asked? (Deshaun looks perplexed and now leans from the edge of his seat) I'm sorry Doctor Jones, what are you referring to? It was made known to me that my wife experienced heart complications that were too unknown to specifically define as a cause of death. The medical examiner's office informed me that some medical complications can be associated with natural causes if it's not applicable to determine any foul play. Not really sure how true that is, but that is what I was told. I'm in so much pain because of her passing so whatever the examiner's office was reporting I didn't hear. I've been in a blurb, a fog, despondent, a paralyzed state. I still am heavily hurting Doctor.

Yes, I understand regarding the examiner's report. However, one year ago your wife was willing to undergo a specific medical surgery trial. She waived her rights to any legal recourse because she desired that scientific discovery be found so that other people would obtain a solution for their heart disease issues. Mr. Smith if not for her, we as medical doctors would not have obtained this breakthrough discovery. This is research that could only evolve until someone was willing to try the surgery. She was willing, and from it, many many lives in the future will be saved. Prior to her surgery, there was only theory available for what could potentially be an outcome. Because of Destiny, we now have proven science that works. She and the other party was willing to undergo this. He donated his heart and blood. Both understood that their life was at risk but for the greater good of humankind, they set aside their own desires in order that life could be extended for all who were willing to undergo this transplant and transfusion. DeVine Shepherd, widely known as God was the donor in this case. God who has a unique, in other words, phenom related to his blood composition, has provided previous blood samples and in some cases, it was either administered not properly or not understood how to practice the surgery with his blood in a more efficient and effective way. Therefore, many medical practitioners avoided conducting it on patients.

How and why did my wife even keep this surgery from me, Doctor Jones?

Many who are facing the crisis of losing their life often hold back from informing loved ones if they can, so that their loved ones don't worry. Such stress could potentially cause both patient and family member health-related problems during operation and recovery time. We're not sure if that was the case but it was set to take about 3-4 weeks for her to experience a full recovery.

Ok, I understand now.

Deshaun. Destiny had blood issues that affected the wellness of her heart. God was sacrificial in providing his heart and blood. Gifting it to Mrs. Smith, and her bravery to allow this trial surgery and post-surgery research was very selfless. We performed what we term as a "reverse transplant." God gave his heart and blood and in exchange, he took Destiny's heart. God's blood composition is one of rare phenom. Totally pure and so we knew by taking her diseased heart, his blood and circulatory system would be able to heal her heart within him. He wanted her heart and wanted her to have his heart. Ultimately, she did not care if death for her would be the outcome. Her focus was to end suffering and be a part of any solution by contributing herself to a medical breakthrough.

That's deep Doc and as painful as it has been to experience her loss, this totally warms my heart.

Mr. Smith, she was bent on being a blessing. As well, she was honored that God would be willing to sacrifice and give up his heart and blood too. We expressed to her how scientists struggled with believing this procedure to be legitimate. We were confident that it could be a success and it has proven to be.

I don't know, as I was hearing Doctor Jones speak, I don't know, my mood began feeling lighter. Shocked, for just a sec, the husband in me wished I could've given my own heart and blood or walked through this terminal health journey with Destiny. Destiny was certainly an open book to me. Of course, I would have liked to be there to dry her eyes, hold her, and speak my encouragement to her but I guess some roads in life are meant for us to go alone, even when it comes to our spouse. She surely was built tough and the kind of person who never complained. Destiny was a lioness, a protector, an advocate, and a very competitive person. My wife took this moment on and persevered through the battle with her disease. Wow, this was a moment I needed. Selfless, Destiny was really on me about treating myself to self-care moments. Work, work, work was my only "M.O." My wife desired a greater goal of success for all. Although her goal was to become superintendent of her educational district, she was willing to test her own self in order that society had a solution to this heart problem.

Mr. Smith, Mr. Smith.

Oops Doc, I went into a fog as you were speaking. Where were we?

Yes, Mr. Smith, despite having a rare chance to survive due to the heart and blood condition that had attacked her body intensely, she wouldn't refuse to do it. Now, what has been made known in the medical field from practically the beginning of time is that all humans have this heart and blood condition. For some, they face sudden attacks with it as Destiny experienced. God's Father's memoir has always stated he was an absolute cure but so much pushback on the validity of the memoir deflected practitioners from trusting him as a healer. As well, no one trusted God's healing plan and sacrificial work to save them from this disease.

God left us a note that he wanted you to have via his Father's memoir. I'll make sure one of our nurses gives it to you before you leave. Mr. Smith will you allow us to name this surgical department after your wife Destiny?

Yes, please do so Doctor Jones, yes Doc.

We thank you so much for your willingness to allow us to establish the *Destiny Smith Center for Surgical Heart & Recovery.* May her legacy continue to make a lasting impact and provide the comfort that she desired patients and families would experience from this medical breakthrough. (They exit the room and, on his way, out, nurse Charita hands Deshaun the letter).

Here's the letter Mr. Smith. Have a blessed day.

You as well Doctor.

CHAPTER 23

"Examiners Report"

(January 7th, 2004)

Interesting details have come out about the death of God. Grap according to the coroner's office God experienced complications related to a transplant/transfusion surgery God had with a local educator. Destiny Smith, a school principal out of the Village Academy School needed a heart and God stepped up to be her heart donor. This happened around the Thanksgiving of 2002. God decided to give her his heart in exchange for hers. And although he could face complications, he chose to do so. Her husband, national investigative reporter Deshaun Smith, who had a controversial interview with presumed alleged murders of God, B. Guyler, and Div A. Den, just revealed those details about his wife on national news station Channel 12 News. For Destiny, it was also a brave move on her part. Knowing the risk could lead to an unfortunate death, as well as knowing that her common heart disease was incurable, she risked her life by allowing doctors to perform this surgery. One major issue that doctors had to deal with was someone who'd be willing to be a Guinea pig per se.

Thump, please explain the details about this shocking twist.

MANY WHO NEEDED THE SAME TRANSPLANT REJECTED THE DOCTORS. IT WAS RECOGNIZED BY STAFF WHO BELIEVED IN THE HEART AND BLOOD SOLUTION. GOD IS NOW BENEFICIAL FOR ANY HUMAN WITH THE SAME HEART CONDITION AS DESTINY. IN ALLOWING GOD TO BE A SOLUTION, ALTHOUGH DEATH OCCURRED DURING TRIAL TESTING. HER TRUST HAS NOW ALLOWED OTHERS TO TRUST WHAT GOD HAS PROVIDED AS WELL IN HIS DEATH. SHE HAS BEEN USED AS A MEANS TO TRANSFER HER FAITH IN GOD'S LOVE BECAUSE NOW OTHERS ARE READY TO DO THE SAME. ONE PERSON'S SACRIFICE IN TRUSTING GOD'S SACRIFICE HAS PROVIDED THE ENCOURAGEMENT FOR OTHERS TO HAVE FAITH AND NOW WILL HAVE THIS HEART CHANGE THAT PROVIDES LIFE FOR THEM. WHAT AN AMAZING SELFLESS ACT OF LOVE BOTH ON GOD AND DESTINY'S PART. UNLESS GOD GIVES UP HIS HEART AND BLOOD, AND UNLESS THIS WOMAN GIVES UP HER RIGHT TO NOT DENY GOD'S SACRIFICE, IT'S FAIR TO SAY NO ONE ELSE WOULD HAVE BEEN BRAVE ENOUGH TO DO SO. THROUGH THIS PROCEDURE, SCIENTISTS HAVE BEEN ABLE TO EXTRACT GOD'S BLOOD. WHICH, AFFORDS A SOLUTION FOR THIS HUMAN CONDITION. THROUGH IMPUTATION OF THE BLOOD INTO WILLING PEOPLE TO RECEIVE THIS GIFT. GOD'S FOUNDATION, PAYS FOR ALL

COSTS FOR ANYONE WILLING TO HAVE THE PROCEDURE. IT'S NOTED THAT SCIENTISTS HAVE CONFIRMED THAT ALL HUMANS ARE PLAGUED WITH THIS CONDITION THAT BRINGS HEART TROUBLE. BUT NOW A SOLUTION IS AVAILABLE BECAUSE OF GOD'S IMPUTED BLOOD AND HEART TRANSFORMATION. THIS SOLUTION WILL PROVIDE EVERLASTING LIFE RESULTS ALBEIT GOD'S FATHER'S MEMOIR. I GUESS ALL WHO BELIEVE THEY HAVE THIS CONDITION AND ACCEPT THIS GIFT FROM GOD, WILL OBTAIN THE AFOREMENTIONED PROMISE. ALL WHO DON'T BELIEVE THIS CONDITION IS REAL AND THAT GOD IS NOT THE SOURCE OF EVERLASTING HEALING, SIMPLY WILL NOT OBTAIN THE PROMISE ACCORDING TO THE MEMOIR. SO, HE LEAVES IT UP TO THEIR CHOICE TO ACCEPT THIS GIFT AND THE RESULTS OF THE GIFT TO ALL HUMANS. YOU KNOW, REPORTS ALSO SAY THAT THIS WOMAN WAS A VERY SELFISH, RUDE, AND MEAN-SPIRITED PERSON. IT'S REMARKABLE THAT GOD WOULD EVEN CHOOSE TO PICK SUCH A PERSON TO OFFER THIS GIFT TO. WOW. I GUESS HIS LOVE WAS UNCONDITIONAL AND THE PREREQUISITE TO BE AWARDED THE GIFT WAS NOT BASED ON THIS WOMAN'S PERFORMANCE. IT'S OBVIOUS TO SEE THAT THE REWARD GIVEN WAS BASED ON GOD'S PERFORMANCE. HECK, WHAT HUMAN DOESN'T HAVE SOMETHING HORRIBLE ABOUT THEIR CHARACTER? TO WALK IN GRACE AND MERCY ALONE, IS SOME MIRACULOUS STUFF AND A PHENOMENAL EXPRESSION

OF LOVE. GET THIS ALSO, THE REPORTER CAME OUT AND SAID THAT ALTHOUGH HE HAD NO CELEBRATORY OR INTEGRITY BIAS WHEN CHOSEN TO INVESTIGATE THIS CASE, HE DID HATE GOD BECAUSE HIS WIFE DIED. GOD HAD SAVED HIS MOTHER BUT NOT HIS WIFE AND BECAUSE OF THAT, IT DREW A DEEP BITTERNESS TOWARD GOD. EXPERIENCING THE MIRACULOUS EFFECTS OF HIS HEART CHANGE. GRAP, WHAT APPEARS AT THE HEART OF THE MATTER—NO PUN INTENDED, IS PRIDE. ONCE HUMAN PRIDE TO BELIEVE THE VALIDITY OF THE PRACTITIONERS CLAIM, IS CONQUERED, FAITH IN GOD'S PROMISE WILL RESULT IN GOD'S EVERLASTING BLESSING FOR ETERNITY, WHICH IS LIFE. GRAP, I BELIEVE THIS IS THE MOST IMPORTANT AND MOST GENEROUS GIFT THAT HUMANS CAN RECEIVE AND EXPERIENCE. BUT, KNOWING OUR HEART CONDITION, MANY WILL REFUSE TO ACCEPT THE GIFT. UNFORTUNATELY, BUT A SAD REALITY. GRAP, IT'S OBVIOUS TO SEE, THAT WHAT KILLED GOD WAS NOT WHAT THE WORLD THOUGHT. IT WOULD APPEAR THAT HE WAS MURDERED BY EITHER B. GUYLER IN AN ACT OF REVENGE AND JEALOUS RAGE BUT THAT WAS NOT THE CASE. IT WAS OBVIOUS THAT B. GUYLER HAS BEEN ALWAYS ON A QUEST TO RULE EVERYONE. B. GUYLER WAS FULL OF LIES, SELFISHNESS, AND EVIL. HE DIDN'T CARE FOR OTHERS AND THEIR WELL-BEING. ALSO, HE ONLY WANTED TO USE ALL, EVEN HIS FATHER, FOR HIS WICKED PLEASURE. IF ANYTHING, WE GET OUT OF THE FATHER'S VISION, IT WAS UNITY

AND SACRIFICE. THE FATHER WANTED EVERYONE TO LOVE EACH OTHER AND IN THAT, HIS PERFECT PURPOSE WOULD RESULT IN COMPLETE LOVE FOR EACH AND EVERY SOUL HE CREATED. THUMP, IT IS ALSO REASONABLE TO BELIEVE THAT DIV A. DEN KILLED GOD SO THAT HE COULD ADVANCE IN STATUS. HE DIDN'T CARE HOW HIS VIEWS WOULD FURTHER HARM THE WORLD. BECAUSE PEOPLE WOULD STILL BE CONSUMED BY THEIR PASSION FOR EXCESS. THIS EARTH WOULD CONTINUE TO FALL IN SWIFT DESTRUCTION BECAUSE THE LOVE OF DIV A. DEN AND THE LOVE OF MONEY AND RESOURCES THAT MANY KILL FOR, IS THE ROOT OF ALL EVIL. IN DIV A. DEN'S SELFISH QUEST, BEING APART FROM THE WILL OF THE FATHER WAS BRILLIANCE. ALTHOUGH DIV A. DEN IN AND OF HIMSELF WASN'T A WICKED RESOURCE TO HAVE, LOVING HIS MONEY MORE THAN GOD WAS DETRIMENTAL FOR TRUE LOVE TO REIGN IN THE WORLD. ALSO, GRAP, CHURCHY TOO WAS A PRIME SUSPECT IN HER LUST TO HAVE DIV A. DEN. IT APPEARED SHE HAD GOD MURDERED IN A PASSION CRIME TO RIDE OFF IN THE SUNSET WITH DIV A. DEN. SHE WAS BLIND TO WHAT THE TRUE PURPOSE OF HUMANKIND WAS. IT WAS NOT IN THEM HAVING AN OPPORTUNITY TO LIVE LIFE APART FROM GOD. THE REASON IS, THAT GOD'S LOVE IS GROUNDED IN RESTORING THE HUMAN MIND AND HEART TO THEIR ORIGINAL PURPOSE. IF WE WERE TO FIND SOLUTIONS TO MAKE OUR LIFE ENDURE FOR ETERNITY, WE WOULD FOREVER BE BOUND TO THIS

CORRUPTED CONDITION. NEVER ABLE TO FIND ETERNAL JOY AND PEACE. WE'D LIVE FOREVER, BUT WE'D HAVE TO LIVE IN A WORLD STILL DESTROYED BY HATRED, FEAR, VIOLDNCE, DRUGS, ADDICTION, DISEASES, ABUSE, AND SO FORTH. GOD'S LOVE AND WILL ARE PERFECT BECAUSE IT WILL REMOVE THOSE THINGS AND PROVIDE A LIFE VOID OF ANY EVIL...

GOD'S GENEROUS KINDNESS IS WHAT KILLED HIM. YEAH MAN, I AGREE, KINDNESS IS WHAT KILLED GOD. NOTHING LESS BUT KINDNESS. HE DID NOT HAVE TO DO WHAT HE DID FOR DESTINY SMITH. NO ONE TOOK HIS LIFE; HE SACRIFICED HIS LIFE. AGAIN, WHAT KILLED GOD? KINDNESS KILLED GOD. AGAIN, HIS GOOD PLEASURE TO BESTOW AND POUR OUT KINDNESS IS WHAT KILLED HIM.

GRAP, THAT'S AMAZING. THUMP, AND REMARKABLE. HE CHOSE TO DIE SO THAT HUMANKIND MAY HAVE LIFE? ONLY GOD IS CAPABLE AND PURE IN SPIRIT TO DO SUCH A THING. APPARENTLY. YES, ONLY GOD. GOD KILLED HIMSELF WITH KINDNESS SO THAT HE WOULD EXEMPLIFY THE EXTENT TO WHICH WE ARE TO DO FOR ONE ANOTHER AND THAT IS TO LOSE OURSELVES SO THAT OTHERS MAY GAIN. YET, WE GAIN WHENEVER SOMEONE ELSE GAINS. A MYSTERY BUT A TRUTH.

SO, BRO, WHY WOULD YOU YELL AT ME THIS ENTIRE TIME TO REPORT THIS? YOU AND INCLUDING MANY OTHERS HAVE DEAF EARS AND I JUST DID NOT WANT

YOU TO MISS THIS IMPORTANT, SO NEEDED TO HEAR, NEWS. OKAY, I FORGIVE YOU, MAKES SENSE. IS THERE ANYWHERE ELSE I KIND FIND MORE DETAILS ABOUT GOD'S LOVE? SURE, READ AND STUDY THE MEMOIR. IT'S FORMALLY CALLED *"THE BIBLE"* I'M CONFIDENT HIS SPIRIT WILL GUIDE YOU AND HELP YOU UNDERSTAND. THE MESSAGE IS SIMPLE. ONCE YOU FULLY UNDERSTAND IT, DON'T MAKE IT SO COMPLICATED TO EXPLAIN IT TO OTHERS. OH YEAH, GO AND GET YOUR HEART FIXED TOO. OR ELSE YOU'LL NOT BE PRACTICING WHAT YOU PREACH. INFORM AS MANY AS YOU CAN AS WELL. PRACTITIONERS REPORT THAT THIS SOLUTION WILL NOT BE OBTAINABLE AND THEY ARE UNSURE ABOUT THE DAY OR THE HOUR THAT THIS OPPORTUNITY WILL CEASE. THEREFORE, PEOPLE MUST JUMP ON IT IMMEDIATELY WHILE GOD'S BLOOD SUPPLY LAST.

NOW GRAP, GIVE ME THAT BAG OF CHEDDAR CARAMEL POPCORN. NO THUMP. PLEASE GRAP. THUMP I DON'T OWE YOU ANYTHING BUT A TOOTHBRUSH SIR, SO NO, YOU CAN NOT RECEIVE THIS GIFT (THEY BOTH LAUGH).

"BE ENCOURAGED!"

(Currently Happening Right Now)

Graciously, I would like to thank you for taking the time out to engage this work. I hope that this writing has encouraged you about the love of God. The great sacrifice that Jesus Christ, Lord and Savior, King and Mediator has made for the world must be made known.

Understand that God has gifted you and made you special for his glory. There is no one like you and no one who will ever be like you. Continue to walk with courage, faith, love, and obedience. Whatever is your calling, gifting, passion, and heart's cry, I encourage you to express it via the Lord's will for his glory. You are loved and purposed. So, walk in power and authority and pray without ceasing. Allow the Word of God to guide you and saturate your soul in worship.

If you fail to walk in your purpose, who will be affected by that failure? Who will suffer? Who will not be free? Who will not know the Lord? I am praying and rooting and believing God's best for you and your family.

If you do not know the Lord Jesus Christ as the savior of your soul, please pray this prayer:

LORD COME INTO MY HEART IN JESUS NAME. AMEN

"Feed your imaginations in order to keep your dreams alive."

-C-Life-

2 Corinthians 5:21 KJV

For He made Him who knew no sin *to be* sin for us, that we might become the righteousness of God in Him.

Romans 5:8 KJV

But God demonstrates His own love toward us, in that while we were still sinners, Christ died for us.

1 Corinthians 13:4-6 NIV

Love is patient, love is kind. It does not envy, it does not boast, it is not proud. It does not dishonor others, it is not self-seeking, it is not easily angered, it keeps no record of wrongs. Love does not delight in evil but rejoices with the truth. It always protects, always trusts, always hopes, and always perseveres.

John 3:16

For God so loved the world, that he gave his only begotten Son, that whosoever believeth in him should not perish, but have everlasting life.

www.ingramcontent.com/pod-product-compliance
Lightning Source LLC
Chambersburg PA
CBHW070216030726
47505CB00006B/1705